WHAT MAKES US

WHAT MAKES US

RAFI MITTLEFEHLDT

CANDLEWICK PRESS

Copyright © 2019 by Rafi Mittlefehldt

First edition 2019

Library of Congress Catalog Card
Number 2019939264
ISBN 978-0-7636-9750-1

LBM 24 23 22 21 20 19
10 9 8 7 6 5 4 3 2 1

Printed in Melrose Park, IL, U.S.A.

This book was typeset in Minion Pro.

Candlewick Press
99 Dover Street
Somerville, Massachusetts 02144

visit us at www.candlewick.com

For Damien,
my reason to be better

DEVORAH

There are no more words. She has said all the ones she wrote down.

She touches the space where more would be, as if searching for them, as if willing them to appear. The paper crinkles under fingers chapped from days of dry air. She smooths it against the fake wood of the podium, flat, light, cheap. She does not know why she lingers, when she wanted this to be over before it began.

She looks up for the first time, at the people standing before her. In those eyes she reads so much: anger, pity, grief, anticipation, disdain. Suspicion.

Her heart aches. There are so many who will still believe what they believe, she knows. In the new silence, now that she's able to measure the completeness of her words together, they feel inadequate, useless, impotent. In desperation, she searches for others, something, anything to communicate what she feels unable to get across, and says the next five that come to her mind.

"This is not our fight."

ERAN

I

My dad only exists in a memory.

I'm so young, barely old enough to stand by myself. Can I walk yet? I'd probably make it a couple steps, stumble, fall back on my ass like Declan's little cousin in the video from New Year's. Maybe the shock would make me laugh like she did; probably I would've cried.

There's light everywhere in this memory: pouring through the windows, from the bulbs overhead, from his smile. He's so much taller than me. I have to crane my head way back to look at him. My neck aches from the strain, but it doesn't bother me enough to stop. I don't know what room I'm in — kitchen? living room? — but it's not the house I live in now or the apartment from when I was little. This is someplace different, a home I only ever see in this memory.

He swoops down and picks me up, lifts me high, and now I'm taller than him. Over his head I can see my mom, and I feel the grin bursting on my face. He spins me around in one great circle, and I laugh and close my eyes, watching the light change through the inside of my eyelids. He kisses me hard on one cheek, on the other, sets me down. He says goodbye as the warmth of those kisses spreads to the rest of my face.

I told my mom about this once, when I was younger. Maybe six or seven. We were eating dinner, and she was reading some old magazine. She didn't look up, just kept picking at her salad. I watched her eyes scanning back and forth across the lines of gray text, and just when I decided she hadn't heard me, she said, "This did not happen."

You ever think about how lonely your oldest memory is? The only one from its time, nothing else to back it up. Those faint images that have been with you the longest at the mercy of your own self-doubt and mistrust.

This memory is hazy now, corrupted by the time that's gone by. I can't tell anymore if it's something that actually happened or what I imagined that something to be.

Or even less, the memory of a dream.

II

My mom's hair is all curls. They wiggle when she shakes her head, even a bit. It's a big, bushy mass, jet black, a bird's nest. I'd have to get close to see the roots, the tiniest bit of brown, probably not even a quarter inch. Eema will dye it again tonight. She won't let more than a couple weeks go by.

"Why do you do that?" I asked her once. I'd watched her as she unwrapped her towel turban, quick but careful, practiced but vigilant, a ritual I'd seen millions of times but never thought about.

When I finally did, it occurred to me how weird it was. Eema's not one to care about appearances more than is absolutely necessary. She's not sloppy, not untidy; she just has no interest in cosmetics. If it's not practical, it's not worth doing. I've never seen her wear lipstick.

She paused in the middle of toweling off her hair, as if she had never considered the question. "I prefer black," she said. That was that.

I watch her now as she reads the *Chronicle*, curls shaking in tiny eruptions. The actual print version, so quaint. I look for the steam above her coffee and don't see it. She almost never finishes her coffee, lets it cool half-full, but still complains about how expensive chicory is.

"Bye, Eema," I say.

"Study hard," she responds, not looking up. I mouth it with her, something I do every time. She never sees.

Declan climbs in, clicks his seat belt in place carefully. I stare at him as he does, at the mismatched three-piece suit he's wearing under a giant overcoat.

He settles in, smoothing down his coat, then notices the stillness. He looks over, sighs.

"Okay. I know. But I wanted to wear my new pants for the first Friday of the school year," he says, pushing his giant overcoat aside so I can see them. "But then my only belt broke, so I needed this vest to cover the waistband, and then I needed a tie if I was wearing a vest, right? But *then* the back of the vest is kind of messed up, so I thought my jacket could cover it." Declan twists around, displaying for me all the things wrong with the pieces of his outfit. "And then my jacket sleeves are frayed, since it's really Don's old jacket he had in ninth grade, I think? So I needed the overcoat to cover *that*."

I wait for him to stop.

"It's ninety-five degrees," I say.

"We'll be inside."

I stare.

And when I have stared long enough, I shift into reverse.

I drive Eema's old Ford Fiesta from the nineties. It has an ancient, musty smell and no air-conditioning, but I'm seventeen and without a better choice. Declan still asks for a ride, even though he has other friends with newer, less shitty cars. I don't mind. Why would I?

"Deck Lehn?" Eema asked when she first met him, trying out the sound of his Irish name on her Israeli tongue.

"Yes, Miss Sharon," Declan said, and I winced.

Eema frowned and shook her hair. "No, no. *Shah-ROHN*," she corrected, as if expecting flawless Hebrew from this kid. "I am not rich Connecticut housewife."

This was in eighth grade.

Declan's looking at his schedule card now, scanning the misaligned print he memorized a month before school even started. We have three classes and lunch together this year, not bad.

We've turned a corner past sunrise, and it's golden out for the last stretch of road before school, that fire directly ahead, low against the ground, light pouring into the car. In a few minutes it'll be blinding, but now it's a warm, thick light, honey colored, sweet. No one ever talks about sunrise, no one my age, but I don't know why.

"Donovan says no one's gonna come tomorrow," Declan says out of nowhere, in a tone I know means he's been thinking about it for a while, has been deciding whether to bring it up. He rubs his schedule card absently between his thumb and forefinger. The ink's smudging.

For a moment, I imagine Avery Park bathed in the light I see now, brilliant and rich and intense as the sound of a thousand voices in our protest. My protest.

"Who cares what Don says? Don is an idiot. Don is maybe the least insightful person on the planet." I drum my fingers on the gearshift. "Are you having second thoughts?" I ask this because I already know the answer.

"No!" he says, a little too quickly.

"It's okay if you are, Declan. Really! That's normal." I try to make my voice sound easy, light. "Plus I know this doesn't sound like the biggest deal to most people, at least at first glance. I mean, we're just talking about speeding tickets here. But it's really about more than just that, and people get it. This is going to take off."

"Yeah," Declan says. "Just, Don said there are more important things to worry about."

"There are." I breathe out, fighting a wave of sudden irritation. "But this is ours, and it's still important."

There's more, much more, that I want to say, now that I've gotten myself worked up. But the conversation has taken us to the school grounds without either of us noticing. I drive past the main student parking lot, not even bothering. The overflow lot is unpaved, and we listen to the crunch of gravel under the tires and the pebbles ricocheting off the underside pipes. I think about the time in ninth grade when we set up a row of cans in the woods near Declan's house and tried to hit them with his BB gun from farther and farther away.

Then I ease into a space, kill the engine, and sigh into the sudden stillness, stifling now with no wind. The heat pulls a drop of sweat from my forehead before the breath is even out of me.

"Well," I say. "Here we fucking go."

When Declan isn't looking, I practice. Drum my fingers on my backpack strap while we walk.

I don't know if it ever calms me down. But it's gotta be worth a try.

I study Mr. Riskin. He's short, a little on the heavier side, bald with a light brown beard. He wears small glasses set over piercing eyes. Pale yellow button-down, sleeves rolled up, narrow tie, black pants. He looks like an accountant or computer engineer. He looks more serious than he is.

Riskin's still using the roll sheet, reading the names he hasn't yet learned. Most people mispronounce my name the first time they see it written, making the first and last names rhyme like I'm a cartoon character. But Riskin guessed right the first day, the first teacher ever to do it.

This year I have World Affairs and Social Issues first period. It's a pretty cool class, actually, even if Riskin is a little off. Mr. Berkler, a wiry guy who looks like an intern but is my counselor, suggested it last May when I was picking courses.

"You need an elective." He looked up, eyebrows raised.

"I dunno," I said.

Berkler looked back at the screen. "Anything in the arts? Choir?"

I snorted.

"How about Home Management?" he asked.

"Is this what you thought you'd be doing with your life?"

I got a laugh out of him for that, smiled to myself in triumph. He leaned back in his chair. "Well, what are you interested in? Any hobbies or clubs?"

I hesitated a moment. "I mean . . . there's Social Justice Club," I said slowly.

"Huh," he said, and I bristled for a second at the surprise. "Which issues in particular are you concerned with?"

"Homophobia, transphobia, racism, misogyny, reproductive rights," I said. "Global warming, Big Oil, rich one-percenters, uh . . . police brutality, death penalty . . . gun control."

"Well, that's quite a —"

"And immigrant rights."

Berkler blinked.

"Also Islamophobia."

Berkler waited three beats, clicked around on his ancient computer, turned the monitor around to face me. "This is a new one we're offering next year for juniors and seniors. Could be your thing."

My eyes went straight to the short paragraph in the middle of the page:

This course will explore current and historical events through the lens of social movements, cultural evolution, and political shifts. Students will learn how issues enter and exit the public conscious-ness, identify which social changes endure, and discuss the differing roles the media has played in the last sixty years. Semester course. Prerequisites: none.

Above that: "World Affairs and Social Issues. Fall Only."

I glanced back up at Berkler. He was looking at me expectantly, waiting for the answer he already knew was coming.

"I mean, of course," I said.

* * *

Riskin's eyes dart around the room. I watch them dance, never resting, landing on one kid only long enough to bounce to the next. I wonder if this is what it's like to look at me.

"What do people mean when they talk about 'acceptable' forms of protest?" he asks us.

He talks to us about violence and nonviolence, and I imagine them as a duality, as one man with two personalities. Like Jekyll and Hyde, like Bruce Banner and the Hulk.

I raise my hand.

"Eran?"

"Why do we —" I stop. Click my tongue. Start over. "Why should people who are fighting for something let other people tell them how to fight for it?" It comes out in a rush, fast but controlled, just the way I like it.

"In what way?"

"Well, like . . ." I try to find the words. "Like if I'm holding a protest." A girl who knows about tomorrow giggles a bit, but I ignore her, already deep in. "Okay, so I'm at a protest, right? And then people on the other side of the issue tell me, you know, my protest is too angry or whatever. Too, uh. Too 'inciteful.' Is that a word?" I look away, distracted suddenly. "Inciteful. Inciting? They say my protest incites violence. Why should I listen to them? They're not against the way I'm protesting, really, they're against the protest to begin with, so they want to undermine it, so they attack the way it's being done instead of the actual message. I mean, even when students protest *actual violence*! The people against them always say they're protesting the wrong way. What's the right way, though? There's not. It's a distraction. They're trying to win on a technicality or something, so that they don't have to have a real debate about the actual issue to begin with. So." I let out a quick breath. "Shouldn't I just protest the way I think is right?"

My knee is bouncing. I wonder when it started.

"What if they are being genuine?" Riskin asks. "What if they truly want to avoid violence and really do believe your protest will cause it?"

I think for a second, only a second. "Sure, but isn't violence okay sometimes? I mean, aren't we cool with it when it's for a good reason? Like when peaceful protests don't work?" Each sentence leads me to another, one thought playing off the next, the words coming more rapidly. "Isn't that basically how the Revolution happened?"

"There have been events upon which history looks favorably, yes," Riskin says slowly. "But who makes that determination in the moment? Is, say, violence by Palestinians toward Israelis justified, if they feel they have no other option?"

This has happened before, lots of times. Because I'm Israeli. But that doesn't mean I think it's cool to murder people who are just trying to survive under a tyrannical, oppressive, imperialist government run by a political party that, by the way, is basically just like the crazies we have here.

"I think . . . it can be, yeah." I lean forward in my seat a little, tapping my pen lightly against my notebook. I know right away what he's trying to do. "I mean, if they've tried everything else, but they're still being killed indiscriminately? What else are they supposed to do? How can they possibly be expected to sit around and try the same thing that hasn't worked for decades, especially when doing the same thing forever is in Israel's best interests but not their own? And anyway, there are *way* more deaths among Palestinians than Israelis, so why don't we ever ask about whether *that* violence is justified? Doesn't that show that it's not really violence in general we care about, only violence toward certain people?"

People are usually surprised to hear that I'd be critical of Israel. Then I ask them if they're never critical of the U.S. government, since they're American. That's when they get it.

It's funny how everyone understands and assumes so much nuance with their own country but not with others.

I watch Riskin closely, trying to gauge his reaction, see if he was expecting this. There are some whispers from other kids in the class, but, disappointingly, he seems unfazed.

"Let's take it further." Riskin's voice quickens, like he's getting more into this conversation, and I lean forward a little, folding my arms on my desktop and resting my weight on them. Maybe his discussion style is invigorating; maybe it's a little intimidating; maybe I don't care either way. "What about people who bomb abortion clinics? To them, their motivations are morally sound, and their options as they see them are limited. Is that enough to say those actions are acceptable, or do you consider these people terrorists?"

I blink a couple times.

"Which brings us back to the original question: Who gets to decide which violence is legitimate and which isn't? Where's the line between justified violence and terrorism?"

For a couple seconds, the only sound is the *tap-tap-tap* of my pen against my notebook, the nervous soundtrack to a light smile spreading on Riskin's lips.

The bell rings, as if out of pity.

That smile widens abruptly, and I stiffen before realizing there's no derision behind it.

"Fascinating discussion, Mr. Sharon, and excellent questions. We'll take it up again next week. Homework!" He gives a sharp wave at the surprised murmurs of the class. "I want you all to go to the Constant Vigilance protest Eran was unsubtly plugging just now. Tomorrow at noon, Avery Park. We'll discuss it Monday."

My pen stops in mid-tap as the murmurs grow immediately louder. I can pick out the individual tones in them: resentment, incredulity, indignation.

"Some of us have plans tomorrow, Mr. Riskin," Marcos says, and those tones shift to agreement, maybe a dash of naive hope.

"We'll discuss it Monday," Riskin says again. He looks tickled by all this. "I'll know if you skip, so don't try it."

Declan tries to speak urgently through a mouthful of tofu burger.

"There's one." He gestures with his chin.

I pass a glance over Jade first, then follow Declan's chin and chance a look. The kid is two or three years younger, lanky and awkward in his oversize backpack. I scan his clothes and movements for the clue that tipped Declan off. My eyes pause at his swoop haircut, but I decide it doesn't stand out enough.

He finds himself accidentally keeping pace with a couple girls nearby, both fidgeting self-consciously. He makes discreet side glances at them when he thinks it's safe, then realizes he should speed up to avoid walking too close.

"He was checking those girls out," I say after they pass by, but already I'm doubting myself.

Bonnie shakes her head, making her sherbet-dyed hair sway. "Amateur."

Declan snorts into his food. "You know how many—" he manages, then gives up. He swallows, wincing, and takes a moment to compose himself and clear his throat. "Girls I looked at before I knew?"

I catch Jade's eyes on the way back. She looks down at her lasagna, but the contact lasts a fraction of a second too long.

"You guys excited about tomorrow?" This from Delia, sitting next to Jade. I've known her since fifth grade, long enough to know she's trying to bring everyone into the conversation. That is her instinct: to want everyone else to be heard as much as she wants it for herself. I wish I had that.

"Does that mean you're coming?" I ask slyly.

Delia's expression is somewhere between sheepish and amused, a resigned smirk. "You don't really take no for an answer," she says, but there's no reproach there.

"I know," I say. I don't mean it glibly. "So that just leaves you, Jade."

She holds my eyes for a couple seconds, considering me while I consider her. Tall with curly hair, light brown highlights to match her eyes, dark brown skin. She speaks like she moves: careful and controlled, elegant and precise. Of everyone, she's the one I know the least. The only one I haven't known for years, really. We've had classes together in the past but never really talked. She's more Delia's friend, brought into our group through Social Justice Club.

But I see a spark of a chance in her hesitation.

"Aren't there bigger things we should be doing in SJC?" she asks finally, almost apologetically.

The words are out as quickly as they cross my mind. "Yes, but doing this doesn't mean we lose out on the chance to do something else. It just means we get to do more. Look," I say, shifting gears. "Think of it this way: You know how everyone cares about the really big elections? The national ones. Everyone talks about the president. But really, it's the local stuff that affects everyone's lives the most."

"We can't vote," Bonnie says through a mouthful of rice.

"I mean local issues." I am unfazed, building speed and rhythm. "We can't vote, but we can protest. We can draw attention to stuff that still affects us, to put pressure on others. Take this Constant Vigilance thing. Sure, I mean, at the end of the day who cares about thirty bucks more for a speeding ticket? Who cares about them pulling people over more? But the point is that the city's just taking for granted that they can do this." I'm leaning forward, balancing my chair on the front two legs and barely noticing. "No one's asking them why, what the money's for, why we should give them more power, what the alternatives are, how we got here, none of that. They're just looking for easy money, and they assume they have the right to grab it whenever they want and through a police force at that. It's sketchy at best and sleazy at worst, and we should just let them know, that's all."

Jade's eyes never leave mine, so mine don't leave hers. My peripheral vision clouds from disuse, and it's like looking into a tunnel, a deep corridor whose walls are made of words, and at the other end is a pair of light brown eyes, cool, unwavering, resolute.

"What are we doing for signs?" she asks after a moment.

I smile.

III

Eema and I eat dinner silently, facing each other across a table too big for just the two of us.

I don't get this table, don't get why we have it. It's always just been us, Eema and me, since I was about two years old.

Eema doesn't talk about my dad much. I used to ask about him, more when I was younger and before I understood what the scowls and curt tones meant. I never got much out of her.

I called him *Abba* once, when I was a kid. "Dad" in Hebrew, the complement to *Eema*. Even back then I was drawn to consistency and symmetry. It made sense.

Eema was writing something for work. She stopped cold in the middle of a word. I watched her pen come to a sudden halt and felt my insides squirm. She placed it flat on the table, looked at me over the rim of her glasses. The chain swooped down from the frames and disappeared into her bushy hair.

She held my eyes for ten seconds before speaking. "Having a child doesn't make someone an *abba*. A man who stays to raise them, to watch them grow — *that* is an *abba*." She looked back down, picked up her pen, went back to scribbling. "He was a mistake. You may call him that instead."

I left, walked outside to the greenbelt near our house, followed the path to the small bridge that goes over the creek. Climbed under the bridge onto a little dry concrete spot where I could sit and watch the turtles. A place I used to go to think, or hide. I tried to make sense of what Eema said. About the *mistake.* I was eight.

I got used to the not knowing, or as used to it as I could get. There was a lot I would never know about him, and eventually my own curiosity faded, the way it does when a question has no hope of an answer. Eema never told me his name, didn't know or care whether he was still alive.

When he left, he took any connection to his family with him. Or maybe they were already dead, I don't know. I only asked Eema once and got a crumb of information, more than I could've hoped for. "No family."

Eema's own family is just her sister, living an isolated life in Tel Aviv. Her father died before I was born, her mother when I was five. Eema and my aunt Talya barely talk. I don't think they hate each other — they're just not close. I met her once; I don't remember it.

So it's just Eema and me, sharing this table meant for more.

Still, there are clues.

My eyes, gray where hers and Aunt Talya's are hazel.

My skin, three shades darker than Eema's. Too much for a tan, too much for a fluke of genetics. Enough to make people look twice when we're together in public, searching for the resemblance.

A rounder forehead, wider fingernails, fuller lips. Remnants of my father she couldn't scrub away.

I used to stare at her when she wasn't looking, taking stock of the features I didn't see. I would watch Eema, measuring her, and find my father in our differences.

"How was school." It comes out like a statement. Eema puts a small forkful of chicken and rice into her mouth, chewing it slowly while she scans the newspaper beside her plate.

I'm not really paying attention. I'm thinking about the protest tomorrow, overwhelmed by equal parts excitement and dread. So I focus on why I'm doing this, what made me want to protest in the first place, silently working myself up to a lather.

I'm getting angry to keep from being anxious.

You should be careful.

This could be dangerous.

I know. But anger can be self-medicating, I've learned. A way to overpower my nerves.

Sometimes the risk is worth it, is all I mean. Sometimes I need just a taste of it, enough to power me through.

I watch Eema for a few moments as she eats and reads, head bent over the paper, just inches away. She looks up after noticing I haven't answered.

"It was fine," I say.

"Just fine?"

"Yeah. Just fine."

She looks back at her paper. "How is the English teacher? The one you say will be so terrible."

I sigh, careful to make it too soft to hear.

"That was Declan saying that, not me."

Eema nods once, not looking up. I stir the remnants of

my chicken and rice, and finish it in three large scoops of my fork.

"Careful. You will choke."

I ignore her and chug the rest of my water, listening to the gulps slide down my throat — one, two, three, four. The last one almost hurts.

I stand up with the glass still in my hand, grab my plate, and head to the kitchen.

"Wait."

I stop at the threshold to the kitchen, turning back to face her. Eema takes a long sip of her tea. I listen to the slow slurping noise, imagining the hot liquid cascading down my throat, and feel a bead of sweat break out on my forehead.

"I thought we could go to synagogue," she says.

My mouth is already open to say no before the last syllable is out of hers. She goes almost every Friday and Saturday, and sometimes I come along. We're both basically atheists, but I don't really mind it. It can be kind of nice. Calming. And Eema, I know, says it's still important to remain connected to the cultural aspects of Judaism. That, and I think she likes meeting her friends there. She doesn't have many.

But tonight? When I'm too worked up to sit still, already half-crazy with worry and a brand of anticipation that leaves me a little queasy? I'll pass.

"I don't think I'd be able to concentrate. I'll probably keep fidgeting and annoy — wait," I say, cutting myself off, a thought coming sharp out of the clear blue. I stare into space for two seconds. "One sec."

I turn abruptly toward the kitchen, putting my glass in the crook of my arm, and pull my phone out with my free hand.

you going tonight?

I hit Send and put my dishes in the sink. Zack texts back before I can turn the faucet on.

Of course.

"Yeah," I call from the kitchen, tapping my fingers against the back of my phone. "I'll come."

Eema and I drive in silence. She prefers it this way, and by this point, so do I.

Our synagogue is a small square box, built in the seventies and not updated since. Cheap vinyl and wood paneling as far as the eye can see. It sits on land large enough for a bigger building, which is what they're planning once they have the money. I dunno why. It's tiny and old and thriving, the Ruth Bader Ginsburg of synagogues, and it is perfect.

Zack finds me near the entrance, rummaging through the little basket of *kippot*.

"They're all the same," he says after a moment.

They are not. Under a maroon cap, I catch a glimpse of seafoam green and make a grab for it. I check the inside. The print is fading, but still readable: *Bar Mitzvah of Eran Sharon. July 17–18, 2015.*

"This one's got history."

Something about the way Rabbi Cassel tells us to turn to page twenty-five, to rise, to read responsively — there's something about his deep voice settling on the refrains I've heard since I was six that works on me like a sedative. The familiarity is soothing.

When we sing, the melodies pulse outward in waves. The words come out of me automatically, committed to memory over years and burned there for good during my bar mitzvah. I couldn't tell you what they mean. Ask Eema.

Everyone moves into the tiny social hall afterward. Zack and I take a thimble of wine and a chunk of challah as they pass it around, washing one down with the other once Rabbi Cassel says the blessings. Then it's over, and the noise rises to the dull roar of four dozen people mingling.

"Eran! I'm glad to see you back here!" Her singsongy voice covers a light tremble: an old-lady voice.

"Hey, Mrs. Persky."

"Usually you make your mother come alone," she goes on. I smile slowly. It's a guarded smile but a real one. I know what she's doing.

"Yeah," I say.

Mrs. Persky smiles back at my nonresponse, then gestures to Zack. "This one comes every week," she says, prodding. "You could learn from him."

Zack looks at her noncommittally. He's not interested in playing.

"I know, Mrs. Persky," I say. I reach around her to grab

a handful of stale cookies from the table and nudge Zack. "Outside?"

The stumpy sign for our synagogue sits in the corner of the lot, far from the building itself. CONGREGATION TIKVAT HADOROT, spelled out in both English and Hebrew letters, facing La Finca Boulevard. The sign is two feet deep with a flat top. We sit on this, eating sugar cookies, watching traffic go by.

"Doing anything tomorrow?"

Zack gives me a sideways glance, warned off by the tone of my voice or just because it's me speaking. He's regularly wary around me, something that makes me feel alternately proud or dejected, depending on the day and my mood.

"The Lord our God commands me to rest on the Sabbath," he says. My lip twitches. Zack's sense of humor turns dry when he wants to stall. My best bet, I know, is just to jump in.

"What do you think of this Constant Vigilance thing?" I ask. "'Cause I think it's dumb as hell."

We're both steeling ourselves, I realize. I try to ease my own tension by kicking my legs a little, shaking the anticipation out of me. Zack takes a contemplative bite of cookie.

"I have no idea what that is," he says.

"Zack, you do. The police thing? Where they're gonna pull people over for no reason and raise fines? We're holding a protest tomorrow. You're coming."

"Ah." He examines the edge of a cookie. "Right."

Four cars pass by. I count them under my breath.

"Yes, it's stupid," he says finally, finishing each word in full before moving on to the next. I tense again. Zack speaks slowly when he's gearing up for something that I'm gonna disagree with. "It's also not the end of the world."

I blink, but I'm only taken off my game for a second.

"Is that the threshold for protest? The actual apocalypse? Or can we protest something before it gets to that point?" There's an edge to my tone now I wasn't intending, but I've gotten this answer maybe one too many times.

"Don't pretend you thought I meant that literally," he says, getting into his own swing. "This kind of protest isn't exactly my thing, if you really want to know."

"Why? I mean it. Why? We pay all this lip service to needing checks on powers so that authority figures don't become authoritarians. Right? As a society, I mean? But it's always in theory. Then when there's an opportunity to actually put those ideas into practice, half the country wants to drag its feet." I take a bite out of a sugar cookie I no longer want. "It's like humans are just drawn to dictators and kings. Why do you think that is?"

"I don't think—"

"It's 'cause we're lazy. We want everything done for us." I point at him with half a cookie. A couple crumbs fall out of my mouth; I wipe them away with my free hand. "Think about it. There's a terror attack: we want the president to protect us by any means necessary, even if we lose freedoms. There's a drug epidemic: we want harsher drug laws. Jesus, even when the crime rate *falls,* we want more police."

I don't like the silence the end of my little speech has created, so I swing my legs harder, letting my heels fall back against the sign while I wait for a response.

Zack finishes his cookie and wipes his hands methodically. He takes a second to inspect his palms.

"Why do you come here?"

Zack does this sometimes. I narrow my eyes, fighting an instinct to course-correct. I know by now that what seems like an abrupt subject change with him isn't always so.

"To the synagogue?"

"Yes."

"I'm a Jew, Zack. Surprise."

He gives me a small smile. "Yes. Technically."

I give him a look. "It's like my mom. She's even more of an atheist than I am, but she comes all the time. It's a cultural thing for her. Or that's what she says." I look at my hand. There's just a pile of crumbs in there now. I frown and toss them into the grass. "I mostly come because I've always come. It's familiar but not stale, I guess. Also for social reasons. Also to talk to you about this protest."

"Ah." Zack follows a minivan with his eyes. "Is that why you're here? Just to recruit Jews to fight the establishment?"

"No, don't be —" My mind changes track. "Or maybe? Wouldn't that make sense? Isn't that kind of what we're supposed to do?" I let my right foot fall back too hard, and it knocks one of the letters loose. "Oh," I mutter, and jump down.

"What do you mean, 'what we're supposed to do'?" Zack asks.

"Judaism *is* protest!" I say. "It's like *all about* protest, not accepting what's in front of you at face value, that sort of thing.

Isn't it?" The black *H* is solid and heavy in my hands, a surprise. I look at the space where it had been affixed to the sign. All the other letters stick out about an inch or so. "Remember in our confirmation class? Remember Rabbi Cassel telling us it was impossible to be a good Jew without questioning authority?" I try to get a good look at the tiny pegs that had been holding up the *H*.

Zack doesn't say anything for a moment. I start to wonder what it means just as he takes a slow breath. "You always sound angry when you talk about your mom." He keeps his voice even, not dull or flat but not charged either.

I stare at the *H* in my hand.

"I am. Usually." I'm startled by the definitiveness in my voice, but only for a second. Then I run with it. "You know how you're super calm and methodical and sometimes a little boring, no offense? That's your dad, right? And then your sense of humor, when it comes through, when you let it, is your mom's. So you're left with two pieces of yourself that both complement each other, that balance each other out, but that can work alone too."

Zack watches me, not sure yet where I'm going with this, but I can feel myself picking up steam, the path to my point clarifying, becoming more solid. I move from a walk to a jog, from a jog to a sprint.

"I just have my mom. I've always just had her. So it feels like I get my entire personality from her. Like my intensity. I know I can get a little wound up and go off the rails, just like her. And I don't think that's always a bad thing either, so get that out of your mind right now," I add, giving him a look. "I think it's one of the best things about me, that I actually care about things instead of just going along with all the bullshit in the world, because going along is how we as humanity get stuck with some pretty awful things. It's just . . ." I sigh. "That intensity gets out of hand sometimes. I get angry easily, just like her, and it's a powerful, crazy, sharp anger, and in the moment the only thing in the world that matters is that feeling."

I look again at the pegs where the *H* was, forcing myself to pause. I try to see if it'll just snap in place.

"There's no complement to my intensity. It's just there, all the time, bubbling under the surface. Nothing to make it less chaotic and more controlled. Or if there is, I haven't found it yet. And I can't help thinking that if my dad was still around, I would have found it by now." I give up on the *H* and rest it on top of the sign. "Like, maybe I wouldn't just be turning out like my mom so much. Maybe I could be more like him, whatever that is. But instead, the only pieces of him that I got, that I even know about, are the ones you can see. My skin color, my eyes, my lips."

I hoist myself back up, next to Zack.

"And thinking about that makes me even angrier. I've asked her all my life to tell me about him. She refuses, just because she never got over that he left her. Which, by the way, part of me wonders if her anger is the reason he left —"

This last part, out before I can stop it, startles me into a full stop. A surge of guilt cuts off my breath, a lump in my throat that blocks any more treasonous words.

Too far.

I cough twice, trying to cover, and try to get back into it before Zack notices anything's off.

"So, yeah. Gleaning what I can about my dad just by looking at myself in the mirror — knowing exactly as much about him as any stranger could guess? Feels like a kick in the teeth." I let a long breath out. "Maybe there are pieces of his personality that are dormant in me, somewhere. Bits that can maybe balance some of the part I get from my mom. But since he's never been around, there's no one to help pull those pieces out of me. 'Cause Eema sure as hell isn't."

Now that it's out, I'm almost surprised how much I told Zack.

Maybe it's because I've already told Declan all this. Or maybe it's just because the protest has made me think about it more often. It's there, a sudden and convenient outlet for my intensity. But the positive kind.

Zack looks quietly at the road. I wait until the silence has made me uncomfortable.

"Anyway, you in or do I have to keep trying to remember lessons from Cassel?"

Zack takes a long, deep breath through his nose, then lets it out all at once. I know what it means before he says anything.

I smile to myself.

Houston is terrible. I'm not kidding. It's filled with awful people and pollution and gross places like Dairy Queen on every block. It's the fourth largest city in America, and there's still nothing to do.

It's pretty diverse at least, which is nice I guess, but we live in super-white Kiley Springs, a suburb on the edge of the city limits.

Kiley used to be its own city, but eons ago, I think in the eighties, Houston straight-up annexed it. I am next to positive that it was a white-flight community a long time ago, when all the white people in big cities moved to these new suburbs so they wouldn't have to live near black people.

Texas is full of places like Kiley. Maybe the state offers a racism tax incentive or something; who knows.

Okay.

Houston is not terrible. We had a lesbian mayor for a while. Not even New York has done that. We come together when we really need to — we kinda crushed it with Harvey and a thousand hurricanes before him. Maybe the only reason I think it's so boring is because I live in the suburbs and I'm seventeen, and that's a hell of a combination.

We're really not as bad as our reputation. I have a love-hate relationship with my hometown, like I bet most people do, like you would probably expect from any kid in any state on any planet. And even I'll admit it's more love than hate.

But.

It is still Texas. Houston can be as racially diverse as it wants and vote for every lesbian in the world, but it's still Texas. And Texas loves its police.

I swing my legs off the bed, bringing myself into a sitting position, blinking away the sleep, fighting off a small wave of morning dizziness. My phone's alarm is still going off. I fumble to my left without looking until it silences.

I take in the warmth of the room on my bare chest and back.

34

Eema keeps the AC at seventy-eight, even in the summer. She gets cold easily.

My feet sink into the carpet. Pale blue, came with the house. I stare at the fibers around my toes, the sea that reaches outward from my feet to meet the four cracked white walls. Those walls are bare except a Longhorns foam hand from a game we went to last year, an old Hulk calendar I kept just for the art, and a *Hamilton* poster Declan got me. It's this last one I look at now, dead in front of me, the silhouette of Alexander Hamilton making up the top point of a black star on a gold background.

Talk less.

The protest is today.

I let these four words float around my mind, trying to use them like I would caffeine. My eyes drift naturally back to the Hulk calendar.

Then my phone buzzes in my hand, and I feel a jolt as I read the notification.

I stand up, fully awake now.

Someone found an old megaphone. It's pretty crude, too small and weak for the size of the crowd. It turns my voice into a mechanical replica of itself.

We got here early. Declan in my car with half the signs; Delia, Jade, and Bonnie in another with the other half. We set up at the edge of Avery Park and for the next hour watched as more and more people arrived. A hundred, then hundreds. Whatever I was feeling before, the sight of all those people took my jitters to a whole new level.

Most of them are because of the *Houston Chronicle* retweeting us, of course. That first buzz when I woke up was followed by others that never really stopped, growing in frequency as the protest time approached and people started reacting with greater urgency. Some angry messages but mostly positive.

In a moment of weakness, I tried to get Delia to do the introduction. To her great credit, she backed away, palms up. "Nuh-uh. This is your protest."

So at noon on the dot, I turn on the megaphone. It gives a short burst of feedback, which helps quiet the crowd, but there's still some chattering here and there.

"Hey! Hey. Thanks for coming today." My voice sounds weird to me, shot out like sprays of static, but people are starting to listen. I swallow. "I don't have much to say, but I did want to thank everyone for coming. And thanks for spreading the word. And thanks to the news for coming to cover this."

I gesture halfheartedly at some of the news vans in the distance. My mouth is dry.

"So, the mayor, or the police chief I guess, is starting this new program called Constant Vigilance, which is a stupid name by the way." There are laughs at this, which encourages me. "And the idea is that the police have to pull people over for barely anything. And if they pull you over by mistake, they won't even get in trouble as long as they say they thought they had a reason. Anyone here ever been pulled over for nothing at all?"

There are a lot of affirmative half-shouts at this.

"Yeah, what I thought. And I don't mean to get all preachy here, but haven't we tried this before? Stop-and-Frisk didn't work in New York; Broken Windows didn't either. All these grand ideas to stop bigger crime by focusing on the small things keep not working, but they keep trying." I switch the megaphone into my other hand. "I have a better idea: Maybe actually focus on the bigger crimes? Maybe leave people who aren't doing anything alone?"

More shouts. They're with me.

"We have murders and rapes in Houston, right? White-collar crime, rich people cheating the poor out of their homes? Isn't this the oil capital of the country, home of Enron, and you're telling me there's nothing worth investigating with those guys? You gotta bother some kid with a broken taillight instead?"

Laughs. I'm raising my voice now.

"Look, I know what we're up against. I know they got donors, I know it's easy to jack up a fine when you need money, I know they want to take the easy way out. Who wouldn't, right? But that's why we're here! We gotta remind them that we still vote them in, and we can vote them out no matter how much money they raise. We gotta remember that we hold the real power here, if we want it!" Full-on shouting now. "But we gotta want it! We gotta keep this up, and not just vote every four years when there's something shiny on the ballot. We gotta vote local, y'all, because local is where the real shit happens!" There's less distinction now between my voice and theirs, a blend of our shared anger. "And until we *can* vote, we gotta keep the pressure on to let them know we're not happy, and when we're not happy, we fuck shit up. So let's fuck shit up!"

A roar of approval as I put the megaphone down, crowd pumped, ready to go. I am surprised by myself but not. Jade grins.

"You're pretty good at this," she says, eyes on the crowd. "The way you talk to people, you're getting them to care about something they probably wouldn't have otherwise."

I watch her watch the crowd.

I'm not always great with compliments, never sure what to say or how to react without it sounding insincere. Normally I just feel a little embarrassed.

But this means a lot, coming from her, for some reason.

"Thanks," I say. She still looks at the crowd but smiles.

You're pretty good at this part, anyway.

But this is what you always do. You get people on your side, make them invest in you.

Then you fuck it up.

Delia and I lead the march, alongside the rest of the SJC members — Declan, Jade, Bonnie, the others. A few freshman members also came, which surprised me. They usually bail after the first meeting. Zack's here too, a little behind us, with one of his lacrosse friends and another guy I've never seen before. Attaboy.

It's electric, the whole thing. Bonnie brought a portable speaker and a beat-heavy playlist, so music follows us as we march, wrapping around our shouts and our bodies. I find myself moving more than I mean to but still not enough, bouncing on my feet as we go, holding my sign high. Everyone else is doing it too, and their energy feeds mine and makes it nearly glow.

We're marching the length of the park alongside the boulevard so that people driving and walking by will see us. A handful of police officers are tailing us in their cars. I guess their being here is just routine, but it still makes me a little uneasy. I wonder what they think of what I said.

I was a bit annoyed about them following in their cars though, since they were obscuring the view of us from the road. Declan shrugged when I mentioned that. "Well, but their lights are on, right? It's just attracting more attention." He had a good point.

Every now and then, we start a new chant, based on the signs we made. The people behind us pick it up, and it flows backward, a wave of voices that build into a unified protest.

I look at one of the news vans as we pass it, my eyes climbing upward along the spire, following the thick wire coil to the top. The reporters themselves are off a little ways, recording in front of their cameras with us in the background. I wonder if they'll interview anyone.

Declan nudges me. "What do you think about that?" he shouts over the noise.

We've rounded a bend where the road hugs the park, and we can see part of the trail of protesters behind us now. Declan's pointing at a group of mostly women farther back, holding a banner that reads: BAY AREA WOMEN'S RESOURCE CENTER SUPPORTS POLICE REFORM.

I hadn't noticed that until we started. There are a couple outside organizations that joined us. I don't really know much about the Women's Resource Center, but I think it's a feminist org. I also saw a civil liberties group and the Harris County Libertarian Party.

Underneath my energy I'm still feeling pretty nervous, and

I think this is part of the reason why. Whatever I said to anyone else, I still imagined this would be a small protest with just a handful of kids. And now here we are with hundreds of people of all ages, news cameras, actual nonprofits, and the police themselves.

Look. If you'd told me two days ago how much attention the protest would get and how much it would spread, I'd have been ecstatic. But it's still pretty intimidating.

"I don't know," I shout back after a minute. "I mean, I'm totally for more exposure. But why'd they decide to come? Are they just here to bring attention to their own groups?"

"The banner only says they're on board with our protest," Jade points out. "So far they aren't focusing on any unrelated causes of their own." Her voice has sort of a lawyerly tone to it. I know that sounds weird, but I don't know how else to describe it. Like she thinks everything through carefully and logically before she speaks.

"Whoa," Declan says after a moment, breaking my train of thought. I look up.

We're coming up against a smaller group of people up ahead, holding their own signs. I can't hear what they're chanting yet, but I don't get why they'd be separated from our march. Then I see what their signs say.

BLUE LIVES MATTER

I STAND WITH POLICE

DON'T LIKE US? DON'T CALL US.

COPS OVER CRIMINALS

I tense a bit, eyeing the counterprotesters warily. There aren't that many of them, but I don't know what will happen when they mix with our group.

I glance at Jade. "It's fine," she says, watching the demonstrators as we approach. But her movements have become more rigid; her jaw clenches and releases.

"Excuse me? Are you Eran Sharon?"

One of the TV reporters is suddenly next to us, walking alongside the march. A cameraman is following her.

"Shah-ROHN," I say.

"Sharon, I'm sorry. I'm Lillian Buskirk, with Channel Six. I understand you're the organizer of this march?"

Lillian Buskirk smiles a little too brightly at me. She's pretty young, maybe in her twenties, but still looks like she's done this a thousand times.

"Uh, yeah."

"Great!" Lillian smiles even wider. "Do you mind if we interview you briefly for a story we're running for the ten-o'clock spot?"

I glance over at Delia. She nods enthusiastically, gently pushing me forward.

"Okay. Sure." I look back at Delia and Declan and the others. "I'll, um, catch up with you."

We step out of the march a few feet. Lillian directs me to what I guess she thinks is the perfect spot, where the stream of protesters becomes my background. She moves over beside her cameraman, leaving just me in the frame by myself. I bounce a bit more on my feet, wishing I could get back to the march. She explains

41

that she'll ask me a few questions, that I should try to answer in complete sentences, and that those responses will be edited into the story later. Then she starts before I can say anything. I'm a little taken aback by how quick she is.

"What do you see as the purpose of this protest?"

Her microphone is two inches from my mouth. My mind is a blank for half a second, and then I start speaking.

"To stop — We're trying to stop the city from raising fines and using the police as a way to grab more money from drivers. And we're trying to stop the police from being able to pull people over without a reason. Because they already have enough power, and it's bad for the rest of us if they can do whatever they want, whenever they want to."

My brain is catching up with my mouth. I can feel my heart starting to race with the thrill of having to evaluate my own words as they're coming out, when it's already too late. But so far I'm not regretting anything I'm saying. It's blunt, but it's true.

"What would you say to those who argue that the police are just trying to stop deadly car accidents?" Lillian continues.

I think only for a moment. "But, like, there are other ways to do that, right? I mean, isn't it convenient that the only way to save lives happens to make them a lot of cash?"

"What about those who say protests like this create tension between police and the community?" Lillian asks.

"Huh?" Her abrupt shift rattles me a bit. "Well, if they don't like it, maybe don't create this new law that lets them get away with illegal stops?" I say. "That's causing tension. I mean, if they can just pull me over, and then say they thought I was speeding even if I wasn't, and no one can do anything about it, like, why *wouldn't* they abuse that? It's just easier to, isn't it?" Lillian's stance makes her look spring-loaded, like she's waiting for the instant I finish talking so she can swoop in with some pointed question. It makes me keep talking out of instinct. "Laws should never create an incentive for people in authority to do the wrong thing. Otherwise they will, every time, because people take whatever route is easier. That's human nature."

Right as I stop, she snaps the microphone back to herself.

"Do you —" she starts, but a loud series of yells from my left, disconnected from the rhythmic shouts of the chants, cuts her off. We both look over.

Our march has reached the small group of counterprotesters. Even from here, I can tell something's wrong. The flow of the march has been disrupted, and a handful of people from each side are close — too close to each other.

I break into a sprint.

Even over the yells and the cheering, I can hear the *thump* of my own feet against the grass and packed dirt. The uneven ground makes my footfalls clumsy and jarring, and I have to clench my jaw shut to keep my teeth from smashing together.

There's a lot going on when I get there, and it takes me a second to register it. But the counterprotesters seem to have almost merged with the front of our group. Which seems dangerous.

There's some commotion from the middle of the mass of people, where the two groups are starting to bleed into each other. I look closer and see Jade and Delia talking to a guy with a beard

43

and sunglasses. He's holding a sign I can't read, but it's at his side, forgotten.

They're not exactly shouting, but it looks pretty tense. I make a beeline for them and overhear the tail end of what Jade is saying to him. She looks flustered but determined to keep her cool.

"— course you can't know, since you've never been —"

He cuts her off.

"If you don't drive like a maniac, you have nothing to worry about. Period."

Jade's voice is ice. "That isn't actually true. Their primary concern is public safety, so from that perspective, it makes sense to stop as many drivers as possible, often multiple times. That is harassment."

The guy shifts his feet. "Uh, not sure why you think public safety's a bad thing. You people just want to be able to get away with stuff without worrying about the cops."

"No," Jade says slowly. "The point is that the police have no incentive to be fair when they operate under an ends-justify-the-means mentality. This is why they need a power check against —"

"Okay, well, excuse me if I trust the police to be fair more than I trust a bunch of thugs."

I am half-aware of Jade's nostrils flaring, of my own rush to get in front of this man, of Lillian Buskirk and her cameraman nearby again, of a couple police officers moving toward us. But an instant later, I'm staring at my own reflection in his sunglasses.

"Get out," I say, inches from his face, my finger on his chest.

"Eran," Jade says behind me, her voice a warning.

"Don't touch me!" the bearded man says, swatting my hand out of the way. "We have just as much —"

I shove him.

It's not hard, but he's not expecting it.

My stomach drops right as I do it. Even in the moment, as he's tripping over the uneven ground and falling backward, I wish I could take it back.

This was a mistake. This was a *mistake*.

"Hey!" This from my left. One of the cops.

"You motherf —" The bearded guy scrambles back up. I tense, not sure if he's about to hit me. I've never been hit before, which is sort of a small miracle when I think about it.

I have a moment to wonder if I just ruined everything because of a stupid flash of anger.

"*Eran.*"

This voice cuts through everything, brings everyone to a halt. Even the bearded guy looks over, confused, anger deflating.

Eema looks at me with a fury I've never seen. She grabs my arm. Harder than I knew she could. I have no idea where she came from.

Lillian Buskirk steps up to us, the only other one moving.

"Eran, could you speak —"

"No," Eema spits at her. "This is not our fight."

For a split second, I think about what a strange response this is as Eema turns back to me. A flash of something passes over her face, making me falter, confused.

Then her anger returns.

"Come."

She doesn't bother to walk around the crowd. She just turns in the direction of her car, parked at an angle on the shoulder, and walks, creating a path through protesters and counterprotesters alike. No one dares stay in her way. My face burns. I try not to imagine how red it is.

"Ma'am . . ." one of the officers starts, taking a tentative step toward us. She turns those eyes on him, not slowing, and whatever he was going to say dies in his throat.

Behind me, a few people snicker. I'm almost thankful when the car door is closed. I stare straight ahead as Eema turns on the car, not wanting to look.

But I do anyway. My eyes lock on Jade's, and I have just a second to register her look of pity and anger before Eema steps on the gas and we speed away, Jade dissolving into the crowd behind us.

IV

This is what I know about him:

He was from Israel too. He and Eema moved to New York from Haifa before I was born.

He would've served in the army. The Israeli army, I mean. Eema too.

Eema didn't have a job when they got to New York, which means they probably moved because he found a job. I can't imagine they'd just pick up and go to a foreign country for no reason, anyway.

That's kind of it, though.

I don't know where in New York. Eema doesn't know that I even know that. But in middle school I learned that social security numbers are organized by state, and I looked up my prefix.

Eema has never told me I was born there.

My heart won't stop pounding. Eema says nothing as we drive, for which I am grateful.

I make the mistake of glancing at her and am overwhelmed by a mix of feelings. Guilt, embarrassment, fear, resentment. Anger, of course, always anger. They pull me in different directions, these feelings, with a force I wasn't expecting, so I shift my thoughts away from her.

I can't get the image of the bearded guy out of my mind.

Hitting the ground at an awkward angle, scrambling to get up, mouth screwed up in sudden rage. The feeling of bracing for impact as I anticipated a punch: a tingling in my gut and chest, a tensing of muscles, skin quivering as I tried to keep still. The cameras on me.

Fuck. Fuck.

That was assault, right? Am I going to be arrested?

Fuck.

I pull my phone out, as if it will have an answer for me. I stare at a black mirror, at a silhouette of my own reflection, then put it back in my pocket.

Eema keeps her silence as we drive, as we pull into the driveway, as we get out of the car and go into the house.

It's only when the door to the house closes behind me that she whirls around, pure crazy coming out of those eyes, that hair.

"What are you thinking, doing this?"

I stare at her, made dumb by competing emotions that cancel each other out, like converging color lights that turn white.

Then one wins out.

"Why were you there?" I blurt out.

"Because I know you, and I know you need to be watched. So I come and watch." I open my mouth to respond to this, but she beats me to it. "You are parading around in front of the news, in front of everyone, getting into fights? You think this is the way people should behave?"

"I wasn't *parading*—"

"This was a parade, yes? A . . . a show for people? What is wrong with you, that you need such attention? What is wrong with you, that you push a man in front of police? In front of news camera? What do you think will happen when this man decide that he will press a charge?"

Eema's accent thickens and her English gets worse when she is at her angriest. When I was a lot younger, I had to keep myself from laughing. Now, in this moment, it grates on me.

I focus on one word to avoid the questions I don't want to think about.

"Why are you so worried about attention? You knew about the protest. You were okay with it."

"You tell me it will be a small demonstration," she fires back. "'Just a few kids,' you say. Not hundreds. Not television and camera."

"It's a *protest*, Eema. Attention is exactly the point! Are you kidding me with this?" I look at her incredulously. "And the attention wasn't for *me*. It was for . . . for the cause." I know how stupid this sounds as soon as I say it. Eema pounces.

"Ah, yes, this cause, these speeding tickets you are fighting against."

She is seething. For the first time, I realize she cares more about the size of the protest than about me shoving a guy. It's baffling, and it throws me off balance, but only for a moment. "It's not about *tickets*, Eema, it's about how much power cops have in the first place."

"Ah! So it is a big problem in this country, yes?" Her eyes glitter.

I stare at her, not wanting to rise to the bait, but she is determined.

"Yes, Eran?"

Slowly, I close my eyes and take a long, deep breath. I resent this.

"Yes."

"And surely then it can be solved by a seventeen-year-old boy."

This doesn't deserve a response. My eyes stay closed. I feel myself wander another step closer to the edge. My heart pounds in anticipation, one part afraid, two parts giddy.

"Stop that," she snaps. "You think you are angry, but that is just covering for your shame."

I open my eyes, gaping at her. Her tone softens, just a little, a subtlety only I could pick up on.

"Eran, you are not the messiah. You cannot solve the world's problems. If you must try, so be it. But do not be so rash and so stupid about it."

It's like peering down the side of a cliff that might be too high, might not. Knowing the cost, knowing the slightest thing could be enough to make a decision for you. Giving in. I jump because I don't resist; I don't resist because I never have.

"*Rash?* Where do you think I *get* that, Eema?" The feeling of free fall is terrifying, exhilarating, awakening. "Have you been listening to yourself at all in this conversation? You say the first thing that pops into your mouth, no filter, same as always. You get mad at me for doing the same thing you do; you get mad at me for *being* you. But you're the adult here, right? What do I do

50

when the only parent I have can't control herself? Where do I learn self-control?"

I watch the anger drift out of her body like smoke. It gives me satisfaction, and even now, even in the moment, that terrifies me, but the part of me that could do anything about it has retreated to its prison, locked up tight, waiting this one out.

"I wish my dad was around." I can make my voice deadly when I want to. It feels powerful in its quietness. "I wish he was here so I had some balance. I wish I wasn't so *rash* either, Eema, but the guy who was supposed to teach me that left you a long time ago. I wish I could be more like him than you, but you're the only one here. If you don't like how I've turned out, think about who's been raising me."

I've never seen this expression on her face. It's not anger, which is what I expected, what I hoped for, what I wanted to do battle with. The force in those hazel eyes is fierce but undirected, like a firecracker turned over, spinning on its side, no target.

She takes a step toward me, her own power like an aura expanding outward.

"You have no idea what that man was." It comes to me hissed through clenched teeth.

She wants to say more.

She doesn't.

She stands still a moment, as if wrestling with something, then lets go of whatever it was she was containing. She has a release valve, I suddenly realize.

Eema turns and tosses her car keys into the key dish in one fluid movement as she walks to the kitchen.

I'm alone ten seconds before I understand I've been dismissed.

Surrounded by the walls of my room, in the middle of my bed, I realize I've been tensing my muscles, my lungs, my entire body. I let myself go limp, fall back on the bed.

I wait. I know it's coming.

This is what you always do.

And it does, like a slow wave, only a minute later. Gradual but relentlessly building. The weight of regret makes it hard to breathe.

I did it again. I got so wrapped up in something, so wound up and excitable—

Then you fuck it up.

—and then overzealous and erratic. I got to my breaking point and jumped clear across it. I lost it, twice. Once with the bearded guy, then right after with Eema.

I wish I could control myself. I can't.

I wish I didn't get so intensely and suddenly angry. But I do.

But.

I mean, Jesus. Fuck it, right? I *love* having my convictions. I love caring about things; I love getting angry. I love that I have so much passion, that I want to change things for the better. I hate that most people don't, that they're so comfortable with the status quo, that they want to live their lives passively in a world where everything happens to them, with no control over it.

But.

It's not like I have much control either.

52

But at least I try!

I force a deep, rattling breath that hurts my chest.

I hate this. I hate this.

I wish I was better.

You have no idea what that man was.

But wasn't that sort of my point?

That I never got the chance to see what he was and learn from it?

I'm clicking around on my laptop a couple hours later, in my room, door shut.

There's a video already up on YouTube, taken with a phone from right behind the bearded guy. Based on the angle, it looks like it's from someone in his counterprotest group.

You can barely hear the conversation between Bearded Guy and Jade. Then I run into the frame. We get right in each other's faces. There's a moment where we're speaking, but the wind covers most of it.

"Don't touch him," says a voice close to the camera. The guy filming, I guess. I don't remember hearing or even seeing him.

And then I push Bearded Guy, and my stomach drops.

It looks bad.

"Whoaaa, dude! *Hey!*"

I stop the video while the guy filming is still shouting and scroll down. The comments are predictable.

goin to jail bruh

press chargesssss

lol "dude"

I follow some links to another video, this one uploaded by Channel Six, and watch myself make the same mistake from another angle.

For a second I was hoping they wouldn't report on the protest and felt immediately guilty about it. I mean, that was the whole point.

The video starts toward the end of my interview. That suddenly stops, in midsentence, with a loud noise from behind video-me that grabs my attention.

My pulse throbs against my throat.

They kept the camera on. I watch myself run offscreen, then it pans quickly back to me and makes a bunch of jerky, hurried movements to catch up. It makes me a little nauseous.

Then I catch the tail end of my brief conversation with Bearded Guy and watch video-me shove him to the ground, and I feel a little more nauseous.

Then Eema steps into the screen.

Close by, you can hear Lillian: "Eran, could you speak—"

Eema turns and glares at the camera.

"No. This is not our fight."

I'm dragged to the car.

I stare at the screen as the video ends, at the grid of suggested videos that pops up afterward. My eyes flick down to the description.

A protest against the new Constant Vigilance police initiative nearly got out of hand during this brief interaction between organizer Eran Sharon, a member of the Social Justice Club at Kiley Springs High School, and counterprotester Arnie Jenkins. Jenkins has said he will not file a police report.

Silently, I bury my head in my hands.

I don't make eye contact with Eema Sunday morning.

But I glance at her, once, when I'm sure she isn't looking.

She has the newspaper on the table in front of her, but she isn't reading it. She's just staring at a fixed point on the table, lost in thought, letting the steam from her coffee wash over her face, flow around her cheeks like swirling liquid. I am surprised not to read any anger in her expression. If anything, she looks worried.

Eema doesn't say much to me all day. Just small things. "Excuse me" when I'm in her way, "Are you hungry?" before lunch, "Please turn it down" when I'm watching TV. All of it muttered, almost impossible to hear. It doesn't feel deliberate, but I find myself wishing it was.

Around two thirty, the phone rings.

I don't usually answer it, because it's almost never for me. But I'm right next to it, rummaging in the fridge to see if we have any yogurt left, and I think Eema might be in the shower.

I pick it up, and right as I'm about to answer it, I hear Eema. "Hello."

She picked up the phone in her bedroom. I start to hang it up and just barely catch a man's voice.

"Hi, I'm sorry to disturb you. This is Benson Domani with the *Houston Chronicle.*"

I freeze. Someone's calling about the protest.

"Okay." Eema is guarded. She must be thinking the same thing.

But then the man asks, "Am I speaking with, ah, Miss Sharon?"

I frown. Why is he asking about Eema?

She doesn't answer. Benson Domani continues, but his voice has changed subtly, become more hesitant.

"How about Devorah Shamir?"

I hear what sounds like a faint intake of breath. A short pause.

"You have the wrong number," Eema says quietly.

"Miss Sharon," Domani says quickly, "I just have a few questions. About your . . . about Eran's father."

I stop breathing. My mind reels.

"You have the wrong number," Eema repeats, more forcefully, and hangs up.

There's near silence on the line. Just the slightest breathing. Then Domani says, "Hello?"

I press the hang-up button instinctively and immediately regret it. I hold the phone receiver in front of me, staring at it with wide eyes, wishing I could undo that button press.

I stay that way for what feels like a full minute, the same question running through my mind over and over. Then Eema's footsteps in the hallway break me out of my trance. I lower the receiver back into the cradle quickly, silently.

I turn around right as she comes in the kitchen and stare at her. Her eyes flick up to mine for a moment as she passes me.

"There is ice cream," she says.

I blink and, after a moment, nod mutely.

There are two more calls. The first comes during dinner.

I look up sharply when the phone rings. Eema doesn't meet my eyes, just stands up automatically. I watch her walk into the kitchen.

She picks up the receiver, and even from the table, I can hear the tinny crackle of a voice. She hangs up almost immediately, walks back, and sits down.

I stare at my Stroganoff.

"Who was that?" I ask my plate. My voice sounds natural, I think.

"It was no one."

The last call comes later that night. I hear it from my room and rush silently into the study. I unplug the phone and pick up the receiver, my hands shaking. When I'm sure Eema's picked it up in the kitchen, I plug my phone back in.

Benson Domani's in the middle of a sentence.

"— ng up, you should know we're running this story no matter what." His voice is apologetic and firm at the same time, regret mixed with determination. "I just wanted to give you the opportunity to tell your side. It would be in your own best interest."

There is a long pause.

Then Eema, just above a whisper: "Please do not."

I breathe as quietly as I can, mouth away from the receiver. "Miss Sharon . . ." Domani begins. "I'm sorry. It's a story, and I can't not run it as a . . . a favor."

"'A favor,'" she says back to him, tasting the word. "I am not asking you to help me with my groceries, Benson Domani. This is not a favor."

"Miss Sharon —"

"I have spent fifteen years putting this man into the past. And you are going to bring him back, bring everything back." My heart pounds. "I moved my son across the country, away from all that I knew, to keep him from this."

Domani sighs into the phone.

"Miss Sharon, I'm sorry."

"No. You are not." I hold my breath, waiting, and then jerk the receiver from my ear as Eema slams the phone down. I hear it both from the receiver and from the kitchen.

"Benson!" I whisper fiercely into the phone. But he's already hung up.

I put the receiver down absently. For a few seconds, I stare at it. Then I turn on my heel and walk out of the study, down the hall, through the dining room. I can't bring myself to cross the threshold to the kitchen.

I watch Eema, her back to me, standing in place, clenching and unclenching her fists, hands shaking. She turns, slowly, and freezes when she sees me. Her eyes plead with me. But I ask anyway.

"Eema, who was my dad?"

Her face does something more than just wince. She reacts as if the question causes physical pain. Gradually, her body seems to lose all of its rigidness, the tension leaving her joint by joint as she gives in.

She lets out a long sigh, releasing the last of her resistance through her breath.

"Sit." Her voice is sandpaper. "We will talk."

DEVORAH

"Are you ready?"

The young lawyer's voice is gentle but sends a jolt through her. Devorah breathes out slowly, holding on to the few seconds she has, and forces herself to tear her eyes away from Avi, still asleep in her lap. Mr. Kelsey's eyes are kind, clear, and deep brown, but they are not her son's.

"No," she says, but stands anyway. This is best, she knows.

Each movement is slow, meant to push the future further away. Her hand closes over the doorknob like a Venus flytrap but doesn't turn it. The contact of metal on skin is soothing but distracting, an excuse for delay. It is too cool for June.

She looks at Avi over her shoulder, at the policewoman who will stay inside and watch him while she is outside. She asked for a woman.

The young lawyer nods at her, once, slow. Go on. She turns back to face the door so he doesn't see her wince.

A sigh of wind on her face; then an eruption of voices, camera shutters, the squeaks of cheap folding chairs. She watches her own feet make the slow journey down the walkway leading from the front door, the cracks in the aging concrete, the clumps of crabgrass shouldering their way through the uneven lawn. Anything to keep from looking up. The camera flashes burn in her periphery.

She can feel the young lawyer behind her, keeping pace; can feel those brown eyes on her, guiding her steps with the force of their compassion. The knowledge of him keeps her upright. He is the only friend she has in this world, this man she's known five days.

They turn with the walkway, climbing onto a raised platform that covers a section of the front yard. Small podium in the center, facing two rows of folding chairs. It is like the bimah *of a synagogue, she thinks. The lawyer's doing, all of this. He guides her gently to the podium, staying close beside her.*

Seven microphones, she counts. She looks at the mesh covering of one, dented here and there, careful not to lift her eyes any farther. She wonders how many others have used these same microphones, for what purposes. How many have stared at this same dent in the mesh, wishing to be anywhere else?

As if rehearsed beforehand, the people in front of her have stopped talking, have taken seats where they could, have become still and quiet except for the occasional snap of a photo.

She releases the beginning of an exhale through her teeth, stopping when she hears her own breath from the speakers near the platform. The rest comes out slowly through her nose. She reaches into her sweater pocket, takes out a single sheet of paper, and unfolds it on the podium top.

She chooses the dented microphone to direct her words.

"My name is Devorah Shamir," she says, and a startled bird flies from a river birch tree.

JADE

V

Sunday nights are for quiet.

Father used to say that when he was feeling wry. The cap to a full day: church, a big lunch, grocery shopping for the week. Mr. and Mrs. DeVos over for games. Football, if it's the season for it.

In the evening, when it is all over, Father will ask how they always manage to pack so much into their Sunday. Not that he minds. But he relishes the quiet of the night, an epilogue to the weekend.

The DeVoses came over today. It is a ritual that started too long ago for Jade to remember: Mr. DeVos with his smiling, shining face, growing redder as the afternoon wore on and his wineglass emptied. Mrs. DeVos, plump and somehow elegant in her casualness, forever wrapped in loose shawls and her Louisiana accent both. Each with white hair, full and bright. Jade looks at that hair sometimes, trying to decide if it is pure white or just the lightest shade of gray, but she can never make up her mind.

Today was Balderdash, so Jade and Sapphire opted in. Mrs. DeVos read some obscure word, and they each wrote down a fake definition to try to fool the group.

Mrs. DeVos laughed long and hard when she read Jade's definition, then doubled over when she learned whose it was. Great big belly laughs, long and slow and indulgent, with seconds between each one — her signature. Mrs. DeVos couldn't take her breaths fast enough to fuel them. It gave away Jade's answer as false, so no one picked it. But Jade didn't care, just counted each laugh-burst as she felt her own small smile grow into a giggle. Nine, a personal best.

Mr. DeVos went next, pointed at Jade with the card he'd picked up.

"Saw you on the news last night, Lady Jade."

Jade nodded at her neighbor, kept cool on the outside even as her heart dropped. She was aware of Ma in her periphery.

Mr. DeVos studied the card, lips upturning as he read, and favored her with a flick of hazel.

"You did great, I thought. Looked serious, respectable. Like you were in charge. Something to be proud of."

"Thank you, Mr. DeVos." In all the years they'd known each other, he'd never asked her to call him by his first name. He was a little old-fashioned with his formalities, Jade thought, but she would respect them.

He turned back to the card. "Shame that young man ruined things."

Here Jade offered a thin smile, lips pressed. "Agreed," she said, and felt a twinge of guilt. But Ma was watching.

Mr. DeVos chuckled a little, then read:

"Okay, movie title: *She'll Be Wearing Pink Pajamas.*"

Sapphire won that round. Jade remembered because of the way her cheeks glowed.

The game went on and on, enough to give Jade the luxury of forgetting the day before.

There were moments, though. Flashes from her mind's

camera, stills from yesterday's mess. Glimpses of Ma's unsmiling face, the almost-angry quality of her worry. Thoughts of other things, firing off at odd times like sparks from a faulty wire.

Those were tiny moments. For the most part, it was a noisy and fun and boisterous Sunday afternoon.

But Sunday nights are for quiet.

Jade watches her reflection in the glass of her father's cabinet and tries not to move. She wants her image to match the stillness of the house.

In the quiet, those spark-thoughts are harder to ignore.

Her eyes refocus and move past the glass, to the rows of books Father hasn't opened in years. Top shelf, she knows. She's looked through it before but finds herself opening the cabinet door and rummaging through those books, pulling out an old photo album wedged behind them, out of sight.

The pictures are still bright, even when the color is off here and there. It was the last of the film her parents used, old disposable cameras they bought on impulse every now and then and developed at the drugstore down the block.

Jade flips through pages of old buildings and streets familiar to her only because of this album. It's always the same photo that makes her stop, that fills her with the same mixture of sadness and frustration. A tiny version of herself, three years old, pedaling a cheap plastic tricycle along the curb. A man passing by, frozen in the act of turning his amused face to watch her go. She's moving too fast for the shutter. The blur adds a fleeting quality to the image.

Jade tries, but she can't remember that street, the man, the homes she passes. She can't even remember the tricycle.

She knows her parents would have different impressions of this photo. Of all the photos of their life in New Orleans. They would look at the same picture and see two different realities, have two different memories for the same thing.

Buried in that thought is a memory. Bringing this photo to Father, years ago, sometime in elementary school when she'd first found it. Him sitting in the living room, Ma on the other couch. Asking him who it was.

Father snatched it out of her hand with an abruptness that startled her, but he was quick to smile. "That's you, honey bunny." His voice the same gentle roll it always was as he stood. "Come on, I'll show you some more." He was already ushering her out of the room.

But when they were alone, he knelt down, and his voice grew quiet. "Don't go looking through that album again, Jade. It'll upset your ma." His serious eyes scared her. "Promise me."

A lot of things upset Ma.

There are more pages to go, but Jade has lost enthusiasm for the album. She starts to put it back, but something stops her hand. Then she makes up her mind and pulls the old photo out of its sleeve.

She closes the door to her father's cabinet, and someone is there in the reflection of the glass, watching her.

Jade's heart skips, then settles. She turns, smiling sheepishly at her sister, at their shared secret.

* * *

Sapphire hugs her knees, back against the wall. Jade watches her sister smooth down the calves of her jeans, bare toes caressing the carpet, and wishes she could draw. Sapphire's hair makes shadows against the wall, a smaller silhouette of Jade's own curly mass. Jade follows the movements of those shadows, thinking about how they will stop existing after this moment, except, maybe, in her own memory. All for the lack of a camera or a pencil and some talent. The thought makes her sad.

Sapphire watches Jade.

"Do you miss New Orleans?" her sister asks. She has asked before.

Jade smiles at the shadows of her sister's hair and plays with the photo in her hands. She knows without asking that Sapphire won't tell. "I was too young. I don't really trust my memories."

"You always say that."

"It's true. Those memories are more like dreams now."

In the quiet of their shared bedroom, even whispers carry weight.

Sapphire traces a line in the carpet with a toe. It leaves a trail of bent fibers two shades darker than the rest. Jade smiles and draws a line next to it, then two more to intersect: a tic-tac-toe board. She looks expectantly at her sister, who rolls her eyes but draws an X in the middle square.

"Father misses it," Sapphire says.

Jade draws an O in a corner. "I don't trust his memories either."

Sapphire giggles and puts another X below her first. "What do you remember?"

Jade considers.

"It was hot and muggy, like here," she says slowly. "But everything felt so . . . rich. Not as sterile."

"Sterile?"

Jade leans back, eyeing the board. She can already see it will be a draw.

"There were no strip malls, Sapphire. Just old, beautiful buildings." She draws another *O* to block her sister's run and wishes she had the words to describe what she can still see, what is left of the first few years of her life.

Sapphire ignores the board.

"I don't remember being upset," Jade says finally. "Or anxious. It felt like home, I think."

It's the best she can do. She feels betrayed by the fragility of her memories.

Jade looks again at the shadows of Sapphire's hair and wills herself to remember that image forever.

She sees Eran from a distance, three minutes before the first bell, and stops. It's only a few paces into the building. She's vaguely aware of the rush of kids from behind, moving around her suddenly still figure like creek water around a dropped rock.

Jade probes her feelings. She's not as angry as she would have thought. But maybe she only expects anger because she knows she has the right to it.

He looks distracted, like he's not really seeing what's in front of him. In their few interactions, he's carried himself with a flavor of self-assurance that flirts with arrogance. She doesn't know him well, but the difference here is still noticeable.

Jade tilts her head, watches him brush his long neck absently, shivers as she imagines the feel of a light hand on her own neck. He disappears around the corner, and she stares at the space he had filled until someone bumps her shoulder.

Delia seems to have settled on resignation. Jade almost asked if she had seen the clips before realizing the question would have been absurd.

"Have you talked to him yet?" Jade asks.

"No, but we don't have any classes in the morning." Delia pulls at the threads of cheap carpet covering the risers. The two girls sit at the top level, backs against the wall, alike and not alike at the same time. Her friend is shorter, fuller, with darker skin and hair she keeps braided. But their shared mannerisms and deliberate way of speaking make them feel like sisters. "You don't look angry," Delia says.

Jade shrugs as Mr. Frasier walks in from his office and plinks the first warm-up notes on the battered grand piano.

"Neither do you."

But by lunch, her mood has soured. She is unsure why.

She works methodically through the last hour in her mind but can't recall any real trigger.

She grabs her tray, jostling a precarious mound of mashed potatoes.

Eran is already at the table. Jade sees him from across the cafeteria and tightens her grip on the tray.

He's on his phone, has it out right in front of him, visible even from her spot. A teacher could see it at any moment and take it away. The lack of discretion bothers her. She watches him for a minute in growing disbelief.

Why hasn't he said anything to them?

The question becomes a catalyst. Jade quickens her pace, keeps her eyes laser-focused on him as she maneuvers around tables, chairs, other kids with trays. If he looks away from his phone, even for an instant, she wants to record the exact moment. But he doesn't, is completely engrossed in it.

Feet away, Eran runs a hand through his hair. It's a tense movement, and Jade falters. Only for a fraction of a second, but it's long enough that Mr. Frasier gets there first.

He comes to an abrupt halt while passing by, eyes snapping to Eran's phone. Jade reads annoyance in Mr. Frasier's expression, but recognizes a hint of reluctance mixed in.

"Cell phone," Mr. Frasier says in a clipped voice. He holds a palm out.

Eran looks up for only a second, giving the choir director barely a glance.

"Huh? No."

Jade raises her eyebrows. For the first time, she sees Declan, who stares at his friend with a mix of disbelief and worry.

A strained moment passes.

"Okay," Mr. Frasier says slowly, face hardening, "then after you give me your phone, you can come with me to the office." His voice lacks conviction. Jade finds herself feeling sorry for her teacher.

He reaches forward.

"No!" Eran shouts, standing and yanking his phone out of reach. Mr. Frasier takes an instinctive step back. Declan puts his sandwich down and stands, slowly and uncertainly. Eran looks wildly around, and his eyes meet Jade's. They are gray, rich, and intense. She wasn't expecting gray. It's unlike her not to have noticed before.

"Mr. Frasier," she says, then shifts toward her director. She can see the surprise as he registers her for the first time, dissolving his mask of forged anger. Even in the moment, she appreciates the tiny phenomenon of real expression replacing fake.

"Jade."

She closes the distance between them, addressing Mr. Frasier. "He's . . . waiting on news about his mom." She packs meaning into the words, stretching the implication with calculated pauses. She lets him read significance into her ambiguity.

It is a strange thing, lying to a teacher she respects. The unfamiliarity of it startles her. Has she never done it before?

But she still feels a prick of guilty pride for how well it was done.

Mr. Frasier will yield, she knows. He gives Eran an embarrassed glance. "Well, keep it under the table, okay?" he says, with the voice of someone for whom firmness does not come naturally. He offers Eran a wan smile before turning to hurry away.

Eran watches him leave, manic energy coming off him in waves.

Jade watches those waves, waiting for them to die down before she speaks again.

They're in a restroom, the three of them, at the end of the hallway that joins the music wing to the auditorium. It's Jade's favorite restroom in the school. Small, too out of the way for anyone but those with a reason to be nearby. A secret shared between choir, band, and theater, a pact between the arts.

She and Declan stand still as Eran paces erratically, neither clear on what to do, how to ask. He moves with no purpose and too much energy, cracking his knuckles, barely acknowledging them. They watch him wander dangerously close to a urinal, then swing sharply to the right. The aimlessness of his movements, the lack of pattern, makes Jade a little queasy.

Declan was the first to speak after Mr. Frasier left. "Buddy?" Low, tentative.

Jade picked it up from there. "Why don't we go talk somewhere?" She was the one to bring them here.

Now that they're away from it, Jade understands the protection a cafeteria full of kids affords, how fully that blanket had enveloped them. She is uncomfortably aware of her own presence, how out of place she is. It feels intrusive. She wonders what compelled her to take charge here, to come with them and involve herself. She is a friend, yes, but a new friend. Eran and Declan are best friends. Alone with them, she recognizes for the first time the buffer Delia and Bonnie normally provide.

She lingers near the door.

"Eran." Declan tries to still him with his voice. "You gonna tell us what's going on?"

Us. Jade shifts her weight to her other foot.

Eran looks back at Declan. His friend's words break through but have no calming effect. Eran pauses only a moment, then turns back around. He looks as though he can't decide where to go or how to get out.

"Found out about my dad." The words come out in quick, uneven spurts, like water from a hose filled with pockets of air.

Jade's lips tighten, and she reaches for the door. "I'm going to let you guys—"

But the door opens on its own, smacking her outstretched hand. A boy walks in, then stops when he sees the three of them. He's taller even than Eran, covered in draping shirts and loose pants. His gaze stops when he gets to Jade. She takes in his clothes and the way he carries himself and decides: theater.

"Uh." The boy waits three uncertain seconds, then turns and walks back out.

The click of the latch makes the silence that follows that much louder. Jade massages her hand where it was hit, counting the spots of peeling brown paint on the door.

"She always told me he just left us when I was a baby." Eran says this to Declan. There is an urgent note of accusation in his voice.

Jade turns but finds herself rooted to the spot.

"But really we left. I used to live in Queens." Eran glances at the trash can next to him before slumping down to sit on top of the closed lid. He stands again a second later. "Can you—? I mean, Queens. Huh. I always—" He runs a hand through his hair. "I always thought it was somewhere in New York, but I didn't know it—well. But who cares! I guess."

Jade has trouble taking her eyes off the frenetic energy of Eran, but forces a glance at Declan. He looks increasingly worried.

"Did you ever hear about a bombing at some Israeli Day parade in New York City?" Eran says out of nowhere, drawing Jade back.

She stills her mind, waiting to see if the question brushes against something in the vague part of her memory that stores once-heards and passing read-abouts. Nothing.

Declan shakes his head too. Slow.

Eran turns away again, takes a couple steps toward the stalls. Stops. Spins back around on his heel. Looks as if some new horror is at the tip of his brain, almost emerging from the shadows to reveal itself.

"Eran." Declan reaches a hand out, as if steadying his friend by will. "What are you . . . What about your dad?"

"The parade." Eran mumbles this, then snaps his attention to the sink to his right. He turns the faucet on. "It was fifteen years ago. They have this parade every year—"

Eran shifts with a start, as if remembering something, and pulls his phone out. He swipes and taps at it for a moment and waits, blinking at the screen.

Jade watches the water pour out of the faucet, focuses on the steady white noise.

Eran puts his phone back in his pocket. Even casual movements threaten significance in this place, in this now.

"There's a parade just to . . . I dunno, celebrate Israel. Maybe it's for their independence day?" He frowns, swatting at the line of water streaming from the faucet. Jade leans against the wall behind her, the door within arm's length.

Eran faces the mirror above the still-running faucet but doesn't meet his own eyes. He runs both wet hands into his hair, as if holding himself in place.

"Someone set off a bomb in the middle of the parade one year. It, um." He shivers. "Killed a few people."

Declan waits, but Jade's heart clenches. Her gaze shifts past Eran, to the row of urinals, the flickering overhead lights. If Sapphire were here, she'd tell Jade later about the faraway look she gets in her eyes when she's sad for others, a look of more than pity, a look of empathy. She tries to imagine what it would be like to learn something so awful after so much time.

"Your father was one of the ones killed," she says, her voice approaching silence.

Eran flicks his gray eyes to her in the mirror. It is the subtlest of moves, but even so she reads something unexpected.

"What? No. No." He lets out a sound that is somewhere between bark-laugh and whimper. "Well, I mean, yeah, he was. But that's —"

His eyes are pleading, terrified, delirious. Jade's breath catches as she understands. She didn't mean to force him to say it. She opens her mouth as if to stop him, but he pushes the words out first, shoving them as one might shove unwanted guests through a front door.

"He was the one who set off the bomb."

VI

Jade counts the seconds. There are eighteen, an eternity.

"Your . . . dad . . . He was Israeli too, wasn't he?" Declan uses the question as a lifeline, trying to hold tight to what he understands.

Eran waves the question off. "I dunno! I mean, yeah, he was. But he was part of some anti- . . . some, uh, some group." He looks down and frowns, as if seeing the faucet for the first time. He turns it off.

Jade slides slowly down to the floor, keeping the wall against her back, keeping her eyes on Eran. She feels the bumps and contours of the painted stone against her spine.

"Eema said he was always super, you know, political, and he was against a lot of the stuff the Israeli government did. Kind of like me." His voice breaks on the last word. Jade watches a half-formed but powerful thought pass over his eyes before he pushes it away.

The bell rings. Declan and Jade wait, neither wanting to be the first to disturb the quiet afterward. Eran saves them.

"It was only a couple years after 9/11, so it was a big deal. I mean, it would've been a big deal anyway, but . . . the way Eema tells it, people were kind of out of their minds back then." He coughs again. "And in New York too."

Declan watches his friend for a few moments, mouth parted slightly. Then he swallows and licks his lips. "How did this . . . come up?"

Eran stares miserably at the tile floor, shoulders hunched. "Some guy from the *Chronicle* saw us on the news. Recognized Eema." Jade feels her eyes widen. "I don't even know how he . . ."

They wait, watching Eran, who watches the floor.

"He said he has to run the story."

"What?" Jade is taken aback by the sharpness of her own voice. Eran looks up from the floor. After a moment, Declan turns to her.

A thousand urgent things run through her mind. She feels paralyzed, not sure which to say first, or whether to say anything at all.

The bathroom door swings open again, so she turns toward it instead. She recognizes the teacher but doesn't know his name.

He holds his hands out, a gesture of incredulity.

"Guys. Really?" He looks at each of them in turn. "Let's go."

"Where'd you guys disappear to?"

Jade hears the hint of annoyance in Delia's voice. They walk through the main doors, caught in the stream of thousands of kids rushing to leave.

"Just needed to talk to Eran," she says. Not a lie. "About Saturday." Still not a lie, but getting close.

"For the whole lunch period?" Her friend is probing.

Jade waits a few beats, trying to run out the clock. "I guess I had a lot to say." This is a lie.

They move toward the parking lot. Delia has a car but lives in the opposite direction. Jade will take a bus.

"It was just Bonnie and me at the table." Delia tries to keep her voice casual.

"We just wanted somewhere private." She can feel Delia's frown and decides not to risk anything more. "I gotta run, Dele. See you tomorrow."

She turns toward the bus circle without looking back, pushing the guilt out of her mind.

There is nothing in the *Chronicle* yet, but it's barely three o'clock.

She scrolls through the app anyway, taking in every headline, her thumb locking into a rhythm, pulsing the news upward. She stops only when she gets to a headline about a new McNugget recipe. If it had been posted, it would be bigger news.

Jade lowers her phone back into her lap. The bus hits a bump, and she and forty other kids rise an inch in their seats for a split second. She looks out the window, away from her seatmate. She thinks his name is Elliot. A sophomore.

Eran didn't know when the story would break, just that it would be today. There was very little else she was able to glean before they were whisked away from the restroom and separated by the crowds. She has no classes with him this year. She could have texted, but it felt invasive. So she spent the rest of the day in anxious wait.

Jade realizes how invested she has become in the family history of an acquaintance.

She thinks about this as she looks back at her phone and types

"Israeli Day parade bombing" into Google, quickening her fingers as her battery ticks from four to three percent.

His name was Dani Shamir.

It was rudimentary, almost primitive. Gunpowder and nails, mostly. But enough.

Five deaths, including Shamir. Eighteen others with a spectrum of injuries. One woman with a bruised thigh; one who lost a foot, an ear, her lips.

He left a backpack on the sidewalk along the parade route. Made his way north a block before it detonated. Two people died in the explosion. One more from his injuries the next morning.

From there, he headed west but was stopped by police trying to control the panicked crowd and evacuate people to safety. They had no idea he was the bomber, but for whatever reason, Shamir pulled out a gun and fired at police. He killed one officer before being shot himself.

Jade gasps when his photo comes up, loud enough that Maybe-Elliot glances over, then quickly away when he sees he's been noticed. Jade ignores him.

The man staring back at her is so young, only a few years older than Eran. So much of him is familiar. Nose, forehead, eyebrows, messy hair. Those gray eyes.

The smile. It's unnerving, like seeing someone you know in an unfamiliar place, wearing unfamiliar clothes. A version of them, not quite right and not quite them, but close enough to be disorienting.

She blinks and Dani Shamir is gone, replaced by a black screen. Jade groans, calculating how much time is left of the trip home.

"You should get one of those portable battery cases. I have one and it's pretty sick," Maybe-Elliot says, then blinks a few times as if his words took even him by surprise. He turns back to stare at the seat in front of him, nonplussed

Jade counts the trees that rush by.

The house is hers for sixty minutes, each one precious. A perk of having a sister in middle school and two working parents. Jade rushes inside, is halfway up the stairs before the front door closes behind her.

The charger is forever plugged into the outlet by her desk, a permanent fixture. She connects her phone. It comes to life seconds later, but her laptop is already on.

Her breath catches when she sees the headline. For a moment, there is perfect silence in her room. The air conditioner almost sounds apologetic when it ticks on.

Ma has taught her to recognize reluctance. She sees it in the courtroom all the time.

"Plenty of attorneys are forced into cases they don't want," Ma told her once. "You can tell by the words they choose, in their written briefs and before the judge. They use sterile language, technicalities, that sort of thing. And that's in a profession already filled to the brim with sterility."

Jade reads this reluctance now, in Benson Domani's words.

His is the voice of someone writing out of obligation rather than want.

Only the headline carries some hint of dramatics: "For a Young Activist, a Dark Past." She wonders if Domani had anything to do with that but doubts it. His article lays out the facts as dryly as possible:

There was a small protest against the Constant Vigilance program in Kiley Springs on Saturday.

One of the leaders, seventeen-year-old Eran Sharon, is the son of Dani Shamir, who killed four people in an act of domestic terrorism fifteen years ago in New York. At the time, Eran was not quite two years old.

Eran's mother, Tamar Sharon, changed her name from Devorah Shamir shortly after the bombing and moved her son across the country. Since she was found not to have been involved in, or known anything about, the attack, interest in her had faded. She was able to blend in.

But the connection was made when she used the same curious expression during a news report about Eran's protest that she had famously used fifteen years before at a press conference: "This is not our fight."

Domani clings to those words, that sentence, like a lifeline. It is his justification for writing his article, for shining a light onto this family's past when he knows better.

She closes the tab with the article and searches instead for an account of the bombing itself.

The first thing she finds is an old blog post, written by a survivor.

There were no clouds.

The parade route went down Fifth Avenue. It was summer, and Manhattan gets hotter in the summer than people realize, so organizers had set up a number of spots to hand out cups of water to marchers and spectators alike.

I stepped off the route near Sixty-Third Street at one of these water stations, mopping beads of sweat from my forehead. I sipped from the paper cup while watching my group, Temple Beyt Elohim, march slowly past. I'd catch up with them in a minute.

Central Park stood vast and open behind me while I drank. The zoo would be right there behind me. The water gave me a small chill. Cold water has a certain taste on a hot day.

The parade inched forward, and for a second I could see through to the other side of the street. There was a backpack sitting there, near the parade line. It barely registered at first, and I let it fade into the background.

Then it clicked. I looked up. It didn't seem like the bag belonged to any of the people standing near it. The woman nearest barely regarded it, maintaining a polite distance.

I watched the backpack and the people around it

over the rim of my cup. I don't consider myself to be a paranoid person, understand. That made me hesitate. But my eyes flicked over to my group, and I thought of all those MTA signs — If You See Something, Say Something, right?—and I made up my mind, even if I felt dumb about it.

"Hey," I said to the lady behind the water table, tossing my cup in the large bin beside her. "Someone —"

That was all I got out before the explosion. I felt myself being lifted off my feet; I could see farther into the park as I rose higher and higher, carried as if by wind, and I thought, *Oh.*

I slammed into the low brick wall lining the park, and my senses slammed back into me. My ears were ringing, muffling the screaming I could just make out, giving it a faraway, non-urgent quality. I was half-aware that my arm was shattered.

Most of the rest I learned watching the news in the hospital. That only a few minutes later, a man named Dani Shamir pulled a gun on police who were trying to evacuate people through Madison Avenue. He was only a block away, but in the chaos, I never heard the gunfire that killed him and one officer.

There were no clouds, so the smoke could be seen from all over the city.

Jade leans back in her chair, studying her laptop screen. She wonders why Dani Shamir pulled his gun. Had he panicked? Did he think he'd been caught? Was he never planning to survive anyway?

She can't make sense of it. The questions distract her, taking up too much space in her mind to think of anything else.

She does not want to be at this table.

Jade lifts a spoonful of creamed spinach, lets it hover an inch above her plate, and remembers a dinner conversation from middle school.

They were talking about barbecue. Comparing favorite dishes. It was a pleasant enough conversation, until Father slipped.

"There was that barbecue place, couple blocks over. You remember," he said then. Jade let her father's slow rumble of a voice roll over her like first thunder and froze. "Some fancy name. The Chesterton?"

Ma's eyes locked on that face. She swallowed a bite of creamed spinach, considering him. Dangling from her wrist, the bracelet she always tugged at absently when Father strayed too close to the subject. Three stones: one blue, one green, and one foggy white with a rainbow burst of colors trapped inside, like a captive nebula.

"Chester's. Just Chester's." Her voice was quieter even than normal, but Father missed the warning.

"Chester's, that's right." The wrinkles around his eyes threatened a wistful smile. "You loved that place. The potato salad."

"Let's talk about something else," Ma snapped.

The wall clock ticked.

"Of course," Father said, chastened. "I'm sorry."

Later, Sapphire asked Jade why Ma was angry. She was still young.

"Ma doesn't like talking about New Orleans, Saph," Jade said, in the bossy annoyed voice she used to use with her little sister. "You know that."

Jade puts her spoon down now as Father laughs at something, a stray comment of Sapphire's she missed. She watches the water in her glass vibrate with each of her father's deep chuckles. At the last ripple, she glances at Ma, finds her already watching her.

The grooves in her face never change, rarely make room for a smile. The lines on her forehead are there so often they're permanent by now.

Jade scowls at her spoon. "Can I be excused?"

She chances a brief look. Ma's eyebrows are raised.

"You haven't finished your pork," she says.

"I'm done." Jade stands and grabs her plate. The creamed spinach sloshes perilously close to the edge.

"Jade —" her father calls from behind, but she's already gone.

She closes the door behind her and stalks to her desk, yanking open the bottom drawer.

It's the only thing in there.

Jade glares at it for a few moments, then reaches down.

The frailty of it still surprises her. She holds the photo by the edges, afraid to smudge it and unsure why. The thought exasperates her.

Whose turn is it to take out the garbage? She thinks back.

Sapphire did it Thursday, so Jade will be asked to tomorrow. She glances at the small trash can by her desk.

There are two light taps, then a third. Sapphire's.

"Yeah," Jade says. Her sister lets the door swing wide open on its hinges, her signature move. But her eyes snap to the photo. She reaches out a hand to catch the door and closes it quietly behind her.

"What was that about?" she asks, eyes on Jade's hands.

Jade sighs. "I dunno. I get tired of Ma being so stern all the time. So worried."

Sapphire rubs her arm and steps closer. "She wasn't worried. Father was laughing."

Jade grimaces, weighing a response. This has touched a nerve with her before. Ma doesn't seem to worry after Sapphire the way she does Jade. Sapphire wouldn't notice Ma's anxieties because she's rarely the focus of them.

But she doesn't want to say this to her sister.

"You have to know how to look for it, Saph," she says finally.

Her sister rolls her eyes. It's an exaggerated move, meant for comedic effect, but Jade doesn't feel like laughing.

Sapphire takes another step and gestures at the photo. "Why'd you take that, anyway?"

Jade's face sags a little as she turns back to the picture of herself, riding a tricycle on a long-forgotten sidewalk. "I dunno."

Sapphire giggles. "Yeah, you do."

A beat.

"You've been acting kind of weird today."

Jade sighs and puts the photo on the desktop.

"Just distracted."

When Sapphire leaves, she closes the door and watches a video.

Eran's mother, gripping his arm, unsteady in the frame of a handheld camera.

This is not our fight.

The image changes, and she stands in front of a podium, microphones nearly covering her face. She looks younger and older at the same time, today's wrinkles traded for yesterday's gaunt and hollow-faced fatigue. She reads from a piece of paper and then looks up. Hazel eyes.

This is not our fight.

Jade takes in a slow breath. The comparison, the then-and-nowness of it, is remarkable.

She wonders about that phrase, its origins and reasons. She wonders if this is simply Miss Sharon's way of putting as much as possible between the two of them and the acts of her dead husband.

Jade stops after this thought, frowning at the wall, suddenly unsure of a name.

Yes.

Miss Sharon, she decides. She would still want to be called Miss Sharon.

Ma's knock. Jade knows it.

She clicks open a new window, hiding her screen.

"Yes?"

Just in time, she remembers the photo on the desk and places her hand over it as Ma opens the door.

"Jade, honey." Ma is trying to make her face inscrutable, but Jade is well practiced.

"Hi, Ma."

"Jade, I wanted to ask you about that boy," Ma says, massaging the space between her thumb and forefinger. She gives so much away.

Which boy? Jade almost asks. But Ma is not stupid; it would just confirm to her that Jade is hiding something.

"The one from the protest," Jade says instead.

"The one from the news," Ma answers. "Jade, how well do you know Eran Sharon?"

The name sounds strange on her tongue, as if she's reading it for the first time.

"Not very. Friend of a friend."

Ma watches her, quiet, long enough to stir Jade's nerves a bit. She worries that her hand looks unnatural resting on the photo. It's an awkward position.

"Might be best if it stays that way," Ma says, finally. "I don't think it'd be a good idea to get mixed up with him."

Jade shrugs and turns back to her laptop. She learned long ago how to ward off further questions. "Sure."

Her eyes stay on a fixed spot on her laptop screen, but her attention is on Ma, marking the moment she turns and walks out of the room.

Jade lets out a slow breath. She moves her hand, uncovering

the old photo of herself. Jade picks it up again as if it calls to her, giving her three-year-old self a glance and then turning it over.

Her eyes flick lazily between the repeating Kodak logo watermarks, a barely visible gold on beige, and then on a string of tiny numbers and letters printed down the middle by some ancient machine.

In the middle of this string:

24NOV2002

Jade blinks twice, and then the significance of this date hits her.

She would've been barely a year old in November 2002.

She turns it back over and brings the image close to her eyes. She takes stock of the blur, of her own face tilted barely away from the camera, looking for things that could obscure her age.

But, no. There's no way she could ride a tricycle that big when she was that young. She is unmistakably an older toddler in this photo.

That's you, honey bunny.

She feels the unpleasant tingle in her gut first, feels it spread outward, to her chest, her waist, her arms, her legs, her cheeks.

Jade places the photo faceup in the empty drawer of her desk, centered, parallel to the edges. She leaves it that way for a while, keeping a steady eye on her tiny young self as if the image might change at any moment.

But eventually she presses the drawer closed, relishing the smooth scraping sound of wood on wood, pushing a secret away from the light and out of view.

DEVORAH

She pictures the man as she speaks of him, holds his image in her mind. She does not know why. She should feel anger, even hatred. Perhaps the seedlings of those feelings have already begun to sprout, but they are young and too small to cast a shadow. This man was her husband, and love is not a switch one can flip.

But she knows she cannot say that.

So her words dance around him instead, reducing his personality to a recitation of facts meant to sound dispassionate. She converts the idiosyncrasies and quirks she loved about him to worrying eccentricities meant to signal the warning signs that she missed. In this way, she hides the love she still feels, the love that shames her. And in this way, she offers apologies she knows she must feel, and perhaps will later.

Dani was a sly man who loved to tease her, who loved to plan surprises over a period of months, dropping false hints and misdirections throughout. Instead she says, "Dani kept many secrets."

Dani was a passionate man who would lose himself sometimes in the turmoil of his own zeal, who would find his highest bliss asserting his convictions. Instead, she says, "Dani at times became intense."

It is dishonest, she knows, but honesty is dangerous.

For her, yes. But more so for Avi.

ERAN

VII

Eema sits at the breakfast table, not meeting my eyes.

"What is the best way to tell you?" she mutters.

Imagine an ordinary day. That is how all great or terrible days start, as ordinary days.

Imagine a father who heads to work. Imagine a boy, just under two years old.

This man kisses his boy as he does every morning. There is laughter, like every morning. Then he leaves.

This boy's *eema* plays with her son. She feeds him; she gives him a bath. She smiles at his squeals, and then at his crying when she changes his diapers.

She listens to the radio while she cleans the bathroom. There has been a bombing at the parade. She is disturbed. She wonders who would want to target people like her here.

She puts her son down for a nap. She writes a little; she tries to do some work. She naps too. When they awake, she takes him to the park nearby. He watches the world from a stroller. Everything is new to him.

She turns on the news when they return. Four people dead, including the bomber. She frets while she feeds her son, wondering what world they have brought him into.

It is late, and the man is still not home. She wonders if there is traffic from the bombing.

She is walking to the phone when several men kick in the door to her kitchen. She screams and runs to her son, scooping him up in her arms, holding him close. More men break down her front door. They are all in black, they are shouting, they have guns.

She is sobbing, shielding her son from them. But they take him from her anyway. She screams for him as they force her to the ground. He screams for her.

She does not know how long she lies there, wailing for her son. Other men have come now, men wearing wrinkled jackets and ties. They tell the men with guns to let her up. They try to calm her. Eventually, they give her back her son.

Holding him, she can feel her heartbeat begin to slow. He has calmed again, is back to normal. The relief overwhelms her. Then the men in jackets and ties explain.

She watches her son, looks at his smiles and gurgles and laughs, as her heart freezes, then shatters.

Her husband will never come home.

Why did he do this? How much did he talk about his political views at home? How long was he planning it? Who else was involved? Was she? What did she know?

They ask her these questions over and over. They look at her with hard eyes. She sees their suspicion. She is so tired and afraid, it does not occur to her to ask for a lawyer.

It is late when they leave. She knows it is a mistake to turn on the television even as she reaches for the remote.

He is smiling back at her. The last time she saw him smile was in person, this morning. The photo the news has is from their wedding, her own face cropped out. This woman lets out a long, low moan, a sound she did not know she could make, and turns the television off.

She locks her windows, moves furniture in front of her broken doors. She is too exhausted to cry, but she cannot sleep. She sits on her couch with her son for hours into the night. In a hospital miles away, another man dies from his wounds while she stays up. She learns this later.

The men come back the next day and the day after that. They ask more questions. But finally, finally it becomes clear to them she was not involved. She watches their expressions change, from suspicion to disdain. This pathetic woman who did not know her own husband.

She cannot see more than a few hours in front of her. What happens now, to her boy, to herself? She has no family here, few friends. She cannot face her sister in Tel Aviv, who has never liked this man, who told her not to marry him. And she cannot return to Israel, where the bombing has become big news in its own way.

She is alone with her son.

Her phone rings all the time: questions from reporters, threats from angry men, prank calls. She always answers it, though she does not know why. And then, one day, she is rewarded. A young lawyer from the ACLU offers to help her for free. It is a sign of her desperation that she trusts him immediately. She has no energy for doubt.

He helps her navigate the police and the prosecutors. He answers questions she has, sometimes well into the night. And finally, he persuades her to speak to the press.

He nudges gently at first, anticipating her fear. But he is persistent, telling her it will help people understand she is a victim as well and will stop the press from hounding her. Exhaustion convinces her to try. What could it hurt?

So a few days later, she stands in front of her home, before a podium filled with microphones. She avoids looking into the faces of the crowd. She does not want to meet their eyes. She reads from a single piece of paper.

Her voice shakes as she offers sorrow for those her husband killed, which cannot be enough. She tells the small crowd she has come to understand that this man was not who she thought he was. She had never known the darkness in his heart. Her only concern now is for her small son, a tiny boy who will one day learn where he came from. She wants to put that day off as long as she can.

For now, she wants only to move on, to let him live the life he deserves. His father committed an act of perfect evil, one that cheated four people of their lives and four families of their loved ones. But that was him, not her son.

She looks up to the crowd for the first time and says the only line that day not written on her paper.

This is not our fight.

She imagines her microphone sending the words out into the world, into space, broadcast forever.

She leaves as the crowd explodes with questions.

Those last five words become headlines. There are mixed reactions. Some see it as indulgent, as self-serving and defensive. Others understand.

She decides that night, while watching herself on the news, to leave New York. She stares into the eyes of her tiny son, plotting out a new future for him she never expected.

It is months of preparation, to change her name and her son's, to find a new city, to look for work, to rid herself of her house and possessions and past. But one day she closes the door behind her in a tiny apartment in Kiley Springs, Texas.

She delays a trip to the supermarket as long as she can. But when she finally goes, no one recognizes her. The girl who rings up her eggs and tomatoes and salt and chicory barely gives her a glance.

Eran sleeps through it all.

There's a long silence. It goes on and on, watching both of us the way an alligator watches a curious fawn approach. Waiting for a mistake, hungry, hiding its anticipation perfectly.

I am moving at two speeds at once: blindingly fast on the inside, mind reeling, flipping out; on the outside, frozen, numb, catatonic almost. I imagine sitting still inside a silent ship hurtling through space, watching stars and planets rush by before I have the time to react. So the reverse of that.

The silence compounds this feeling of duality, making it unbearable. So I break it and feed the alligator.

"What was my name?" It's the first thing that comes to mind. Immediately after asking, I realize how badly I want to know.

Eema looks up for the first time.

"Avi."

Avi.

Eema's eyes search mine, and then she looks away again.

"It is short for Avshalom," she says, her face turning sour. "It means 'father of peace.'"

This woman watches her son ride his first tricycle in Texas. She teaches him how to use the toilet, how to dress himself and tie his shoes. She moves them from the tiny apartment to a little house. She sends him off to his first day of school by herself.

It is not how she imagined it.

One day he asks who his father was. She stares at this young boy for a full minute, her heart racing, and tells him his father left when he was a baby.

"Is he coming back?" the boy asks.

"No," she says.

He is still so young.

She watches him grow older, knowing one day she must tell him. But she can't bear it, every time he asks. She shuts down, withdraws into herself. She tries to warn him off with short responses and scowls. She tells herself: Not yet. Not now. Next year.

Her blood boils the day he calls the dead man his *abba*. She snaps at him. How dare this man try to take back her son from beyond the grave, beyond the grave of four others? Her anger is at him, not her son, she knows.

The next morning she takes her boy to get ice cream. He is

confused but accepts it happily. She watches him eat and wills him to understand.

He grows older and older, into his awkward years. Soon he is a teenager. He asks about his father less and less, but looks like him more and more. His energy grows with him; he finds so much to care about, so many things that move him so deeply. This woman watches carefully. She is terrified.

She must tell him. If for no other reason, then as a warning. But she can't.

And then one day, she understands she has waited too long. The choice has been made for her.

Eema drums three fingers on the table, a slow wave from ring to index finger. I never noticed it before.

"You do not have a father, Eran. You have the memory of a man, a shadow that follows us both."

I stare at her for a long time, thinking about too much at once. I can't remember ever trying to process so much at the same time; I can't remember being so mentally exhausted so quickly. In my head I am running around, quarantining questions, stamping out sudden realizations and worries, cordoning off sections of my brain from one another, closing all the doors I find until there's just one left open.

I let this last thought take all my attention, focusing on it to keep the other doors closed, and think about my name. My almost-name. How I would've been someone else. Avi Shamir, some kid in Queens with a different life and a different identity and a past that stayed where it should've.

I look at the lines on Eema's face, the brown roots of her dyed hair, the shadows under her eyes.

I wonder how everyone would've mispronounced Avi.

Then I say, "You could've picked any name for me, and you picked Eran Sharon?"

She looks up again.

"What is wrong with Eran Sharon?"

I don't know why I'm picking this hill. Maybe because it's in front of me. "Everyone mispronounces it."

Eema blinks several times.

"This is the least of your worries now, Eran."

VIII

I don't remember exactly when. Some point Sunday night.

In my room, sitting still, no sound, door closed. I'm staring at a blank spot on the wall, featureless white and lightly textured.

I'm adrift in a slow-moving stream, but the sluggishness of those waters is tense, not lazy: more reluctant than relaxed. Until a thought bobs to the surface and nudges my raft subtly in another direction. Another thought, then another; the raft bounces off floating debris and hidden rocks, cascading toward an unexpected realization.

I sit up, suddenly, eyes wide and alert. I stay that way a moment, two, then grab my phone.

His name feels wrong, typed hurriedly by the blunt ends of my thumbs.

Dani Shamir.

Forever I've wanted to know about him, and here he is. More than I ever imagined I'd be able to learn.

The first result is a photo of him.

It freezes my heart but not my hand. I click on it, which leads to others. A wall of Dani Shamirs. Many of them the same photo, but each subtly different from one another in color or size or crop.

There are others, though, lots. My dad looks back at me, wearing different outfits, sometimes smiling, sometimes serious, sometimes clean-shaven or not, alone or with others. There are some of Eema, younger. One or two of me as Avi. Google Images is the closest thing I have to a family photo album.

I lower the phone, and in the blank white wall I see the negative of his image, inescapable now.

I move automatically. The bedroom door opens and closes; the hallway glides by. The bathroom lock clicks. I turn the fan on after a moment's hesitation, because the added noise feels like a buffer.

My face in the mirror is tense with anticipation, excitement smothered by fear. I look at that face, taking in the rattled eyes and dumb parted mouth. Then I slowly bring my phone back up, pressing the back flat against the glass.

I have to get closer to the mirror to see my father clearly, to compare his features to mine. My eyes shift back and forth, flicking left and right between the photo of him and my own terrified reflection.

His forehead, his darker skin, his lips. His gray eyes. All mine too.

If I could grow more facial hair, this photo could even be mistaken as me. I stare at it for what feels like hours, at the origin of so much of myself. Getting that confirmation now, like this, is the punch line to an awful joke.

Still.

Someone else with my eyes.

The photo takes it out of me, the curiosity to learn more. At least right away. I leave the bathroom and turn off the light and don't really look at my phone anymore the rest of the night, the search I started now forgotten.

The article comes out the next day.

Declan calls me Monday after school. His voice is excited, tentative, afraid. He asks if I saw it.

The day was a blur. I was barely there. I don't remember anything about Physics or English. I think we had a quiz in Government. Did I even take it? Did I just stare at the paper and turn it in blank? Was I just on my phone the whole time, checking it under the desk every two minutes? It's a miracle Mr. Klesko didn't notice, but then he's in his eighties, isn't he?

Of course I saw it, I tell him. Nothing about my voice sounds familiar to me. I wonder what Declan hears in it.

There's just quiet on the other end. A long pause that neither of us wants to end. Then:

"What . . . should I call you now?"

I pull the phone away from my face for a moment, trying to understand what I'm feeling, what I'm supposed to feel now.

I put it back against my ear.

"My name is Eran. I'm still Eran."

Eema picks up the remote in one swift motion, looking at the TV over the tops of her glasses as she turns it off. I listen to the tingle of static, then the house is totally quiet again.

I don't look at her. I get up and walk out and down the hall and close the door to my room.

She was watching an old *Cheers* rerun. We both were. Neither of us are fans; she was just a kid when it was running, and I was two decades behind her. But it was on, and that was enough of an excuse, escape for her and background noise for me, something to keep away the quiet of the house and the roar of our own thoughts.

It wasn't just that. It wasn't just the promise of distraction.

Honestly, I didn't want to be in the same room as her. But I heard those opening piano trills and that weirdly soothing voice, and there was just a moment where I really saw her and how worried she was. She looked up at me from the chair while the theme played, saying nothing, watching to see what I would do. It was just that she looked so helpless.

I never see her looking helpless.

So I sat, and we watched it together. We didn't say anything until halfway through.

"Why Texas?" My voice, croaky from disuse. I didn't want to speak, but the woman on TV looked like Eema, hair and all — especially the hair — and I wanted to say something about that, but this other question came out instead.

Eema kept her eyes on the screen, fingers splayed on the armrests of her recliner, not moving or reacting. But I can tell when she's going to respond to something and when she's not.

"Because it was different and unfamiliar and far," she said finally. "Because it was disconnected from our lives and didn't leave a trail of bread crumbs to tempt us back home." The studio laughter from the show sounded a million miles away, the auditory equivalent of seeing a glimpse of movement through a far-off dirty window. "And it was warm."

"Who's that?" I asked, pointing my chin at the TV, because there was too much else I wanted to ask but didn't want to hear.

"Rhea Perlman," Eema whispered. "She's Jewish, you know."

That was all either of us said though.

And then it's over, and Eema's turning the TV off, and I'm leaving the room.

I watch Declan closely while he walks around to the passenger side. I wouldn't admit it to him, but I'm looking for signs that something's off. He has a loping walk, one that carries him upward with each long step. I follow him through the frame of my windshield. The grime on the glass obscures his face.

"Hey." He seems normal. Mostly normal. As normal as I could've hoped for, I guess.

"Hey. Why am I picking you up here?" I ask. We're outside the tiny convenience shop three blocks from his house. It's gone through maybe six names since I've lived here: Stop-N-Go, U-Stop, 7-Eleven, Marty-Go-Round, a couple others I can't remember. But inside, it's never changed.

He waves two giant Kit Kat bars at me as he turns to put his seat belt on.

"Got you one too."

I'm not hungry, but I take it.

I don't know if people are actually staring or if I'm imagining it. Every quick turn looks furtive, every moment of eye contact looks wide-eyed and prying.

How many kids even follow the news?

I focus on that. This is all I'm thinking about, but that's because it's about me. It's my own past; it's my dad I've wondered about all my life. It's a huge goddamn deal to me.

But would anyone else really care that much? I mean, I'm sure it would grab their interest. But after they remember whatever homework they have to do, or plans to meet up with friends, or whatever else they're worried about or thinking about or interested in, wouldn't they just go on with their regular lives? I grasp on to this and try to calculate how long until life goes back to normal. Three days?

But every eye is on me when I walk into first period. Just as I decide to pretend not to notice, Riskin turns to me.

"Mr. Sharon."

He sounds a little surprised. I grip my Kit Kat a little tighter. My fingertips push into it where their heat has melted the chocolate.

I give him a little nod. I walk to my desk. I add a couple days to my calculation.

He motions to me when the bell rings, just the smallest jerk of his head. I grimace and take my time gathering my books. I want the room empty.

"Mr. Sharon," he says again, lower this time, as I approach his desk. The last kid to leave — pretty sure her name is Alexa — shoots a quick look over her shoulder, fleeting and unsubtle.

He studies me with his sharp eyes, searching my face. I glance away after a few seconds of it.

"How are you doing?" His voice is gentler than I expected.

I look back up. There's nothing hostile or threatening there, just frank curiosity mixed with concern. Or what I hope is concern. I feel a surge of something like gratitude, unexpected and white-hot, and choke it down to keep my eyes from watering.

"Fine."

One eyebrow twitches upward, just a hair.

"Been better."

He holds me with those piercing eyes a few seconds longer, then nods.

"I expect so. I have to say, I'm a little surprised to see you today."

My stomach drops. "Why?"

Riskin tilts his head and looks away, as if thinking how to word what he wants to say.

"You would be forgiven for needing some time off," he says finally.

As soon as he says it, I wish he hadn't. It's just that little bit of confirmation that I'm not the only one thinking of who my dad turned out to be. My heart starts pounding.

"They don't give us vacation days to use up," I say, trying to keep my voice steady, cool, calm, collected. But those eyes are just so piercing, and I clutch my books harder.

"I'm fine," I say, giving him a look that's just a notch below a glare, daring him to respond.

"All right." He looks at me sideways a hair too long before nodding his dismissal.

*   *   *

That look stays with me through PE.

I barely remember what we did. Some kind of circuit training, I think.

Is this a big deal to everyone else too? Should I have stayed home? They don't exactly make a handbook for what to do when you find out your dad was a terrorist at the same time your whole school finds out too.

But I still see it, every time I make eye contact with another kid: the same open stare, unconcealed and unashamed, like I'm being led away in handcuffs. One or two look away when I catch them, but most don't. They just watch.

So I avoid their stares, or try to. It's unnerving, knowing those eyes are on me or that they could be at any moment.

I'm changing in the locker room afterward and suddenly realize I don't remember getting there. The whole period was like this: blips that went by, staccato leaps from one moment to another, a flea making its way across a table. I just blink and suddenly my gym clothes are laid out on the wooden bench in front of me. My jeans are on, my shirt's waiting to be.

I blink a few more times, pull the shirt on over my head, and someone knocks me hard on the back. Just in time I reach a hand up to grab the line of clothes hooks and only keep from falling by landing a knee on the bench.

I yank the shirt down and turn around. I don't know the guy. Keith? Kyle, maybe? We've never spoken before. But he looks back over his shoulder as he walks past, just enough to let me know it was deliberate.

I don't move, even after he's gone, because I don't think to. It's like I've forgotten how, like the pieces of my brain that control this or that muscle are walled off suddenly, and I'm left just staring at my limbs, thinking at them *Go, go, go* while they hang there, useless and dead.

Then the bell rings, my paralysis fades, and I remember what it means to move. I grab my bag.

Outside the hallways are crazy, the usual jumble of kids and noise and laughter and worry. I walk slowly, looking at nothing, taking nothing in.

I don't know him.

I replay the moment of contact, the feel of his shoulder or hand or whatever it was on the top of my back, the shove.

Don't even know his name. It begins with a *K*.

When I reach the cafeteria, I stop.

Hundreds of kids keep moving around me, in my now-panoramic view. A swarm, going in dozens of different directions. It's dizzying.

"What am I doing here?"

I realize a second later I actually muttered this, actually said it out loud, and that realization moves my feet for me, but not in the direction I need to go. I have Pre-Cal next. Norsworthy hinted at a quiz, I remind myself. But my feet still bring me past the main office, toward the three sets of double doors leading outside.

I'm yards away, the sky already visible through the glass, the promise of freedom.

"Mr. Sharon!"

I stop; I turn. The principal leans out of the doorway to the main office.

I've never talked to him. I didn't know he knew my name. It's a big school.

But I mean, I guess a lot of people know my name now.

"I was actually going to call you in next period. Where are you going?"

"I dunno," I say. The truth sounds like an obvious lie sometimes.

"You don't know," he repeats, frowning.

We look at each other across forty feet of hallway.

"With me, please," he says finally, and turns back into the office.

"Did you drive today?"

I look at Dr. Pham warily. He's almost completely bald, with just a few gray hairs struggling on the sides. Deep wrinkles cut across his cheeks, leading down to a thin and disconnected goatee. He has a permanent look of firmness, but there's something else under that.

"Yeah," I say.

"Good." He clasps his hands together on his desk and leans subtly forward. "We need to discuss your behavior at this protest of yours. What were you thinking?"

I'm a little taken aback by his sudden combativeness, if only because for all that severity, I didn't see any anger in his expression.

"He — I barely pushed him. He just lost his balance."

"It was assault, and you're lucky you weren't arrested." Dr. Pham regards me with hard eyes. "You do not go around shoving people, Mr. Sharon. It is unacceptable under any circumstances, but made all the worse when one is representing this school, as you were."

My heart starts beating faster. I make eye contact with a Houston Astros bobblehead on the cabinet behind Dr. Pham. It's wearing one of the old uniforms, red and yellow and orange stripes. It stares back, completely still.

"You are suspended for two weeks, effective immediately."

I snap my attention back to Dr. Pham. "*What?*" The rush of adrenaline is so familiar. I love and hate it at the same time.

"You will be expected to keep up with your schoolwork. Your teachers will create a packet for you each day, which —"

"You're suspending me for pushing —"

"Do not interrupt." Dr. Pham's voice, sharp and direct, cuts through my will to keep talking. "Plan to arrive here between two thirty and three each afternoon to pick up the day's packet."

There's a pause while we both consider each other.

"Someone just shoved me into the changing room bench in PE. How is that different?"

Dr. Pham frowns at this.

"Someone shoved you? Who?"

The something else under his firmness comes out again, slowing my heartbeat for a moment.

"Some kid. I don't know him." I glare as much as I think I can get away with. "Even if you found out who it was, though, would you do anything? Would he get suspended too?"

"Yes," Dr. Pham says, so immediately and so matter-of-factly that I'm at a loss to respond. I watch him sense that he's disarmed me and move on.

"Eran, to be frank, the next week or so may be difficult. It's enormously taxing to become the sudden center of attention even when that attention is positive, which this most certainly is not." His tone has shifted with his role: first a disciplinarian, now an adviser. Even in the moment, I can appreciate the self-control it must take to do this. "You're going to see and hear a lot of unpleasant things directed at you. You may come to welcome this time away from school." He favors me with a searching look. "To let the dust settle."

I look down at his desktop, at the neat arrangement of some hand-selected items, at the persona he's chosen to make visible. An old-fashioned nameplate, a container of hand sanitizer, a mouse pad made to look like an afghan rug. I reach forward and pick up an Astros snow globe because it's there, because it's a distraction, because it fits nicely in my hand, because it is outward-facing and therefore meant for visitors. It snows in Houston maybe once every five years.

"You mean I'll be a distraction to everyone else," I mutter, turning the globe upside down.

Dr. Pham shrugs lightly. "Yes, there is that too."

I blink, not expecting him to be that honest.

"Will it?" I ask after a while, righting the globe.

"Will what?"

I watch the snow swirl, then slow, then still. "The dust settle."

Dr. Pham leans back, studying me. "Yes," he says after a while. "I don't think it could get much more stirred up."

* * *

Outside, it's bright and crisp and quiet. Dry, for once. The shock
of loud and fast to silent and still is jarring but pleasant. I think
about the first time a doctor tested my reflexes as a kid, the light
knock to just under the knee, the tingle that shot up my leg, the
delight that this wasn't just something that happened on TV. Me,
giggling; Eema, allowing a rare tiny smile.

The gravel on the overflow lot crunches under my shoes.
There's barely any other sound.

It's always so weird being outside in the middle of a school
day. Everything feels off, like I'm not supposed to be here and
everyone knows. It's disorienting. Like being at a carnival after it's
closed or on the beach during winter.

I'm at my car. My reflection in the driver's-side window,
warped by the glass. I look at my giant chin and tiny forehead,
and then I open the door and get in and turn the car on and drive
out of the parking lot, and I'm gone, gone.

The drive home is relaxing, soothing, but it also gives me time to
collect thoughts I don't need, time to lower the walls I've erected
to keep those thoughts at bay.

I'm breathing harder by the time I pull into the driveway,
shaking by the time I'm at the front door. The key in my trembling
hand scratches the metal around the keyhole until I bring a second hand in to help steady it.

I drop my bag down near the front door as I feel my energy
click over from frenzy to fury, from adrenaline to rage, wondering

but not really caring in the moment why this transition always feels so deeply satisfying even as it scares me.

Maybe *because* it scares me.

Sometimes I imagine having a superpower, like in a comic book, like one of the X-Men, the kind that manifests during adolescence, when you can't control it but also don't want to. I imagine this rage as a precursor to my own manifestation and clench my fists and wait for the fire to fly. And it doesn't, of course, which only fuels me more.

I slam the door to my room.

I'm suspended. Suspended because this asshole thirty-something got in our faces, wanted to argue with kids half his age and then snowflake the fuck out when I put my finger on his chest. I'm suspended because some douchebag wanted to be smug and racist but didn't want to be called out for it. I'm suspended because he's a clumsy idiot with terrible balance and felt emasculated and needed to cover for that.

But that's not even it, right? That's just the scum floating on top, the bit that hit the air and congealed. Underneath that is the real filth, still rotting away in the bowl.

I just found out who my dad was.

I've wanted to know my whole life. Even after I was old enough to understand he'd be far from perfect, that there would be a reason Eema hated talking about him. But I let myself believe his leaving us was the worst of it. I let myself imagine a man who made mistakes he would be ashamed of now, a decent man with flaws.

Instead it was . . . this.

Instead, my dad was a murderer. Instead, I'm the son of a murderer.

Already some other kid wanted to blame me for it, needed to shoulder-check me to let me know what he thought, to put me in my place before I even have a chance to figure out what that place is myself.

"FUCK!"

I scream this into the enclosed cube of my room because I need the release, but it's still not enough. I grab the first thing I see, an old plastic Snoopy coin bank I got as a kid, and I turn around and hurl it at the wall.

It's still in the air when I wish I could take it back.

Like the shove. Like the fucking shove. I always do this. I'm always past the point of no return when I feel first regret.

I always sober up just in time to watch my mistakes unfold.

I follow its flight through the air toward the wall, my outstretched hand still pointed at it but now desperately trying to pull, praying that this will be the superpower that manifests, that I can stop it in midair and reel it safely back.

It smashes against the corner of the wall and explodes, splinters of plastic and old change — precious when I put it in, forgotten until now — spraying in all directions. It's so crazily cinematic that my rage is instantly erased, drowned out by this shock of theatrics.

The last of the plastic shards rains down around me, a muffled putter on the carpet. The force of it knocked out the paint and a layer of drywall, leaving an egg-sized crater that will need repair. I've had that Snoopy bank since I was eleven.

I always do this.

The focus of my anger shifts, as it always does at this point, as if on autopilot: at Eema for making me like this, for giving me only one person to help shape my personality, for ensuring her worst traits aren't offset by —

And for the first time, those thoughts break down, run into an obstacle that hadn't been there before.

Offset by who? The guy who killed four people?

Two beats of my pulse pounding in my ears, but no other sound.

What if this isn't Eema?

What if I'm not getting this rage from her, like I always thought?

My breath catches. I stare at the chunk of wall I just knocked out, eyes wide. Next to it, six inches to the left, the old Hulk calendar.

What if I get this from my dead father?

Don't you always pride yourself on being so quick-thinking?

You'd never say that to anyone else, not even Declan. But haven't you told yourself it feels like your brain works a million miles a minute when you really get going?

And here you are just getting it.

My mind reels. I play back every memory I can find of Eema's anger, grabbing at them wildly from the library of my mind, a half-mad and desperate archivist.

The fire Zack and I started in the garage when we were ten.

When I gave the principal the finger on a dare in eighth grade.

Just the other day, when I shoved that guy at the protest.

All of those times, wasn't that anger controlled, if considerable? Palpable but contained? I was afraid of her, but she didn't scream. There were no explosions. The opposite, actually: it was always her deadly silence that scared me most.

What about those few times she did lash out? What about the cutting words, the bouts of meanness?

I think about these, piecing together the events that led to them. When I asked about my dad, when I called him *Abba*. When I said I wished he was still around.

All things that involved him.

Jesus.

Eema's always been strict. Hypercritical, reluctant to smile, curmudgeonly. But it's always been a slow-burning temper, hasn't it? A quiet anger.

How did I never see this?

How did I conflate her hushed severity with my furious outbursts? Even as it slows, my breathing is impossibly loud against the backdrop of my thoughts.

What if Eema was the source of the patience I'd always hoped my father had? Only, what if her patience wasn't enough to overcome what my father passed to me?

What if all this time I was worried about turning into her, I was actually turning into him?

I'm sitting on my bed, I realize. The small part of my mind forever occupied with such everyday thoughts wonders how long ago that happened.

*   *   *

You do not have a father, Eema told me.

You have the memory of a man, a shadow that follows us both.
Eema told me.

At some point, after the misery sanded itself into a rounded, blunt
end, I lay down on the bed, kicked my shoes off as I did, letting
them thud onto the carpet.

It gets quiet in the suburbs, even during the day, and there are
times that can be a relief.

Outside. But it gets loud online, and I can't help myself, so
I'm on Twitter.

I got a notification a minute ago. A light buzz that seemed
harmless at the time but was followed by more buzzes. Someone
has connected the dots: my protest was at its roots anti-police; my
father shot a policeman.

I regarded the initial tweets with a sort of dull resignation.
It's just, there were more.

> good thing you didnt have a gun w u at ur i hate
> cops rally @eranaway

And then more.

> Sounds like @eranaway is training to be just like
> dad, this is why we take them out when their
> young

called it. lol theyre always "i dont hate police,"
but then, why are you they always the ones killing
them? gtfo @eranaway

srsly zionists are terrorists, we've been sayin it
for years

My thumbs hover over the screen, waiting for me to make up my mind. The will to respond comes and goes, comes and goes, a swiftly advancing wave that breaks and retreats to regather its courage.

I hear Eema's car door slam just as my thumb presses down on a letter, and I freeze. It's not even eleven o'clock.

I follow the sound of her movements, carrying her from the garage to the back hallway, listening to doors open and close as she makes her way through the house.

Outside my room, her footsteps pause. I stare at the single *S* I've typed on my phone, the beginning of a response I've already forgotten, as she knocks twice.

"Yeah."

She opens the door, and I look at her.

"You are home," she says. Her voice is small and short.

"You too." She doesn't respond, just watches me, and I realize I'm no longer dreading telling her. "I was suspended."

"Suspended."

I nod. The casualness in her voice makes me weirdly uneasy.

"I was not-fired," she says.

"They fired you?" I ask, shocked.

"No. They not-fired me." Her fingers rest lightly on the door-knob. "They asked me to resign, which is less messy."

I just stare at her, not sure what to do or say, absorbing this news on top of everything else that's happened. Outside, a dog barks, and a faraway airplane makes its way across the sky. The sounds of the suburbs.

Then Eema turns around and heads to the living room, closing the door to my room behind her, and I'm left in still silence again.

IX

I find Eema in her bedroom, kneeling, rummaging through her socks. I'm standing in the hallway so that she's framed in the doorway, as if I'm removed from the scene, watching a screen showing someone else's story. A rectangle of quiet torment, a miserable woman going about her day anyway.

"What did he believe?"

She looks up as she sits slowly on her legs and hesitates.

Her instinct is still not to tell me anything, I realize. Out of habit.

"He was more religious than me," she says finally. "He would read the Talmud and show me passages he likes. He believed these passages built Israel, but he believed the Israeli government strayed from their teachings. It made him angry."

I wait, expecting more, but she just looks at me.

It's not much. Barely anything, really. A toe in the water, neither of us sure if we should get in or let it be for now.

I open my mouth to ask another question, but the urge seeps out of me, abrupt but not unexpected.

So I turn around and head back to my room.

When two thirty approaches, I'm waiting for it in my desk chair, rotating slowly and watching the minutes tick by on my phone. School is out.

Reporters called twice. Eema answered the first and hung up without saying a word.

I picked up the second one. The woman's voice came in a breathless rush, before the phone was even all the way up to my ear.

"Hi this is Joanne Aderholt I'm calling for Eran Sharon is he in please?"

I considered it. I could think of a thousand good reasons to take this call.

Instead I followed Eema's cue and put the phone back in the cradle as lightly as I could. It made a gentle and satisfying click.

That was the most exciting thing to happen all day. I mean, besides me being kicked out of school and Eema losing her job. But the hours have worn away the sharpness of the morning's despair, that stabbing pain replaced by a dull, constant throb. It still hurts; it comes in waves now and still makes me feel sick. But it's like carrying a heavy backpack around for hours. You don't exactly get used to it, but it starts slipping more into the background. Until you try to run or squat down or jump, and it reminds you it's there.

Now it's midafternoon and I've been stuck in the house all day with nothing to do. It's weird how fast feelings can . . . not normalize, I guess. But take a backseat, even if just temporarily.

I give it another twenty minutes and call Declan. It takes him three rings.

"Hey?"

"Hey. Did you get my text?"

"Yeah, checked at lunch when you weren't there." He has that same tentative, careful voice. I hate that voice. It's like he thinks I'm about to blow up or something.

I wait for a second, but then realize he's waiting for me to talk.

"Yeah. So. That's why I couldn't give you a ride," I finish lamely.

"That's cool, I took the bus."

Pause.

I don't know what I was expecting. I mean, Declan is usually pretty high energy as it is. I figured he'd be flipping out about everything, maybe even more than I have. But he just seems weirdly subdued.

"Listen. I'm gonna come over, cool? I gotta get out. I've been stuck in the house with just my mom and my own thoughts and I'm going crazy."

"Uh . . . yeah, that's . . . fine."

Pause.

"You okay?" I ask with a little too much force.

"Yeah! Yeah. Come over. For sure," he says, recovering. "Wait, why is your mom home?"

"She got fired."

"She — what?"

"No. I resigned," Eema says, walking past my room. I stretch a leg forward and close the door with my foot.

"I'll tell you about it there," I say.

We go walking with his dog through the woods behind Declan's subdivision. He brought Sky at my insistence.

Almost the minute I get there, he's pushing me out the door.

He says his mom's kinda mad at him because he and Don had a fight, so he doesn't want to be there when she gets home.

These aren't real woods, understand. Like, not an actual forest or anything. Just a huge area full of trees that's still on the subdivision property. At some point they're going to expand his neighborhood and clear the trees and build more houses on this land.

But for now, it's pretty undeveloped and wild, and goes deep enough that we can get some privacy. Kids come in here all the time to smoke and drink and have sex. Every now and then, we run across a small collection of empty cans and condom wrappers.

This far in, Declan can take Sky off the leash. She's old and doesn't stray off the path much, but you can tell she loves being out here.

Declan's parents got her when he was eight. Blue heeler mix, speckled gray fur. The shelter manager thought she was probably abused by her last owners. She's skittish and wary around new people, but once she sees that Declan trusts someone, she'll come up and reluctantly offer a paw in greeting.

That's what I love about her: she confronts her fears. She's my Patronus.

I look at her, searching for her big doleful brown eyes, but her attention is on the trees and the creatures they might be hiding.

"What was school like?" I ask, looking back up.

"It's . . ."

He's being shifty again. I can already tell I've hit on something. My stomach drops a bit.

"Declan, come on. Just tell me."

He sighs and kicks a rock. Sky traces its path with perked ears.

"You know it's not like people are going to tell me directly," he says finally. "They know we're best friends, so they'll be talking behind my back too." Declan kicks another rock, trying to hit the same spot, and misses by a few feet. "But. Yeah. Everyone's talking about it, and now everyone knows you've been suspended, and people are giving me weird looks in the hall."

Weird looks in the hall.

"What about Delia and Bonnie? Did you and Jade tell them?"

"Yeah. I mean. They heard about it before we got a chance." He shrugs. "I think Delia was surprised Jade already knew. But mostly they're just, you know. Shocked. Like everyone else."

"Like everyone —"

"I don't mean like that," he says quickly. "They seemed pretty worried about you."

Something about that word quiets me a second. They're *worried* about me.

We walk a little farther on. "What did your mom say about all this? Oh God, Don, did he say anything?"

"No," Declan says, a little curtly, but switches gears before I can follow up. "Have you been checking your phone?"

I swoop down to scratch the back of Sky's neck. Her ears turn outward at the touch, and she gives a perfunctory flick of her tail, but she stays focused on the world around her.

"I turned notifications off," I tell him. The last time I looked, the number had gone up by another few dozen.

"Well . . . not to freak you out, but there were some reporters at school today."

I get a twinge from turning to him too quickly, and clench my teeth and close my eyes until it passes. "What the actual — They let them in the school?"

"No, they were outside when the last bell rang." Declan picks up a stone, aims for a pinecone. "They interviewed a couple kids in the parking lot till Pham stormed out with campus cops and threatened to have them arrested. Never seen him that pissed," he adds, with a bit of reverence in his voice.

I pull out my phone. "Has there been anything yet?"

"Nah," Declan says. "But . . . you know, maybe check later tonight? Or not."

I scroll through a bit but, when I don't see anything, shove the phone back in my pocket.

"I'm tired of reading about myself."

Declan nods and puts an arm around my shoulders. His way of showing sympathy, but taking the edge off by pretending it's a joke.

It's awkward trying to walk like that and messes up my balance, but I don't mind.

We stay out wandering for a couple hours but head back when we notice Sky slowing down. I keep forgetting it's harder for her to keep up now. She's been around forever.

A few houses away from his, Declan stops suddenly, looking ahead.

"Shit," he mutters.

"What?" I ask, following his gaze, heart already pounding. It's been a tense few days, and I feel like I'm on edge for almost anything.

Declan nods ahead of him. "Don's home."

His brother's car is in the driveway. It's their dad's old Jeep from like twenty years ago. Faded red, zip-up windows. Donovan hates it because it has this weird smell, but it's his own fault because he never cleans it out and leaves trash all over the floor. I think it's kind of a kickass car. At least the AC works.

I'm confused by the intensity of Declan's reaction, and maybe a little put off by the scare. But before I can ask anything, he starts reluctantly toward the house again.

I take a detour on the way home. Declan insists I shouldn't stay, since his mom could be home any minute. But it's only six o'clock. I don't want to go home yet.

So instead I drive around Kiley, just to be out. It's kinda peaceful actually, even if it is a little hot. Outside, I watch the strip malls and elementary schools and neighborhood signs roll lazily by. I think about how these gross chain stores and cookie-cutter brick houses are the only things I've ever known in my life.

I wonder what I'm doing right now in another universe, where I'm still Avi Shamir. Do I have a car in Queens? Do I take the train into Manhattan after school and, like, get lit or something?

I guess not. It's not like I'm a big party guy or anything.

But what if Avi is? Like, how much of me is whatever I was born with, and how much is because of what I've lived through? Maybe I'd have a totally different personality. Maybe I'd be quiet or shy or really bratty or super cheerful. Maybe I'd be into baseball, or love Dunkin' Donuts or something. Maybe I'd have a thick Queens accent and wear cargo shorts all the time.

Or not. What if you are born with your personality?

What if it's all hereditary? I frown at this.

It's minutes before I realize I've gone down a familiar rabbit hole. I shake my head to clear it, feeling drops of sweat trickle down my temple, and see that I've driven up to Avery Park while on autopilot.

I slow down as it slips by on the right, tracing the path of our march with my eyes. Lingering on the spot where I shoved that Arnie guy.

Jesus, if I hadn't pushed him. I guess I'd still be living my regular Eran life, no one knowing I was the son of a terrorist. Heading unaware toward some other point in the future where it would inevitably come out.

A thousand more universes split out in front of me. Different mes living parallel lives, then diverging at different moments from one another —

I exhale, letting it out long and slow. It is more than a sigh.

I've been avoiding going home because I didn't want to think about all this, and I believed home had become the place where I think about all this.

But more likely, it just happens when I'm alone, wherever I am.

I breathe out again, blowing my thoughts away, and turn my car in the direction of home.

* * *

The wind has dried the sweat on my face by the time I pull into our driveway.

I take my time. Even though it won't do any good, I take my time.

Eema's in the living room, the TV on mute. She ignores it in favor of her Sudoku book. She gives me a small nod when I walk in through the front door, then goes back to her puzzle.

The phone rings before I've made it two steps. Eema doesn't react, just peers down her glasses at her book and makes a delicate mark.

"Are you gonna get that?" I ask. The phone is inches away on the end table.

Eema's pen hovers over a page as she decides on the right box to fill in, then swoops down and makes another mark.

"No."

A small green light at the base of the phone flashes. It means unopened voicemail.

"Eema?" I call out, staring at the light.

"Ignore it," she answers after a moment. "They are reporters. They pretend to be your friend while they try to trap you."

Her tone floats somewhere in the space between bitterness and resigned amusement.

"When did they start calling?" I ask. The light blinks five times before she answers.

"About an hour ago."

An hour ago Declan and I were still in the woods but heading back. I've been avoiding looking at my phone since then.

The phone cuts out in the middle of the fourth ring. Eema pays it no mind.

I let out a sigh through my nose, turn on my heel, and head to my room to watch the other shoe drop.

Kristen talks about me like I'm a stranger. That's the weirdest part.

"I just never expected that there would be someone like that in one of my classes," she tells someone offscreen. We've been in those classes together, off and on, since sixth grade. I sat behind her in Life Science, and we worked on a *Romeo and Juliet* project together freshman year. Last year she interviewed me for some story in the yearbook about the dress code. She has three older sisters. The oldest two are twins who hate each other. "It's just strange that he could be sitting a few desks over, and all this time he had this violent past he didn't tell anyone about."

T.J. talks about "the signs." About how I've always been really into protesting and always angry about something going on the world. I try to recall any conversations I've had with him that went beyond just SAT scores.

Only Jillian seems a little nervous talking to the reporter. She sits two seats behind me in Riskin's class.

"Well, we were talking about rioting and stuff," she says.

The reporter pushes, and Jillian fidgets.

"Like, our teacher asked if it was okay to be violent in a protest, like with the Israel and Palestine thing, or with police. Since sometimes in history that's happened and like now we're cool with it. Like the American Revolution."

What'd Eran say?

"Just that . . . I guess, that sometimes violence is okay."

Does he want a revolution?

This question especially seems to make her uncomfortable.

"I mean . . ." She cracks her knuckles, one by one. "I dunno. He didn't say anything about that, just that, like, it's okay to be violent if you're desperate." Reluctance makes her voice trail off at the end.

I grind my teeth, wishing there was a way I could respond to all this. That's not what I said.

Or at least not how I said it.

These are kids I know on sight. They've been around since elementary school. We're not exactly friends, but we've always been friendly.

And now it's like they don't even know me.

I watch Eema closely. She spends most of the evening sitting in the living room, alternating between reading and staring at but not really watching the TV. For dinner she mixes canned tuna with pasta. Something she does when she's busy or tired.

The phone rings two more times. It takes everything in me not to answer it.

At eight o'clock she finally tells me she's going to take a shower.

I force myself to wait a full minute, until I'm sure I hear the water running. Then I grab the phone from the living room and turn the ringer volume to the lowest it'll go.

The phone in the study is older. I unplug it and hope Eema won't notice.

In front of her bedroom door, I pause, hand hovering over

the knob. I move as slowly as possible, satisfied when I've turned it all the way without making a sound. I push it open, then creep into the room and toward her nightstand, eyes on the door to the attached bathroom. The shower's still on, but I don't know for how long.

I turn the ringer off on her phone, then silently pad out of her bedroom and close the door behind me.

Back in my room, I shut my door and slump into my desk chair, leaving the living room phone next to my laptop.

And I wait.

It's another thirty minutes before a faint ring drifts meekly from the desk. My hand flashes forward, faster than I expected, heart lurching as I press the Talk button.

I stay perfectly still, phone away from my head, listening to the rest of the house. Eema is long out of the shower, but I hear water running. I think she's washing dishes.

Then a tinny voice from the receiver: "Hello?"

I bring the phone to my ear.

"Hello."

"Hi . . . Is this —"

"It's Eran Sharon."

The other voice quickens.

"Eran, thank you for picking up. I'm Justin Gils, I'm a reporter with the *Post,* I just had some —"

"Yeah, ask away," I cut in. There's a moment while Justin collects himself on the other end. Then he recovers and launches back into it.

"Okay. Can you explain your views on Houston's Constant Vigilance program and on police in general?"

"Yeah," I say, not missing a beat. "Constant Vigilance is stupid. Why are we giving police power to pull us over any time they want, for any reason, even when we haven't done anything, and then even saying they won't get reviewed or punished or whatever if it turns out they pulled us over by mistake? Like, we're all supposed to follow the rules, right? So shouldn't police have to follow their rules too? If not, isn't that basically a police state, where they have total power and there's no, uh, oversight? And isn't there a little thing called the Fifth Amendment, or maybe the Fourth, I don't remember"— my face grows a little warm —"but I mean the one about no unreasonable searches, and needing warrants, and that kind of thing? I don't have anything against police. I just think that if we give them more and more power, without any oversight at all, of course they're going to abuse it. Anyone would, right?"

My voice gets faster and louder, taking on a life of its own, then gives way abruptly to the distant sound of furious typing. I give Justin a few moments to catch up.

"Okay. Some of your schoolmates have claimed that you've made some statements in class advocating for violence. Can you —"

"No, I didn't. I just said that sometimes protests become violent, and we've been okay with that in history. That's just fact."

"Are you okay with violent protests?" Justin asks.

"I —"

I drum my fingers on the desk, forcing myself to wait three seconds.

"Okay, what about Stonewall? Or the riots that happened because of, like, segregation and stuff?" I ask, more slowly. "Does anyone today think those were not okay? Because the police were racist and homophobic. Or what about the Revolutionary War? I mean, people started shooting actual muskets and shit at authority figures, the British, and now we celebrate them on the Fourth of July. So what's the difference?"

Justin types, but I can hear the next question ready to burst out in the seconds it takes him to catch up.

"Isn't that what your father believed? What do you think about what he did?"

I was waiting for this question, expecting it, but that foresight does nothing to keep my heart from skipping.

"I dunno, what do you think about it?" I snap. "Why are you asking me? I didn't know him any better than you did. He was just some guy."

No typing now.

"Just some guy?" Justin asks after a second.

The steady background noise of water in old pipes shuts off. I glance at the door, turning my desk chair side to side, and lower my voice.

"Yeah. I never met him. I mean, not since I was two. I have no idea what he believed." I wonder if my voice has actually taken on the urgent quality I hear in it, if Justin can hear it too, or if it's my imagination.

"Do you think you might be like him at all?" he asks.

My face burns, and I'm thankful he can't see me. I shift the phone into my other hand and try to keep cool. "No. I never knew the guy. Listen, I gotta go."

"Eran, what about —"

"Gotta go, bye." His voice cuts out with a muted beep. I give myself three seconds.

Go, Eran.

But I can't move just yet.

Go!

Something finally clicks, and I stand abruptly. My desk chair's still spinning slowly behind me when I head out of my room to sneak the phone back to its cradle.

DEVORAH

Her finger caresses the words she speaks, as if coaxing them to be more gentle.

She pauses, just for a fraction of a moment, at the end of a paragraph halfway down her sheet. She is nervous about the next sentences, the pieces the young lawyer said would be necessary but would have a mixed reception.

Some people won't be happy unless you admit to things you didn't do, *he told her.* You're the only one who can protect yourself. And your son.

The last three words carried intent, meant to push her, she knew. But they were effective. He is a persuasive man.

So she continues.

"I understand the anger directed at me," *she says. She has to pause again as the microphone picks up feedback and the speakers squeal, as if in protest of her words. It lasts only a second.* "I understand people are hurt, and I understand if that hurt turns to hatred."

She clears her throat and forces out the rest.

"But these were Dani's actions. He committed them without me and without my knowledge. He lived in a world inside his own head that he never revealed to me." *Her voice lowers on its own.* "I wish he had. I wish he had confided in me, so that I could stop him. And so that I could know."

The small crowd is even more still, somehow. Without looking up, without seeing them as she speaks, she feels alone.

"I realize now that I never truly knew my own husband," she says, and swallows a deep, aching misery at the truth of those words.

ERAN

X

The sudden rumble and acceleration is unexpected, so Eema unbuckles his seat belt and puts him in her lap, holding him close. The flight attendants are already seated; from here they are unseen. There's no one to object. The old lady in the aisle seat smiles at them both.

The pressure builds in her son's ears almost immediately. He puts his hands over them, face scrunching from the discomfort, so she points to the window to distract him.

He looks, watches the water and the buildings and the highways, the cemetery and towers and the few trees, getting smaller and smaller. For the first time, he has a glimpse of the size of this world he inhabits. It's not about having the words to describe it — he has so far to go before that vocabulary begins building itself with its first clumsy, lurching words — it's that he's still years from even the capacity to understand what he sees, what the implications are. But still, on some basic level, he recognizes its importance. It is a glimmer of pre-understanding how much there is unknown. It comes in a flash and is gone just as quickly, too intense an unrealized promise for his young mind to cope with. He has never felt humility before.

"Big map?" he says after a moment, voice muted and far away, hushed by the background noise.

Eema looks out now too, watching everything she knew slip away, feeling her new world shrink and tighten around her as it opens wider for her son.

"That was home," she says softly.

"Keens?"

"No, more than Queens. The whole city." She pretends to count the endless spires of Manhattan, crowding the tiny island like rows of sharks' teeth, no room even after the loss of two towers. Beyond it, Jersey City attempts a lame imitation, gives up halfway through, and gradually descends into the lesser buildings and then labyrinthine waterways to the west. "We are leaving."

"Go 'way?" her son asks.

Eema imagines what he looks like from the outside, tiny face framed by thick glass and rounded corners. Shock of dark hair, already coming in fast, spilling down over the tops of his ears.

"Yes," she tells her son. "Far."

He stares out that window, lost now in the enormity of something he cannot grasp, watching his expansive world grow ever larger, and still reaching out to the horizon forever. He watches those buildings, the largest things he'd ever seen before this day, as they shrink into toy versions of themselves, and then tiny dots, and then into nothing, swallowed entirely by a land that has no end, until even that land is swallowed by clouds and the world turns white.

Then the discomfort in his ears turns to pain, and he cries.

* * *

My ears still hurt when I wake up. I yawn to try to pop them, but the pressure buildup isn't real. The phantom pain fades away with the dream. With the memory.

I hear Eema's voice, from another time.

This did not happen.

How many other lies?

I let out a quick breath through my nose, short and humorless, and stretch.

We both sit at the breakfast table, me eating cereal, Eema having just her coffee and a piece of dry toast. She takes mouse-size nibbles out of it periodically, stopping for a break every few bites, like it's the only food we have and it has to last her a month. I'm eating even less.

We don't really look at each other or talk to each other or acknowledge each other. We're both just here.

I feel squirmy today. I felt it a little last night, actually, after the adrenaline wore off and I was left with just the quiet of my own thoughts.

The first creep of doubt came fifteen minutes after the call with Justin Whatever from the *Post*. The first little tingle that made me wonder if I'd made a mistake. I ignored it, pushed it out of my mind, and went to bed. But those doubts hardened overnight, congealed into something firmer and more unpleasant that puts me off my breakfast every time my mind turns to them.

The phone rings three times while Eema nibbles and I stare at my food. I hate that sound, always have. It's jarring and annoying to the point of being almost physically uncomfortable. It's like having someone clap right in your ear as you're falling asleep.

Each time, I jerk in my seat, wanting on impulse to answer the phone just to cut off the sound.

Eema doesn't even flinch, like she can't hear it.

The rest of the time, we just sit and eat in silence. I wonder if this is what it will be like now. If this is how we'll spend our days, around each other but not, occupying the same space without interacting.

Maybe it's that thought that makes me speak.

Because it's the little bit I can control.

Still, it takes me two full minutes to work up the courage to ask.

"What were the passages?"

Eema is in the living room. I'm sitting at the dining table, my back to her, separated only by a low railing that divides the two rooms. I hear her put her pages down, but I don't turn around, stay still and focused, watching the wall that hides the kitchen. Bracing myself for an answer.

"There is one he showed me many times. It says if someone has power to prevent injustice but does not, then he is responsible for this injustice." There is a moment's pause, and I wonder what Eema is doing, what she is looking at as she thinks what else to say. "He would want to talk about this passage endlessly. Sometimes into the night. 'There is injustice everywhere, Devorah, and we are commanded to stop it,' he would tell me."

The wallpaper in this room is a tangle of flower-covered vines on a beige background. It's ugly and old, something left over from the last owners. Eema always said we would change it, but it's aged along with us, untouched and time-proof.

It takes me a moment to realize that name is hers, was hers.

"I asked him how we could ever stop the injustice of the world," Eema continues. I thought she was done. "He would say it is up to us to try."

I find where the pattern repeats in the wallpaper. Eema picks up her pages, and this time her pause doesn't end.

You're thinking it.

Maybe you wouldn't say it, wouldn't dare. But you're thinking it:

He wasn't wrong.

There's a knock around noon. I hear it from my bedroom and walk toward the front door, curious.

Eema's in the living room, watching the door as if she expects it to burst open.

I move toward it.

"Do not," she says.

Then, from the other side: "It's just me, hon!"

Mrs. Redwood, across the street and one house over. I open the door.

She smiles when she sees me, a real one that stretches the wrinkles across her face.

"Jeanie had me bake these for you," she says, shoving a large Tupperware container into my chest. "They're chocolate chip pecan, and they are *very* good. I'm sorry to see them go. How are you two doing?"

Eema stands at the threshold to the living room now.

"Hello, Olivia," she says. "Come in."

Mrs. Redwood waves her off. "I can't, amiga, there's a church group I'm heading to with all the other old crones. Just wanted to drop those off and make sure you're both sane, still."

Eema nods. "Of course. Thank you."

Mrs. Redwood smiles and turns to me.

"You too? Sane, yeah?"

"Yes, Mrs. Redwood."

Her smile falters, just the tiniest bit, and she regards me for a split second longer.

"Well, that's good to hear. But you come to me if you need anything, okay? Both of you."

"Of course," Eema repeats.

Mrs. Redwood gives me one more appraising glance as she leaves.

My room is both comfortable and oppressive. I keep the door closed for a while, then open it when the walls start closing in. Then close it to keep the rest of the house out.

It goes back and forth like that for the better part of an hour, until finally I settle on just leaving the door ajar a little.

My laptop's in front of me. Just sitting there. Waiting.

I don't know if I want to do this yet.

I eat a cookie.

But.

I have the entire Internet in front of me. All this time, my entire life, I've wanted to know more about my dad, and all I had to do was Google him. And now that there's nothing stopping me, I'm still not doing it.

It was looking at him the other day that did it, I know. Seeing him, studying my own face in his, snuffed out the will to find out more right then. I've put this off for three days.

That thought flips a switch somewhere in me, and I scowl at myself.

What good does running ever do?

Dani Shamir.

I scroll past the photo this time.

The first several results are all articles from the last couple days. Most from the *Chronicle* and other local outlets, but a couple from statewide media and one from the AP. My stomach lurches at the last one. This story is spreading.

But what did I expect?

I keep scrolling until I come to some older articles from the actual incident and the immediate aftermath. Reference sites, links to books, "On This Day" remembrances. A sidebar headlined "People also search for," with head shots and names underneath: Omar Mateen, Jared Lee Loughner, Dzhokhar A. Tsarnaev. There's so much, and I'm not sure where to start.

Now that I'm here, now that I've pushed aside my own barriers, I'm surprised by the strength of my curiosity, the way my hunger to learn more brushes aside, for now, the deep ache of shame I feel.

I settle on the Wikipedia page, and I read.

* * *

This is how I learn more of my family history than I've ever known. This is how I discover that my father was born in Jerusalem, that his parents emigrated there from North Africa and died when he was young.

This is how I learn I am half Algerian. This is how I discover why I look the way I do, how a part of me comes from a country I've never thought of, a place I couldn't point to on a map.

This is how I learn my grandparents' names.

From Wikipedia.

I find an old *New York Times* article. Then another. And more. In each one, I pause at the photos of Dani Shamir.

I drink it all in, reading and seeing as much as I can, playing catch-up to a dozen years of stonewalled questions and dead ends.

It's almost two hours before I finally close the laptop.

I sit there, in silence, not moving. Door still ajar. Three minutes pass.

Then I take out my phone. School's been out for an hour. I'm halfway through a text to Declan when I stop. My thumb floats there, then presses down on the backspace. I watch the cursor eat my text in reverse, word after word disappearing.

I still have Jade's number, from the march.

Jade's lost the uneasiness she carried with her in the bathroom on Monday, when I told her and Declan everything. Now she's more like the girl from the march, the girl from the first meeting of SJC. Confident, calm, collected.

Or she's close to that, anyway. Every now and then, I catch a whiff of some edginess, something at the back of her mind. But for the most part, she walks next to me with a sure stride, a steady one-two, one-two of heel to toe. Slow but solid. You could set a metronome to that walk.

I'm relieved but still surprised. Now, looking back, I can see how weird it was that I unloaded in front of her when we barely knew each other, in that restroom with Declan at school. I think in the moment I was barely aware of her being there. I was just freaking out.

I don't know why I texted her. Why in that moment I had an overpowering urge to hang out with her instead of Declan. I wonder if she'll ask.

"Here we are again," she says. She barely raises an arm, covered in a thin, loose sweater too warm for the weather, then lets it drop. A half gesture of welcome for Avery Park, all around us.

I shrug. "I just wanted somewhere quiet. This place keeps pulling me back." I picked her up twenty minutes ago. I'd never been to her neighborhood before, but I remember that it used to be zoned for another school, until they built a new one and restructured the map. Three years earlier and we would never have met.

I let my car idle while she climbed in, watching the house and the face of her sister framed in the upstairs window, thinking about that near miss. *How much of life is dictated by random timing?* I wondered, then remembered that everyone my father killed was a victim of bad timing. My stomach lurched while Jade slammed the car door closed.

She shakes her head now, bringing me back to the present. "I don't mean the park. The path."

We're walking along the perimeter, along the march route. I don't think either of us meant to retrace our steps; it just felt natural and automatic. She chuckles, reading my mind.

"It's like me and my sister. We always sit in the same spots in the car, no matter who's driving. I'm behind the driver's seat, Sapphire's behind the passenger's." She swoops down and picks up a long, thin stick. "Why? Just where we happened to sit the first time, when we got the car five or six years ago. And from then on it was habit."

Jade drags the stick lightly in the grass and dirt between us, making a line.

"My mom and I always sit at the same spot at the dinner table," I say.

Jade nods. "We are creatures of habit." I don't know if "we" means me and her, or everyone.

I don't know if this is small talk. I don't know which of us is supposed to start.

She does. "Where's Declan?"

Despite everything, I make room for the tiniest smile, hidden behind a turn of my head where she can't see it.

"At home, probably," I say, trying to sound casual. "I didn't text him."

She lifts her head, holds it, then nods. Her stride is unbroken.

This time of day, there are only a few other people in the park.

An old couple sits at a picnic table on the other side, closer to the water. I watch them talk to each other, silent from this distance, pausing occasionally to tear off small pieces of bread and toss them at a gathering of ducks. The ducks waddle over with each throw, moving as fast as they can on unsteady bodies. The waves just barely cover their quacks.

"How are you doing, anyway?" she asks.

"I dunno." I follow the line she's drawn in the dirt with her stick, her on the right of it, me on the left. I turn back to see the trail it's made behind us. "I mean, it's weird. I'm just home with my mom, since she got fired." I watch for a reaction to this, but Jade doesn't look surprised. "So I'm just dying to get out all the time. I didn't think I'd miss school, but here we are." I kick a stone. "Not that I'd really want to go back right now."

"Okay," Jade says, "but I mean how are you doing with . . . with everything you've found out?"

The low bushes between the park and the road have been trimmed. I brush my fingers along the flat top as we walk by, feeling the prickle of leaves and twigs.

"Right." The way I say it makes it sound like an admission. An acknowledgment that I was stalling. "I don't know. I don't know what to think. I —"

Jade is patient while I wait for the words.

"I was looking him up today. Researching my own dad on Wikipedia. Which is weird enough, right? But you know they have a 'View history' button to see every time a page has been edited?" I pause to let her respond, but she thinks it's a rhetorical question. "I clicked on that, and it brought up a list of dated links, each one an earlier version of the Wikipedia entry. There were fifty, which kind of took my breath away. Dani Shamir was so well-known that the account of his life and death had already been edited fifty times.

"But then . . ." I take a deep breath, as if recalling the oxygen I lost, as if reclaiming it back. "Then I noticed those fifty edits only went back a couple months. That's when I noticed I could look at five *hundred* at a time. And that still wasn't everything."

My voice is rising, the words coming faster. I let it happen.

"There were pages and pages of cached links, each one just days apart from the ones above and below. The oldest one was from June 2004. There was never a break, Jade. The entry on my dad has been edited thousands of times by hundreds of people every couple days for *fifteen years,* nonstop. Since the day it all happened."

I kick another stone, harder than I mean to, wincing when it just barely misses a duck. She flaps her wings as she scuttles off, chiding me with her quacks.

"All these people who knew so much about my own father, years before I'd heard his name. You get it? This wasn't someone they just read about passively — it's a life and an incident they've studied for years. They are experts on Dani Shamir, and I'm just playing catch-up to a bunch of strangers who've been chronicling every detail they could find about him since the day he killed everyone."

All at once I hit the brakes, and we run into a wall of sudden silence.

Jade is quiet, and I know she's soaking this all in. But I'm not really looking for a response, I realize.

"Anyway. That's just one small part of the whole shebang. More than all that is, uh . . ." I start to scratch my elbow, then stop when I worry it looks timid. "I just — I don't know what it means that I'm related to this guy."

"What do you mean?" she asks.

"Well, like, I never knew him anyway. He didn't raise me. He didn't teach me anything. He could've been anyone, right? A doctor, a plumber, a mountain climber, a rapist. Would it make any difference?"

Jade stays quiet beside me, sensing that there's more. It's a little unnerving, and I think that's why I keep talking.

"But then I think, how much is genetic? You know, nature versus nurture, right? I've always been really, uh"— I make a set of air quotes —"'impassioned,' as I've been told. I get worked up easily. I know that." The path curves away from the bushes as my words run away from me. "So is that just a coincidence? Or did he pass on some weird worked-up-ness DNA to me, and that's why he got it in his head he needed to kill people, and I have the same thing?"

"Whoa, whoa." Jade comes to a full stop. The sudden halt tugs at me, like I'm tethered to her, and I almost lose my balance as I turn to face her. We look at each other for a bit. I'm breathing hard.

"It's not —" I breathe through my nose, a trick Eema taught me once when I was ten. "I don't think I'm a terrorist," I tell her.

"It's just . . ." I shove my hands in my pockets, trying to find the words. "This whole thing has made me think a lot about my name, who I am, who I could've been, that sort of thing. And this part of it makes me wonder how much of what I care about is just, you know, biology."

She's beside me again but says nothing.

Her silence makes me suddenly angry at myself, for divulging so much again to someone I don't know well. Here I am, spilling everything, and there's no reaction, but really, what did I expect?

"What color is Bonnie's hair?" I ask, changing the subject.

"Robin's-egg blue," she says, voice guarded. "Purple highlights."

"Declan told me school's been kind of weird."

"Yeah," she says. "It is."

I run with it, grateful for the distraction. "How?"

She thinks.

"I guess I wasn't expecting to hear about it everywhere," she says finally. "Between people we know, sure. But I overheard a couple freshmen talking about it."

I blink a few times, processing this bit of news, and glance over to the right absently. A middle-aged man sits alone at another picnic table a ways off, smoking from a crushed pack of Marlboros. He finishes one, stubs it out on the table, then pulls out another and lights it. I accidentally make eye contact with him, then look away. I can still feel his stare.

"That, and Mr. Riskin." Jade sighs. "Though Ma said that wasn't surprising."

"Huh?" The mention of Mr. Riskin snaps me back to attention.

"Mr. —" Jade starts, then turns to stone when she realizes I don't know what she's talking about.

Now I stop in my tracks. I stare at her for a minute, until she gives up.

"Mr. Riskin was fired," she says reluctantly.

"What!"

"I thought you'd heard."

"Why!"

She draws in the dirt, moving her stick in a listless figure eight.

"I'm sure it was the interviews they did on campus," she says. "They were kind of damning, Eran. They made it seem like he was encouraging violence and riots."

"He wasn't!"

"I know, but —"

"He was just . . . He was leading a class. He was just talking about the history!"

"Right, but —"

"Like, what the fuck are they even talking about? He was just asking me what I thought was okay, he wasn't saying anything ab —"

"Eran. I know." Jade is able to make her voice cut through mine even without raising its volume. There's something about it, some power, that takes possession of and holds the floor. "But it doesn't matter what actually happened. Think about what it *looks* like. Then imagine legions of angry parents calling the school. Does it matter if they're right or wrong?"

I let myself take a couple breaths. We turn the bend toward the parking lot.

"Wait. Who took over his class?"

"The basketball coach, I think," Jade says.

I glare at the ground. Coach Flynn? I run through the last twenty-four hours in my mind. It's a second before I can be sure it's Wednesday.

"That was . . . That was yesterday," I say, mostly to myself. The days are running together. "They only posted those interviews yesterday."

I make eye contact with the smoking guy again, who puts out another stub and rises from the picnic table. Then Jade catches my eye with hers.

"Yes," she said. "It's happening fast." Maybe it's that quiet power in her voice, or maybe it's because of what isn't being said, but the way she says "it" makes me shudder a little. I glance over her shoulder, at my car waiting for us.

And then.

I feel the confusion and fright giving way to anger. Like clockwork. The relief that it brings is intense and familiar and comfortable. Anger is something I know better, something I can hold on to, something that makes me get to work.

It's just that now, mixed in with the anger, is a pinprick of unease about what that anger means. But I shove it out of my mind anyway, clenching my jaw.

I open my mouth to say something, not knowing yet what it is, but my voice dies in my throat when I see Jade's eyes flick over my shoulder and widen.

I turn around and almost bump right into Marlboro Man. I try to cover, but having someone right behind me while I'm already so on edge makes me almost jump out of my skin.

"What." It's the first thing that comes out, pure instinct.

His face gives nothing away. Up close I can see the deep grooves that carve out his features, sprinkled with day-old gray stubble. "You're that boy."

There it is. My first sighting. I'm recognizable.

"I'm that boy." There's a waver in my voice that I hate when I hear it. It turns what I want to sound unflappable into something scared and defensive. But I can't help it, which makes me hate it more.

The grooves in his face, so still and set before, become unlocked, sliding and repositioning into a new expression: hard, angry, dangerous.

"Why don't you go back where you came from?" he says, taking another step toward me.

"Why don't you mind your own business?" I shoot back, heart pounding.

"You wanna say that again?" He is right there, nearly pressed against me. Close enough to smell the menthol on his breath, a sheer layer of sweet on rank like air freshener sprayed on dog shit.

This feels like last time, with Arnie, the bearded guy with sunglasses. With a jolt, I realize we're almost in the exact same spot.

He's right there. Inches away, waiting like me for the moment to boil over. I make some calculations and realize this could hurt, but find myself bracing for impact as my mouth opens.

"Why don't you get the f—"

I'm half-crazy now with fear and anger and anticipation, intensified as I sense a subtle but building movement — Marlboro Man tensing, bringing an arm up — but a sharp tug at my arm cuts me off, makes him hesitate.

"Let's go." Jade's grip is firm, unyielding.

"Smart to listen to your girlfriend," Marlboro Man jeers, and turns away.

I watch him walk away as Jade pulls me toward the car, but my anger stays. For just a moment, I'm at an edge I find so familiar it's almost comforting. The dividing line between an act I can't take back and a passiveness I will regret later.

I fell on the hasty side of that line with Arnie. I realize this just as I make the same decision again.

"*Fuck* you, you fucking inbred—"

He swings around and my heart skips. Marlboro Man charges toward us, face contorted. We both scramble instinctively the last couple steps and climb in the car.

I slam the door a half second before Marlboro Man reaches us. He pounds a fist against the driver's-side window, making us both jump at the bang.

"*Get out of here!*" he yells.

I fumble with the keys, hand shaking and heart pounding. I see him in my periphery as he bangs on the window a couple more times, and I wonder how strong the glass is.

I aim wildly for the ignition and miss. The keys slip out of my hand, fall to the floor of the bar behind my foot.

Shit shit shit shit shit!

I bump my head on the steering wheel bending down to find them, wincing against the pain. I tense as I grope around blindly, bracing for the sound of fist on glass, but nothing comes.

"Eran . . ." Jade says, pleading, urgent.

I'm flooded with relief when my fingers finally brush the keys, but when I sit up, I can't help looking out the window.

For a second I don't see him, but a movement in my sideview mirror catches my eye.

Marlboro Man is a few feet away now, standing still, a giant chunk of concrete in his hand.

"Jesus!"

He lifts the concrete up, behind his head.

"Go, Eran!"

I throw the car into reverse and peel out, turning into a pivot. I put it in first gear and floor it just as he throws the concrete. It flies into my blind spot and I clench my teeth, waiting for impact. There's a dull thud, too muffled to be coming from the car — he missed, by inches. I see him in my mirror scrambling in the lot for another chunk. But we're already gone.

I drive too fast for half a mile, then see I'm still shaking, my vision getting blurred, and pull abruptly into a Starbucks.

I stop the car. For just a moment there's quiet, and then I look away from the steering wheel, at Jade, as the direction of my anger turns with me. There is poison on my tongue, waiting to be used against someone.

"Why the *fuck* did you —"

"Eran."

She looks at me with the fullness of her being, and my eyes

are no match for hers. My words trail off, and I look straight ahead to avoid looking at her.

My anger, paused, restarts, focuses back on its cause, swells to a climax in the space of two seconds. The acceleration gives me heartburn.

I punch the wheel, relishing the hot pain in my knuckles and the beep of the horn.

"He knew who I was." I can hear my voice shaking.

"Eran," she says again, softer now.

I force myself to look at Jade. Those light brown eyes are speckled with green, like saplings in turned soil. The anger eases enough for me to breathe but stays, skulking in the background, watching for its turn.

"Let's go," she says.

Ten seconds, fifteen, while I press down on my rage. It's stopping a sneeze just as you feel it build. It's clenching your teeth and keeping silent when you burn a finger. I swallow a bitter lump and step down from the ledge.

Torn vinyl, faded Ford logo, stitching in the steering wheel coming undone. I stare at these while waiting to stop shaking, and then I give Jade one quick nod and turn the car back on.

Once you were nine. You skipped a report on a book you hated, and Eema grounded you.

You didn't just yell. You screamed at her, at the top of your lungs. You said things normal nine-year-old boys don't say to their moms.

That wasn't anger. That was something else.

When you were calm again, when you were done crying from frustration and guilt, Eema sat down with you. You two needed a code word, she said, something to remind you that you still love each other even when you're in your red zone. The word should be funny-sounding. *Kalamazoo,* she offered.

She had to say it less than a week later, and it set you off.

SHUT UP! you screamed at her.

There were signs, even back then.

Sia is playing on the drive home after I drop Jade off. It's "Dressed in Black," good head-clearing music. I crank it up, but I don't sing along — I never sing along. I hang my arm out the window, slapping the side of the car to the beat, reveling in the buildup and each false climax. I feel the wind in my fingers. I try to ignore the dangling mirror, the way it swings on its wires and hits the door with every bump in the road.

There's a car parked on the curb in front of our house. Newish tan sedan. I tell myself this isn't really that out of the ordinary, that everything has made me paranoid, right as I pass by and see a young man sitting inside. He's looking down at some papers in his lap. Our eyes meet for the tiniest fraction of a second, just as he glances up and I look away, and for a moment I think maybe he didn't notice.

But if I noticed, he would have too.

I turn into our driveway, leaving him in my blind spot. The engine growls as it slows, bouncing off the pavement beneath me. Sia goes mute just before I turn off the car, and it's quiet enough just then for me to hear his car door slam.

"Hi there!"

He says it as I stand up. I turn around warily.

He's maybe ten years older than me. Or maybe one of those young-looking thirtysomethings. I stare at him over the roof of Eema's old Fiesta, waiting. He goes on when he understands that's the extent of my hello.

"Hey, I'm Roland Stoops, *Southeast Texas Sun.*"

It takes me a second to parse this, to understand that he's talking about a newspaper.

"Okay," I say stiffly, and roll up the car window, bending at a slight but awkward angle to reach the handle.

"I was just wondering if I could ask you some questions." Only now do I hear the drawl, either because it's slight enough or I'm used to hearing it around Kiley Springs. He ambles over, leaving the car between us.

I look him over to stall for time. He's wearing a navy blazer over a light pink button-down and khakis that even I can tell are cheap.

I don't mean that as a dig; I'm just trying to get a sense of where this guy works. Roland Stoops is young; he doesn't make a lot. I take a little comfort in that. This isn't the *New York Times.*

I close the car door, out of time now. I open my mouth to say something — *I've never heard of that paper,* or, *What was your name again?* — anything to win a few more seconds. But the door connecting the garage to the house opens, and Eema is there.

"I told you to leave," she says. There's a lot of force there.

Roland holds his hands out. It's meant to look deferential without actually giving anything up.

"I'm sorry, ma'am, I just wanted to see —"

"Leave," she says.

"Ma'am," he says, pretend-apologetic, "I'm sorry, but the sidewalk is public, and I'm afraid my editor —"

"You are on our driveway. This is not public."

Roland looks down at his feet, then allows a concessionary laugh. "You are right about that, ma'am, fair enough, and I am truly sorry." He takes a few steps backward until he's on the sidewalk, his safe zone.

"Eran, do you think —"

"No." Eema says it a mile before I have a chance to react.

I glance at her for just a second, trying to get a read on the level of her anger, then back at Roland. "I gotta go, sorry," I tell him reluctantly.

Eema steps aside as I walk toward her, holding the door and her glare. I feel it scald the side of my face as I pass, before she turns those eyes away.

"You talked to a reporter." Her voice is calm and even and full of poison.

"Yeah," I reply, and hope my voice sounds defiant.

She glares two seconds, then turns and heads to the kitchen. I listen to her footsteps, angry and quick even on a carpet that should muffle them. I hear the sound of a newspaper being grabbed and swung around. Eema holds it up as she approaches again, shaking it at me.

She still gets the physical newspaper delivered. I don't get why.

"Front page. Congratulations," she spits.

I take it from her, but casually, as if I can't be bothered.

And there it is. Front page, yeah, but all the way at the bottom. Plus it's the *Houston Post,* not the *Chronicle.*

"*Constant Vigilance is stupid.*"

I get the same feeling I always get when confronted with something blunt I said. A blip of uneasiness, the sort of second-guessing I think most people do, which fades immediately once I realize that, yeah, what I said was actually fair. Constant Vigilance is stupid. Unchecked power is *stupid.*

But there are more quotes. I read them and feel my face hardening with each one.

compared the program to a police state

"*of course*" *police will abuse power*

listed past examples of violent protests, "*racist*" *police*

"*Now we celebrate them on the Fourth of July*"

And then, about my dad:

"*Why are you asking me? I didn't know him any better than you did. He was just some guy.*"

How do they keep doing this? How do they keep taking things I say that are objectively reasonable and making them sound worse than they are? It is a *fact* that humans abuse power when there's no one around to stop them. It's a *fact* that society is okay with violence sometimes. It's a goddamn *fact* I didn't know my dad.

I mean, all they're doing is reporting me saying these facts. But I can read the tone in all of this. It's meant to make me look extreme.

And people will pick up on that tone and ignore the facts I'm actually saying.

My lips are tight and my eyes narrowed when I look back up at Eema, and the anger I see in her face doesn't improve my mood.

"Why did you do this." There's no question mark at the end.

"Because I'm tired of reading all this bullshit about me and not being able to tell my side!" It comes out with power and conviction. Good. "I mean, come on! They can just write whatever they want about me, and I'm just supposed to sit and take it?"

"This is not about whether to 'sit and take,'" Eema hisses. "Fighting back like this will make it worse."

"How could it? Do you know what it's like to have an entire city talking about you? Or having thousands of strangers acting like they know everything about you because they read something written by other strangers? Do you know what it's like to have to just let them do that and not be able to defend yourself?"

Eema tries to scoff, but her frustration makes it sound manic. "You are asking me what it is like to be the center of attention and not be able to say anything?"

"You could've!" I shout. "You just didn't, for days, until you gave your stupid little press conference and ran away!"

Eema takes an urgent step toward me. She's a lot shorter than me, so she has to tilt her head back to maintain eye contact.

"I 'ran away' to take you from these people. I kept my silence to keep their cameras off of you, Eran. Do you think I did not want to speak? Do you think I didn't ache to tell everyone everything on my mind? That I didn't want to scream it?" She stabs my chest with her finger, the paper between us. "What do you think would have happened if I did this? Do you think they would have been understanding, sympathetic for the poor wife of a murderer? These same people who thought I was part of his crime, many who still do?"

Eema takes a step backward, eyes moving back and forth between each of mine.

"It would have been more fuel for them. Some people do not have interest in being convinced of a thing. They want a response because they want to shout." She sighs and speaks more gently. "I would have made it worse, Eran. Sometimes you must do what is better for yourself and your family, not what is easy. You have to use good judgment."

Almost. I was almost calmed down. I could feel my pulse slowing, could feel the anger ebbing even as I grasped blindly for it, wanting to hold on a bit longer.

And then, her last few words. A gift.

"Easy? I think staying inside and hiding from the world is pretty *easy*, Eema!" I explode. "I think crying about it and giving yourself excuses not to stand up for yourself is easy. I think what's hard is confronting people when you're right and everyone thinks you're wrong. I think *that* is 'good judgment.' You're gonna talk to me about having good judgment? *You married a fucking terrorist!*"

Eema stares at me, one eyebrow barely raised, face frozen mid-expression. Then she blinks once, slowly, and takes the paper from my hand.

She walks past me, down the hallway, toward her bedroom. And in the doorway, she stops but doesn't turn around.

"You have no self-control, Eran."

She lets the unspoken part hang there in the space behind her as she walks into the bedroom and closes the door.

Your father didn't, either.

XI

My room is darker than normal when I wake up.

I like to leave the curtains open when I sleep, at least this time of year. My bed's right near the window, so at night I watch the stars and the moon arc across the slice of sky I can see. The nearest streetlamp is a few houses down, so the pinpricks of light show up crisp and undiluted. I fall asleep watching them, and then the sun rises right around seven. It's a more gentle and gradual wake-up than an alarm.

Last night I left the curtains closed. It was a clear night with just the thinnest wisp of cloud, pierced by the stars behind it even before it evaporated into nothing. But you can see the street from my window. Just barely, at a sharp angle, but enough to see the cars parked out front.

A woman replaced Roland Stoops yesterday morning, tagging him out like they were wrestling partners. The other reporters came toward the evening. Whether out of a sense of duty or optimism, they each rang the doorbell at their arrival to try for an interview. With each, Eema and I stopped whatever we were doing, which was nothing anyway, and looked up. We sat still, waiting for the moment to pass, until we heard whoever it was retreating back to their car.

I peek out now, exposing a sliver of glass in the curtains, just enough for one eye to see through. There are three old sedans and one news van. I think one of the sedans wasn't there last night. I try to make out faces in the windows, but give up after a minute and let the curtain fall back. The room gets subtly darker.

I guess it's nice to sleep in.

Eema mostly watches TV and works on puzzles. Crosswords, Sudoku, random word games on pages she tears from newspapers and one-a-day calendars. I don't get how she's not driving herself crazy, just sitting around and being.

I try to picture our house in Queens.

From faded stills of what I used to think were dreams, from Eema's description of the day my dad blew everything up.

I can see part of one room in my mind. The room with all the light.

The rest I make up, filling in the holes of my own history, like I've done all my life.

I never realized how small this house is. There is nowhere to go.

So I sit in the backyard.

It's outside, at least. Fenced in, out of view, private. The prison yard for our house.

But at least it's a yard.

I'm leaning against the wishbone tree. It's one of six trees that line the back wooden fence, each one different from the one next to it but all evenly spaced, all lined up like hastily assembled army recruits.

We used to live in an apartment before this place. It was a tiny thing, cramped and suffocating, but at age five I didn't know that. I just knew it didn't have a backyard and a chimney, two things that TV had taught me all homes must have. When we moved, I told Eema I'd only live somewhere with both.

I was with her when we looked at this house, amazed by what to me was an enormous amount of space, more rooms than I'd ever known. Seeing the fireplace, the wooden mantel over white bricks, sent a thrill up my spine. I don't know why. Maybe I associated chimneys with Christmas. We've never celebrated Christmas, but there's no escaping it when you're a kid in the U.S.

But then I looked through the doorway into the breakfast room. Behind it, cheap vertical blinds hid slices of a glass sliding door and, beyond that, what looked like an endless field. It wasn't — it's only a few yards to the back fence. But to me at that age, having come from our little apartment, it was all the space in the world.

I ran out, leaving the vertical blinds swaying and the glass door open behind me, and stopped dead when I saw the wishbone tree. I named it that in my mind at first sight, because of the way the trunk split into two thick branches near the ground. The split was an easy foothold for a five-year-old, and I understood immediately this would be the first tree I would be able to climb. Those six feet were the most I'd ever scaled in my life, and I was still climbing when Eema called me back in to go.

*   *   *

Look, I know it's a real sweet story, blah-blah-blah. But right now this place is just a prison yard with grass.

The wishbone tree's leaves are broad and flat, three wide lobes on each.

You have no self-control, Eran. I always knew this. I've always said it.

Eema says they remind her of the leaves of a fig tree, like the one she had in Israel growing up. They're still green and it's still summer, but a few have already fallen. I pick up the ones nearby, tearing them into thin strips and scattering them around. There's a breeze, at least, and shade. It's better than the house.

I've spent so long trying to understand my anger, thinking I got it from Eema. Even thinking that was why my dad left her.

I grab a clump of grass absently and rip it up.

But so what? So what if I get angry sometimes? Isn't anger useful?

The fence is to my left, running out in front of me, making vertical lines that, as the posts go farther out from my vantage point, get closer and closer together. I follow along with my eyes until the wood changes: a section of older fence, a sad collection of porous and rotting slats, deeply textured by years of heat and rain.

Why should I be trying to tamp this down, if it's who I am? Anger is the only way to get things done sometimes, to force yourself out of passivity and into action. Isn't anger sometimes the only thing that separates the driven from the complacent?

At the very end, in the corner of the backyard next to a balding willow, the bottoms of several posts are missing, a gap-toothed grin running along the ground. I look at them absently, watching a squirrel slip through them into a neighbor's backyard.

Can't anger be a virtue?

I think this just as it clicks what I'm looking at. I get up, quickly.

There's some give to these fence posts when I pull on them.

I turn around, hand resting on the rotting wood. In front is the window to the kitchen. She's not in there, not in the breakfast area through the sliding door either. Last I saw her she was in the living room.

I pull at one of the posts. There's almost no resistance.

I glance over my shoulder again, then pull as much as I can from the bottom. It's almost chest level when the old nails sigh their way out of place, and the fence post comes away in my hand. Old wood dust, damp and musty, covers my palms. I brush it away absently on my jeans.

I pull away at another post, quick and quiet as I can, and then I slip through the hole and into our neighbor's backyard.

I look around. I've never been here, because it's a weird thing to break into someone's backyard, and I don't know these neighbors. Their yard is enormous — there's a lot of open space to be seen. It's the middle of the day, but a lot of our neighbors are old, and I bet a bunch have guns.

Also they probably think I'm a terrorist.

There's a brief moment where I reconsider, but when that's done, I carefully lean the two fence posts back where they were.

I hug the perimeter of their backyard, keeping an eye on their house as I get nearer. Straight ahead is the gate leading to the front yard. I duck under the windows I pass by.

On the other side of the gate, I pause only long enough to make sure no one's coming, then make a beeline for the sidewalk. It's hard to act natural while you're hurrying. I'm pretty sure I don't pull it off.

But no one's there. Only when I can see that for sure, after the furtive glances that finally convince me, do I breathe easier.

A beat, where I listen to the still sounds of the suburbs.

Then I go left.

The neighborhood's pretty quiet.

I take a roundabout way, giving my street a wide berth in case any of the reporters are coming in or out. I wish it were cooler already, hoodie weather. Something to hide in. In my thin T-shirt, I feel so exposed.

But there's really no one around. I get that out-of-place feeling again and think about how rarely I see these streets this early on a weekday afternoon. School is only just now ending.

The sidewalk ends at a row of shrubs running perpendicular to it, guarding the border of our little subdivision. I squeeze past them, onto a sliver of well-manicured grass that abuts a boulevard. A car zooms by and I half turn away, listening carefully to its passing, trying to detect any deceleration. He just keeps going, though. I hunch my shoulders and look down while my heartbeat slows, trying to look anonymous but probably calling more attention to myself. I wait three awkward seconds, then hurry across the boulevard.

These houses are newer. Eema complains about our homeowners' association, how much power they have, shifted to them because Houston has no zoning laws. Basically a group of people who get to dictate what your house can look like. There's a specific color palette they say is acceptable, and anything too blue or too bold can get you a fine. Trees can't go past a certain height. Front-yard fences must be in good repair; grass has gotta be freshly cut.

But, man. This subdivision next to ours, Creeks Hollow, is something else. I'm pretty sure they're only allowed three shades of red brick. All white trim, no exceptions. I've never — and I mean never — seen grass that has gone more than a week before being buzzed back down to earth level. They don't even let you park cars on the street overnight.

Creeks Hollow is Declan's neighborhood. Newer, yeah, but still something like twenty years old.

It's massive, though. No grid pattern like ours, just winding capillaries that end in culs-de-sac, because cul-de-sac houses sell better. Huge sections of these differ subtly from one another in character and style, but tastefully so. Like themed sections of a super-upscale amusement park. Each one with its own yard and pool.

Normally it's a three-minute drive to Declan's. Eight-minute bike ride. Twenty-minute walk.

I make it there in twenty-five, since I had to detour.

* * *

I feel a buzz in my pocket right as I press the doorbell.

It's Eema:

You are gone.

My thumb hovers over the notification. But I decide it's not technically a question so I don't have to respond.

Donovan opens the door. He looks at me blankly for a second, then his face relaxes into its usual default smugness, and he leans against the doorway. Sky pokes her snout into the space between his leg and the door frame, wagging her tail.

"Well," he says.

"Donnie," I reply, reaching down to scratch under Sky's chin.

"Anything strapped to your chest?" he asks.

"Fuck off, Donnie." I hope my voice sounds bored.

He snorts. "I'm just messing with you." He gives me a look I've never seen him give, something more than the passing contempt he usually favors me with. It's not unfriendly, which takes me by surprise.

"Declan!" he calls, turning away and walking off. Sky sits in the space he left, lifting a paw in greeting, tail still wagging. I smile a little as Declan pounds down the stairs.

"Hey!" he says. There's an edge to the cheerfulness in his voice. He moves past Sky, closing the door behind him, and keeps going, half pulling me down the walkway leading from his door.

"Um," I say.

"What's up!" Declan stops us in front of his garage, off to the side of the house.

"Can I come in?" I ask after a second.

"Ahhh, not now, Mom's home and she's in a bit of a mood —"

"Well, let's go somewhere, then." I nod with my chin toward the front door. "Get Sky."

Declan twists the lip of his jeans pocket in his hands. "Mmm, I got a lot of homework I need to catch up on."

"What are you talking about? It's Friday." I look up from his jeans pocket. "Come on, I've been stuck inside all day. All week. Get Sky and let's go walk in the woods or something."

"Well, it's gonna be a busy weekend, so now's my only —"

"Dude." He stops fidgeting at my look. "What're you doing?"

Declan is trying to decide how much to tell me.

Finally he sighs. "Mom. She said it might not be a good idea to hang out with you too much."

"What." I can barely hear myself.

"Well . . . It was more of her telling me I couldn't, not just suggesting it. And, uh, and she said I couldn't talk to you either."

A light breeze travels down the street, tickling tree leaves as it passes. I hear it before I feel it, and let it take my breath with it as it goes, brushing the tips of the grass in front of Declan's house. They bend in the direction of the wind, just slightly, blades quivering in the fluctuations too small for us to feel, before the wind evaporates and the grass is still again.

Then my eyes snap back to Declan's.

"You know I was two when it happened, right?"

Declan senses the force in my voice at the same time I do.

"Yeah, she —"

186

"Like, I didn't kill anyone. Or even do anything. You get that my dad and I are different people?"

"Eran —"

"So why the hell are you avoiding me? You think I'm gonna, like, try to seduce you with ISIS propaganda or something?" I'm almost shouting now.

Declan looks at me like he can't believe what he's hearing, which is pretty laughable actually, given what he just said. It fuels me even more.

"We've been best friends for, like, four years, and suddenly you don't think you know me?"

"Eran, Jesus, chill out, buddy." The impatience to get a word in sharpens his tone. "It's not me, it's my mom! I've been fighting with her all week, defending you —"

"You don't need to defend me! I didn't *do* anything!" Now I am shouting. I'm near panic, I realize. Whatever this is, it's more than just anger. It's a flavor of disbelief that melts into desperation.

"I. Know." Declan talks with his hands when he's agitated. "Eran. Listen to what I'm saying. This was Mom, not me. You get she and I are different people too, right? I've been telling her the same thing you're saying now, trying to convince her —"

"Doesn't seem like you've been trying that hard," I butt in. "I mean, come on, there's zero reason for her to be afraid of me, and you know it. It can't seriously be this difficult to make her see that."

Declan opens his mouth, and I can see in his eyes he has a ready response for this, but the front door opens instead.

"Declan." Mrs. Knowles's voice is sharp, staccato, like a snake-bite. We both turn in the direction of the door, waiting until she takes the three steps that bring her into view.

She stops short when she sees me, and even though I was expecting it, the thin set of her lips is like a punch in the stomach. Sky trots up half a second behind her.

"Don't worry," I spit. "I'm leaving. Been trying all week to convince him to blow up a church, but he's not as easy as the third-graders I normally recruit."

Mrs. Knowles's expression doesn't change, but Declan rolls his eyes a little. Neither is that satisfying, so I look at Sky instead. Her ears are down and her tail wags a little too hard, which I know means she can sense the tension. She locks eyes with me, and her tail wags even harder as she finds what might be a receptive audience. This is her pleading face.

"Tell it to them," I mutter at her.

Then I turn and leave.

I've known that woman for four years.

It's not like she's ever super cheerful or anything. She's got that reserved suburban Catholic mom thing down. But she's always been nice to me, and that niceness always felt genuine. Not the bless-your-heart kind of fake southern niceness. It was real.

It felt real.

The wind picks up again, dropping a still-green leaf onto my shoulder. I pluck it off absently, tossing it back on its path.

And the way Declan just let it happen?

For the first time, it really hits me what it might mean to lose friends over this. It's already occurred to me that it could happen, that it probably will, but I sort of brushed it off at the time.

Didn't Eema tell me once that there's a difference between knowing something and really understanding it? I don't think I got that at the time. When I thought of the possibility of lost friends, it was an abstract thing. I imagined faceless friends and nameless relationships. Maybe because of everything that was going on, I couldn't let myself imagine more.

I didn't imagine Declan.

I kick a pinecone out of my way. It skids across the sidewalk, then bounces into the grass of someone's yard.

He's the guy who knows me best. It's not just history; it's not just a friendship we keep up for old time's sake — it's all right here and now. And his mom thinks it's the kind of thing you can just drop like that.

Yes. That part hurts. But I'm not friends with Mrs. Knowles.

I just would've expected Declan to put up more of a fight. I don't know what it means that he didn't.

The street I'm on curves to the left and intersects with another. I turn right, vaguely in the direction of where I know the subdivision exit is. I've been coming to Declan's house for years, but it's still easy to get lost in the winding roads.

Jesus, even Jade is willing to be seen with me, and I've only known her a couple weeks.

It's another hour before I'm where I think I should be.

I look again at the address painted on the curb, compare

it number by number to the one on my phone screen. Still a match.

Riskin apparently has a landline and is apparently listed in the white pages. Seems like a misstep, but I'll give him a pass since he's old.

It's a small house, older even than ours, in a neighborhood closer to the highway. Not something I'd normally walk to. But desperate times.

The grass looks pretty freshly cut, clear of leaves. The tiny porch, supported by thin metal beams, has been cleanly swept. The vinyl siding is a pale green, outlined with white trim. Tasteful without being too boring. It's a level of care not met by a lot of the other houses on the block.

Seems pretty Riskin to me.

I look again at my phone anyway for one last confirmation, brushing away another text from Eema. I'm going to have to respond to these pretty soon.

Then I walk up to knock on the door.

It opens just before the fourth knock. My knuckles hit thin air, rattling my balance and startling me at the same time. I take half a stumbling step forward, then automatically lurch backward to compensate, but overdo it so I lose my balance for real and barely catch myself with a flailing arm that connects with one of the porch beams.

It makes a protracted *DONG!* sound, bone against metal, that reverberates for what seems like a full minute, growing softer and softer even as it makes me feel more and more conspicuous.

Riskin looks at me the way someone might examine an

avocado at the grocery store. He's wearing a polo shirt and chino shorts. No shoes, just socks. It's weird seeing a teacher in shorts and socks, but what was I expecting? He's at home.

Plus they're still chino shorts. It's not like he's wearing yoga pants or something.

"Hey," I say after I collect myself.

"Mr. Sharon," he responds.

I rub my elbow where it hit the beam. This was sorta the extent of my plan.

"Well, come in," he says after a moment. "Don't suppose it could do much harm at this point."

"Something to drink?" he asks. His socks make a soft shuffling sound on the carpet, and I imagine the static electricity building up through his feet. I stay in the living room, wondering if I should take off my shoes, as he disappears into the kitchen. "I have beer, though it's old . . . a little rosé . . . Oh, I recommend some of the ten-year Bulleit, if you're a bourbon fan."

"Uh," I say.

He pops his head into the doorway. "That was a joke, Mr. Sharon. There's soda or water."

"I'm fine."

I reach down to unlace my shoes.

"Actually, can I have some Coke?"

The hiss from the bottle is powerful, even from the next room. He must be opening a fresh one. I listen to the clink of ice in glass, the *glug-glug* of liquid poured from a two-liter, the crackle of fizz that in my mind I can see rising to the edge of the glass and then retreating. Then there's a higher-pitched clink of ice in another glass and a smoother, shorter pour.

Riskin walks into the living room carrying both drinks and hands me my Coke. His glass is squatter, with only about an inch of a flatter, light brown liquid.

"What's that?" I ask.

"The ten-year," he says, as if it's obvious.

I blink. It's weird to watch a teacher drink.

"Can I try some?"

Riskin takes a sip, eyes on me. "Don't be ridiculous."

He turns and sinks into the couch, one fluid motion, then gestures to the recliner. It's upholstered in yellow fuzz, well-worn and fading in spots.

I take a seat. It rocks more than I was expecting, but it's still pretty comfortable for such an ancient chair.

There's a silence. It lasts one minute. Riskin is looking at me. I can see it in my peripheral vision as I avoid looking directly at him. Finally I get tired of not saying what isn't being said.

"Why'd they fire you?" I blurt out.

"Because they felt they had no choice." Riskin says this without missing a beat, as if he's been waiting for this question. His eyes don't leave mine.

"What are you talking about? Of course they had a choice."

"I said they *felt* they had no choice."

I give him the kind of look I always imagine when an author uses the word "withering" in a book.

"Come on. I'm seventeen and I was able to figure out on my

own that they didn't have to fire you, but the principal, who is an adult professional who's probably devoted his whole life to education —"

"This didn't come from Dr. Pham; it was a school board decision," Riskin says. "If that helps."

I snort. "No. That doesn't help. 'Cause now it's a dozen adult professionals who are complete asshats, not just one."

"Not exactly." Riskin takes a small sip and sets his bourbon down. "Mr. Sharon, imagine you have gotten yourself elected to the school board of a small suburban district outside a large city. Depending on your personal trajectory, you are either a bored senior hoping for an uncomplicated but prestigious post-retirement activity, a career educator looking for a last hurrah, or an ambitious politician seeking a low-risk starting point. A quiet, boring, mostly white suburb is the ideal place for you, regardless of which persona you inhabit."

He takes his glasses off and polishes the lenses with the tip of his shirt, then repositions them.

"And now imagine your world, where the most exciting thing to happen is the occasional school bond vote, has been disrupted by the revelation that a member of your student body is the son of an infamous terrorist"— I wince —"and the backlash to this is swift and powerful. You need to respond to the anger surrounding this entirely unprecedented event, this sudden crisis that ballooned out of control before you were even able to get a handle on what was happening, and you have almost no time to craft your response. You have state and, it appears imminent, national media breathing down your neck, which means inevitable political pressure. Not to mention thousands of parents who want an answer."

Riskin reaches for his bourbon.

"Then you discover this student made some comments that, given this new context, could sound damning. And his teacher seemed in fact to engage with him, rather than push back. Now what do you do? Ignore this new complexity in the story, which will likely add to the considerable outside pressure you're facing? Or eliminate the threat? Remember: you are first and foremost self-interested and conflict-averse, and you have no experience with large-scale media exposure."

I discover I'm leaning forward.

"You're *defending* them?"

Riskin sighs and takes a sip. "Does this sound like a defense to you? I thought I was laying the cynicism on a bit thick." He swirls his drink, looking at me over the rim of the glass. "I am talking about a cost-benefit analysis. School officials are very protective of their institutions. They have to be, because they don't get much support from the outside. If there is something that they perceive to be a threat, they are more likely than not to choose the easiest path to mitigate it."

For the first time, I realize Riskin holds a conversation the same way he teaches.

"Sure sounds like a defense."

"It is not. Quite the opposite. Firing me was a foolish move, a Band-Aid solution that exposes them to liability in the future.

But desperation breeds short-term thinking and rash action. I'm just explaining their thinking, not endorsing it."

Riskin's tone is always sharp by default, but now it gets almost imperceptibly sharper. In a less controlled way. I let the ice melt in my drink.

"So what are you gonna do?" I ask after a moment.

"I . . ." He leans back, pulling his glass with him. "Am going to wait this out, I think."

I open my mouth to reply, think better of it, and then say what I'm thinking anyway.

"You're not going to fight it?"

Riskin bobs his head a little, side to side, like I've seen him do in class.

"For one, in all honesty, I'm not sure how I would go about 'fighting it.'" I can hear the quote marks in his tone. "I have neither the fortitude nor the funds for legal action. But I don't think it's necessary in any case. Chaos has considerable destructive potential, but often, once the dust settles, people instinctively revert back to order."

"What are you talking about?"

"I mean that right after the shit hits the fan, all you see is shit everywhere, and it seems like too much to clean up." He crosses one leg over another. "People go a little berserk in crises. But nothing lasts forever, and they eventually grab a rag and some bleach, and get to work. Which brings us to you."

Outside, a car alarm goes off. We both ignore it.

"What about me?" I ask cautiously.

"How are you handling all this . . ." Riskin pauses, searching for the right word before he gives up and settles. "Attention?"

I shift my glass from one hand to the other. The movement disturbs the condensation that had been collecting on the sides, which runs down and drips into my lap.

"I understand there are a lot of reporters in front of your house," Riskin presses.

"How'd you know?"

He raises an eyebrow. "Because they're broadcasting and I'm old. I've been watching the news. You know you can set that down, if you like."

I put my glass on the coffee table, on a little coaster that, weirdly, has a picture of one of the Golden Girls on it. I don't really know them, but she's the short one with the bushy hair and eyeglass chain.

"So?" he asks after another moment.

"So what?"

"How are you dealing with these people hounding you for a story?"

"Oh. Right. I dunno."

He waits.

"There were half a dozen of them out there this morning. Probably more by now. I think they know that we're not going to answer the door. I didn't see them broadcasting, but we've been keeping the windows closed."

"Smart."

"But they call a lot. Every hour or so, pretty late into the night. I don't know why Ee — why Mom won't just disconnect the phones. She never answers them, just lets them ring, and it kind of drives me crazy."

"What does?" Riskin cuts in.

"Huh?"

"What specifically drives you crazy about their calling?" he asks. "The relentlessness? The sound itself?"

I think about this. "I mean, the sound, definitely. I've always hated jarring noises, like phones and alarms. But . . ."

I consider how much I want to say.

"Mostly it's because my mom won't let me answer it."

Riskin raises his eyebrows. "You want to talk to the reporters."

"Well, yeah. I mean, I've been hearing all this stuff about me for a week, and it's all pretty heavy, and I haven't been able to tell my side. Wouldn't you want that?"

He looks into the corner of the ceiling, as if thinking how to word it. "I could see wanting to tell my side, yes."

I narrow my eyes a little at how slowly he says this but decide not to say anything.

"And the only time I got to, I basically had to go all stealth mode, behind my mom's back, and then when she found out, she flipped," I add, a little bitterly. "She kept saying I'd make things worse."

"Did it make things worse?"

Riskin's matter-of-factness is starting to get to me, honestly. "No."

He smiles. "Okay, maybe not a fair way to phrase that. But, was the result . . . not quite what you hoped for?"

I watch two pieces of ice in my glass become unfused with

a tiny pop, the surface rippling as they break away into separate free-floating chunks that clink lightly against the rim.

"Yeah," I say finally.

"Perhaps your mother was trying to prevent that," he suggests.

"I know she was. But what am I supposed to do? Just stay quiet and not at least try to set the record straight? Is that what you'd do, if people asked for your side of the story?"

"No," he says, not missing a beat, and even now I'm still surprised by how up-front he is. "How did you get here, by the way?"

The sudden change in direction disorients me. "What?"

"Here, to my house. How did you leave yours without the reporters seeing you and following you?"

"Oh." I shift in my seat. "I snuck out through my backyard, into our neighbors'."

"That seems dangerous." He says this conversationally, not at all in a chiding or nagging way.

"Yeah, well."

I let that hang in the air, and he doesn't answer. The conversation seems to have fizzled. I look at the layer of melted-ice water at the top of my glass, the chipped wood of the coffee table, the bald patch on the fuzzy recliner. Anything to avoid looking at Riskin.

"Eran."

I flick my eyes to his in response. My name sounds wrong in his mouth, and I can't figure out why. It's like hearing a nun swear or some Hill Country grandma talking about Passover.

"Is there something else that's bothering you?" he asks, giving me a sly look. "A question you've been asking yourself?"

A million possible answers run through my mind. My instinct is to pick one. Any one will do. I could say no, I could play dumb, I could turn it into a joke, I could be vague, I could tell him to mind his own business, I could deflect, I could change the subject completely, I could pretend to be reluctant but candid, I could ignore him, I could come up with any number of other responses, each of them plausible, all of them quashed by the understanding that he will see through any lie I tell.

And then I realize this was the first time he's called me by my first name.

"Am I like my dad." It comes out flat, monotone, quiet, not a question. Something said at gunpoint.

"Ah." Riskin doesn't exactly look like he's enjoying this, but there's some other spark in his eyes anyway. Something that says we're headed somewhere. "The short answer is: that's the wrong question."

I stare at him. "What are you talking about?"

"Eran, I understand the concern, and why you might obsess over that question. But the one you should be asking is: Do you *want* to be like your father? You'll find this easier to answer, and perhaps more comforting." He swirls the ice in his cup again. I wonder if it does anything for the taste or if it's just a tic. "More importantly, it's a more accurate question. You're not predestined for anything, if I'm reading your worries correctly."

Riskin looks at me for a moment, then throws back the rest

of his bourbon, placing the glass with a *clunk* on his own Golden Girls coaster. It's the tall one with the deep voice.

"Come. I'll drive you . . . well, within a few blocks of home. Probably wouldn't do for you to be seen getting out of my car."

I glance at his empty glass. He smiles.

"Fair enough. We can wait a few minutes."

I don't look away, letting my eyes relax, letting the glass dissolve into a blurry something that loses its edges. I stay that way for a moment until I start to wonder what my expression looks like. My face sags, feels heavy.

Then I snap out of it and look over my shoulder, to the window near the front door. The skies are blue and bright.

"I'll walk," I say after a moment. "But thanks."

Do I want to be like my dad?

It sounded so calming when Riskin phrased it that way, so easy to answer.

But the farther I get from his house, the closer to mine, the more time I have to think, the more I wonder.

"Would it be so bad?" I whisper it under my breath, as if afraid a passing bird will hear and condemn me.

To care about something that much? Would it be so bad?

The question makes my stomach drop. It cracks the dam of guilt I've erected, floods the basin of my conscience, washes over me, makes me feel every drop.

Of course, I think. Of course it would be bad.

* * *

But that guilt doesn't erase the nagging doubt I have.

I think about the passage in the Talmud that Eema told me about.

If someone can stop injustice but doesn't, then he's to blame for that injustice.

It's up to us to try.

Isn't it?

I pause at the entrance to my block. I'd have to go the next street up to get to the house with the backyard that sits against ours.

But our house is far enough down that none of the reporters will see me from where I am, and I want to check if I can see anything.

I can. A lot more than I expected. There are police cars now, flashing lights on, overseeing a number of new reporters. Cars are lined up and down the street, with a group of people milling about between them, carrying equipment and setting up. Even from here, it looks like a mess.

I turn to walk up to the next block but stop after two steps.

This is my street.

Why should I have to break into someone's backyard and risk getting arrested or shot just to go home? This is where I live. I should be able to just walk up to my house.

The thought is weirdly exhilarating, if only because once I think it, I know I'm going to do it.

Our house is the tenth one on the right. I keep my eye on the mass of people and cars and lights ahead of me, wondering which step will be the one where they all notice me. How far will I get before they swarm? What will the police do?

"Hey, Eran."

I falter just half a second, glancing to my right, where an older man is sitting in a lawn chair, drinking a beer and reading a tattered paperback. Tom Clancy. I can see the cover from here.

"Hey, Mr. Wallace," I mumble at him without stopping.

"This a good idea?" That voice is low and thick, a heavy bag dragged across the ground. He's lived here all his life.

"Dunno."

He takes a sip. "Welp. Good luck t'yuh." I keep my eyes ahead.

Two more houses and I see that some of the people gathered aren't reporters or cops. I'm confused for a moment before I hear chanting and realize: protesters. The cops are here for them.

I stare at them. No one I know. Mostly older, mostly men, mostly white. Don't these people have jobs?

I'm still watching them, walking on the sidewalk on our side of the street, when I bump into someone's arm. I turn and there's a cop there, holding out his arm in front of me. I'm a house away from mine.

"Protesters can't go up to the door or anywhere on the lawn," he warns me. "Gotta stay on public property."

"I live here," I tell him.

The cop doesn't have time to react to this, whether he's surprised or doubtful or indifferent, because one of the protesters overhears me.

"That's him!" he shouts. I turn and there's a group of them, not far.

"Go back home, terrorist!" another of the protesters shouts.

"I'm trying to, fuckwit," I say automatically. There's an indignant rumble from the crowd at this. I mean, are they surprised by my response? "Why don't *you* go home? I'm the one who lives here."

"Yeah, 'cause you moved here to kill Americans." This one comes from some guy wearing a Trump hat.

"I was born in America," I tell him, incredulous.

By now reporters are surrounding us, snapping photos and trying frantically to ask questions. I look around. The police are watching us tensely, calculating the point at which they should intervene. A few neighbors are peeking through windows or watching from their lawns. I wonder how long they've been here.

This is getting weird. The protesters are starting to crowd around me, so I move past them, toward my house.

"Anchor baby!" shouts Trump Hat, and I can't help it. It's just too bizarre. I whirl around.

"Hey, Someone's Crazy Grandpa, I was a toddler when it happened. You think I was sitting there in diapers, helping my dad build . . ."

The guy flicks his eyes over my shoulders, and I trail off. A few others look, and then there's more angry commotion from the protesters and an excited buzz from the reporters.

"Miss Shamir!" one calls out, so eager his voice cracks. "Can you give us —"

I turn just as Eema stalks past me, toward the guy in the Trump hat. He towers over her tiny frame, but her bushy hair is quivering. I recognize in an instant he doesn't know how much danger he's in.

"Well, well, if it isn't the Whore of Bab —"

That's as much as he gets out before she reaches her right hand across her front and back behind her left side, almost comically far, and swings her arm in a wide, upward arc. I see it in slow-motion. The crack of her backhand against his cheek is so loud, it echoes against the house across the street. Her heels raise an inch above the ground, pushing her to her toes, so she can reach.

Trump Hat's head snaps to his left, jaw crooked from the impact, spittle flying.

There's a moment — it feels like forever, but it's gotta be only a second — where no one moves at all, no one makes a sound, except Eema, who turns to start walking back to the house. I can hear the scrape of her shoes on the sidewalk.

Then the world goes to hell.

Everyone shouts at once. The guy in the Trump hat lunges forward, face purple, stopped immediately by three cops who hold the rest of the crowd at bay. A reporter trips over himself trying to take a photo. Mrs. Redwood from across the street, who is like eighty, is doubled over from laughter — I can hear it from here — while her wife holds back a light smile.

Eema grabs my arm as she passes, but I go without a fight.

It's a dozen steps to the house, and then we close the door on the chaos outside.

Eema walks past me.

"Now we both have made it worse," she says.

I stare after her.

She stops before she gets to the hallway and turns back to me. We make eye contact.

Her lips are tight, but she doesn't look angry. Just tense. She studies me silently for a long time, weighing whatever it is she wants to say, me just waiting.

"You are sneaking out."

It is a fact, not an accusation. I wait.

Then her hazel eyes change. It's subtle, but the difference takes them from piercing to pleading.

"Be careful if you must do this." The low growl of her voice is gentle, rolling, soft.

I don't react for a moment. Then I nod. It's the least I can do.

She nods too, but the worry doesn't leave her face. She turns and walks into the hallway, toward her bedroom.

I just stand in the living room. It's artificially dark, curtains drawn, closed off to the rest of the world, a room of isolation and retreat. Those curtains are rough to the touch, nearly threadbare. They came with the house when we moved in.

I stand there for a minute, watching a pulse of red light that shines through the cracks in the drapes, making frantic shadows on the far wall.

XII

The world outside threatens constantly to seep in.

We have curtains drawn, doors and windows shut, but this is a small suburban house, not a fortress. There are cracks, seams in the door frames, places where light bleeds through the fabric. Our home isn't airtight, and the chaos outside is poison gas.

When we stop moving, when we stop talking, when we stop making sounds of our own — then we hear the noise that's there, underneath it all. A dull moan that builds to a roar when our defenses are down. We hear the men outside, the chanting, the yelling, the fury from our appearance a few hours ago, and soon we can't hear anything else.

These walls are no match for all of that.

So we don't stop moving. We leave the TV on, even when we're not watching. We sauté onions for an early dinner, we run the dishwasher, we stream light classical on a loop. We use our own sounds as a secondary barrier.

And in that way, we keep what's outside mostly outside. For now, at least.

I watch Eema folding socks in front of the TV and wonder if this was what it was like for her in the days after her world blew up too. Did she fortify our house in Queens? Was it us against the world, again?

But.

No. It had to have been worse, right? She'd just lost her husband. She'd just found out her son's father was a monster. And she was alone, or close enough to make no difference. I was there but I was no help, just a toddler.

I turn away, frowning, feeling the slow-rising tide of guilt. Despite everything that's happening now, despite everything we've been through already, this is still much easier than the worst days of her life.

Even if they're mine.

Then I shove the thought back out.

Fuck that.

I didn't marry the guy who brought everything down, did I? I didn't have a choice in that. Or in any of this. She did.

I give her a parting glance over my shoulder.

She did.

She folds a T-shirt with practiced hands.

But even so, the guilt won't go away, not entirely. It sits at chest level, waiting its turn, buoyed by my doubts.

Eema stands at the open doorway to my room. She doesn't bother knocking, just waits for eye contact.

I look away from my laptop and at her, taking one earbud out, leaving the other in.

"I thought we could go to synagogue again tonight," she says.

I watch her while Rihanna plays into my left ear. She stands still at the threshold to my room, arms at her side, waiting. I think of the throngs of people outside our door, what they will do or say if they see us a second time in one evening.

"Yeah," I say. I'm simultaneously surprised and not by my response.

I give it a moment, reevaluating at a furious speed, considering and reconsidering.

"Yeah."

We leave through the back door, into the garage. It's dark, closed off, just a square of light coming in through a grimy side window. From in here, the noise outside is a low thrum, a wasp's nest waiting to be stirred.

"Don't look at them," Eema says before she presses the button.

I face forward in the passenger seat as the garage door slowly opens behind me, new light and sound rushing in to fill the space.

"Do not look at them." She backs out slowly into the driveway, waiting for the surprised police to clear a path for us. There are people all around us; I can feel them inches to my right, shouting, taking pictures.

Eema presses the button again, making sure no one slips into the garage.

The drive normally takes twelve minutes, almost exactly. I used to time it in the months before my bar mitzvah. It was a way to calm my nerves. By dividing the day into measurable sections, I felt more in control. I could quantify each piece, give myself markers to split up the stress, make it manageable.

I still time it in my mind, out of habit, making note of landmarks that have come and gone.

The Shipley's Donuts we pass on Space City Boulevard means ten minutes left. The Mormon church — used to be Baptist — is two minutes after. The Valero station is just past the halfway point, and the right turn onto Highway 6 begins the final ninety-second stretch.

I turn to look behind us every now and then. There are at least a couple cars that followed us from our block.

Eema pulls into the Valero station, disrupting my silent countdown.

"We need gas," she says, an unnecessary explanation.

I get out when she does. I hate staying in the car when we're filling it up. It's the only time I feel claustrophobic.

The air outside is sharp, cut by the smell of gasoline. I love that smell, love most pungent odors, the way they sting the inside of my nose. Blue cheese, rain dust, dead skunks on the highway.

A few cars have pulled into the station with us. Men get out, start snapping photos. But they keep their distance.

I lean against the passenger door and close my eyes, breathing in slowly. Behind me I hear Eema locking the nozzle in place and the traffic on the road beyond.

When I open my eyes, there's a man yards away, walking toward us. I turn around to see where he might be headed, but there are no other parked cars behind us.

I turn back, tensing now, and my stomach drops as he gets closer. He moves with purpose, carrying himself with the flavor of anger I saw in the man at the park, in the man outside our house.

"What do you —?" My voice sputters, though, as he walks past me without a glance.

He walks around the front of the car. Eema turns, hearing my voice and his approach.

"You wanna slap me too and see what happens?" he snarls at her.

Eema gives him an appraising look, leaning subtly back. "What do you want?"

"I want you to get the hell out of our city, is what I want." He takes another small step forward. "No way you didn't have something to do with the parade bombing. You mighta fooled the FBI, but you don't fool us."

"This is not true." Eema mutters this, and for an instant I get a glimpse of the impossible dread she feels: the need to respond to this, the fear it will make things bubble over.

It seems to. He steps forward again.

"Hey!" I shout. It comes out garbled, strangled by a moment of agonizing uncertainty. Two competing instincts hit me: to run toward them, and to stop and grab something—anything—as a weapon. But there's nothing around me, nothing in the car I can think of in the cloud of my rising panic. The indecision brings me only a couple lurching steps closer. The men with cameras snap their photos.

"You gonna tell me you didn't know *exactly* what your own husband was up to?" The man is yelling now, eyes bulging, enraged. "You gonna lie to *me* too?"

He takes one more step, and my panic breaks. I close the distance between us, not knowing what I'm doing till I'm doing it.

"Hey!" I yell again, but clearer this time, and grab his wrist.

He rips his arm easily out of my grasp, so hard that I nearly lose my balance, as he pivots toward me and away from Eema. An angry bear turning from one threat to a new one.

Caught now in the reckless fury of those eyes, I have just a moment to remember the flashlight Eema keeps in the glove compartment. Heavy, long, solid. It would've been perfect.

The man grabs both my arms.

"You too, little shit."

I hear a wet sloshing sound from somewhere, but it barely registers, like a far-off dog bark.

He takes a step toward me, still holding my arms, forcing me back while keeping me immobilized. I fight to stay upright, nearly tripping over my feet. My stomach drops again as I feel my balance loosen, a sense of vertigo, the anticipation of colliding backward with something I can't see.

Then a spray of water.

A windshield squeegee smashes against the man's temple.

He yells out and lets me go, and now I fall back, down on my ass.

Eema takes another swing as the man turns around to face her, knocking him on the chest. It doesn't look like it hurts, but the water — filthy, brown, and sudsy — gets in his eyes.

"You *get*! Out of here!"

Her face is set, cold and furious, but not without fear. I can actually hear the photos being snapped even though I can't see the reporters anymore. Why the hell aren't they doing anything?

He grabs the squeegee on the third swing, yanking it out of her hands and tossing it aside.

"You fucking little bitch!" he screams, pure rage now, and shoves her on the chest.

My breath catches as she falls back, knocking into the hose, ripping it out of the car. She grunts at the impact. Gasoline pours out of the nozzle, soaking into Eema's pants.

"Fucking bitch!" he screams again. He looks huge against her tiny frame, towering over where she lies on the ground.

"Stop!"

This from a ways off.

"Hey!" A little closer now. "We're calling the police!"

The man turns left, and I peer around the tire. I can just make out the station manager and one of the reporters hurrying toward us. Another reporter hangs back, watching us as he speaks into a cell phone.

Fucking finally.

I look back. The man blinks twice, as if realizing where he is. He glares once more at Eema before turning to his right, walking around the gas pumps toward the road. He doesn't look back, just hurries his steps, picking up his pace.

I watch him go, staring because I can't think to do anything else. For a moment, everything is quiet, like the world is waiting for the next thing to happen.

Then I hear a noise in front of me and turn to see Eema struggling to disentangle herself from the gas hose, and a sharp and sudden rise of anxiety threatens to suffocate me. A thousand things suddenly become apparent: the dull pain in my tailbone where I landed, the feel of hot cement on bare palm, my pulse pounding in my ears, the fresh grime on my pants.

Seeing her stop to unwind the hose from her ankle, careful to point the nozzle away from herself and her clothes — it's the proof that what happened happened, the thing that carries us from surreal to real. It makes it inescapable. In the span of two seconds, I'm shaking, choking in a surge of white-hot anger that leaves me almost light-headed, blanketed by a smothering layer of shock and fear. I can barely breathe.

But Eema.

Her mouth is a thin line. She doesn't look afraid or angry or embarrassed. She looks, if anything, annoyed. As if something unpleasant but inevitable has come to pass, and she's impatient to put it behind her.

She catches my eye, but only for only a fraction of a second.

She doesn't say anything as we get up. The manager asks if we're okay. Eema mumbles a yes and a thank you at him as she puts the nozzle back in its place and grabs the receipt and opens the driver's-side door.

She doesn't say anything the rest of the way to the synagogue. Eema speaks only out of necessity, another thing I didn't get from her.

I wonder, for a moment, if my father talked as much as I do.

You gonna tell me you didn't know exactly what your own husband was up to?

But I don't say anything either while we're in the car. Because I'm still in shock, because I'm trying desperately to keep myself calm and swallow the kind of rage that feels like hate.

Maybe because I'm still angry at her. Maybe because she should be the one to ask me, not the other way around.

Are you okay?

I imagine it said, by one or the other of us. I imagine the grunted response, curt and resentful: *fine.*

Instead we're both quiet. Me, fighting with everything I have to stop from shaking. Eema, stony but placid.

She has such control, I realize, seething.

The inside of the car smells like gas, still soaked into Eema's pant leg.

We're late, but not by much. They're in the middle of "Ma Tovu," the first song. Still, it means I can't talk to Zack till after. The reporters followed us to the synagogue, shouting questions as we walked toward the building. But they didn't dare follow us inside.

Rabbi Cassel catches Eema's eye as we walk in, holding it a beat too long.

With everything that's happened, I'd forgotten until right this second that this is the first time we're seeing everyone since the news broke. Since the world found out who we are.

I almost freeze in place right there, in the aisle between the two blocks of chairs. But Rabbi Cassel offers a small smile and nod, continuing the song.

Others in the congregation notice and turn. I avoid them and find Zack in our usual row, an empty seat next to him.

"Hey," I whisper as I sit down. I can't wait — I need to talk about it, about everything, so I decide I'll tell him a little of what happened, decide I will whisper it urgently between lines of prayer. But he turns to me before I can, eyebrows raised, and his look throws me off.

He's surprised to see me but also uncomfortable.

Zack tries to recover, but his expression's already betrayed him. I face forward, motionless, as if I've forgotten what to do. A moment passes, and I open my siddur just as the song ends.

Services have never felt this long.

Twenty minutes in and I can't stop squirming. I want so badly to talk to Zack, and not being able to do that while I'm sitting right next to him is killing me.

"Please turn to page eighty, and read responsively with me in the English," Rabbi Cassel says, and I see my chance.

He clears his throat before starting.

"*Sing to the sound of the ten-string lyre, with voice and the music of the harp.*"

I follow along, mouthing the words I memorized years ago. As he nears the end of his line, I lean subtly toward Zack, waiting.

Now it's the congregation's turn to read. They jump into the line seamlessly. An effortless, practiced move.

"*Your works, O Lord, bring me gladness. Of Your deeds, I joyously sing.*"

And while they read aloud, I speak into Zack's ear, my voice covered by everyone else's: "I need to talk to you. Now."

Zack almost jumps at the sound of my voice in his ear but, to his great credit, recovers almost immediately. He gives me a look, half warning, half worry that I'm serious.

"*How great are Your deeds, O Lord,*" Rabbi Cassel continues. "*How profound are Your designs.*"

I time my breath with the end of his sentence.

The congregation picks it up. "*The simple cannot comprehend . . .*"

"Meet me in the bathroom. It's important," I say to Zack, following the rhythm and cadence of the group voice around me.

"*The foolish cannot grasp this,*" they finish.

I turn to Zack as the rabbi begins his line, regarding him coolly, communicating in every way I can that I will do this the whole rest of services if I have to.

"*Though the wicked may thrive like grass, and doers of evil seem to flourish.*"

Zack finally turns to me for the last few words, anticipatory. He takes a breath as the rabbi finishes, and I realize immediately I have to get in before him to cut him off.

"*Their doom . . .*"

"Someone attacked me and Eema," I say, probably too loudly, probably too out of rhythm, probably too easily overheard.

"*For Yours is the ultimate triumph.*"

"Fine," Zack whispers into the half second of silence before the rabbi's next line. "I'll meet you out there."

The bathroom linoleum is older than I am, I'm pretty sure. There are ancient dents in it from dress-shoe heels, dropped things, whatever. The walls are a yellowed beige, for some reason. The trim is dark brown, for some reason. The one stall door doesn't lock. I love this building.

Zack leaves me in there alone just long enough to wonder if he's really going to come in.

Then the door creaks open and I turn.

"So." He looks at me two seconds too long. "What's up?"

There's a clipped quality to his voice I don't like.

"Some guy," I say. "He . . . attacked us. Just came up and fucking shoved us both to the ground." I realize I've started from the middle and take a step back. "At the gas station on the way here. Someone followed us from home, ran up to us when we stopped for gas. He tried to grab Eema, so I ran up to him, and then he was like shoving me, and then Eema hit him with a squeegee —"

I take a ragged breath. I'm all over the place.

"A squeegee." He sounds . . . not dubious, exactly. Just like someone taking a lot in at once.

And I see it.

The main thing, the only thing on his mind right now, is who I am, who Eema is, who we've been revealed to be. Not what's happened to us since; not the guy at the gas station, not the guy at the park, not the guy in front of our house. He's starting from the beginning because we haven't had a chance to talk yet.

What does he hear when I speak, when I sound urgent and anxious? Who does he see? An old friend who needs help? Someone he trusts, someone he's grown up with and laughed with and been in trouble with too many times to count? Someone whose bar mitzvah was the week after his, with whom he made a mutual pact to be the first to clap after the speech, so neither felt nervous?

Someone who started that garage fire with him, who microwaved a Styrofoam cup in the synagogue kitchen five years ago and had to explain the black smoke to angry parents, who snuck out of the house with him at a sleepover in middle school?

Or an impostor? Someone he thought he knew, someone whose entire identity changed since the last time he saw me?

"Zack," I say, hating the vulnerability I hear in my voice. "It's been some week."

Zack looks at me as if making a decision.

"Yeah," he says finally. "It has." He looks at the bathroom door, as if he wants nothing more than to walk through it.

"Look." He turns back to me. "Some of the stuff you guys said . . . You have to understand, it's not a great look."

It feels like a gut punch, enough to knock the wind out of me. It's the moment of thinking I know where things stand, and then realizing I had no idea to begin with.

"What."

He hears the ice in my voice. But he's used to it by now, and tonight he is immune.

"About violence toward Israelis," he explains. "That wasn't smart."

It takes me a moment to understand what he's even talking about.

"That interview? With kids from my class?" I almost yell. "Are you kidding me?"

Zack hesitates.

"Stop it," I snap. "I don't need to be *handled*, Zack. Just say what you're thinking."

His face turns to stone. "It was a really stupid thing to say."

"It was out of context!"

"So what?" he fires back, ready. "You know what the last thing Jews need is? One of our own saying we deserve what we're getting."

"I didn't mean —"

"It doesn't matter what you *meant* — it matters what it *sounds* like to everyone else!" I'm surprised he's shouting at me. "You've noticed you're not just getting attacked by right-wingers, right? That some people are making this about Israel? Those people don't see Jews as an oppressed people. How do you not get that your comments play right into that?"

He keeps his eyes locked on mine but doesn't stop speaking, barely even pauses for breath.

"Jews don't get to speak without thinking, Eran. We don't get to say the first thing that pops into our minds. When we do, we put every other one of us at risk. We are always, constantly, every freaking day representing Judaism to everyone we talk to and everyone who sees us. *Especially* in Texas. It's not fair, but there it is." He holds up a hand, cutting me off before I begin. "I know you don't have a filter, and, Jesus, please don't get started again on questioning authority. I'm not talking about that. I'm talking about having some self-control so you don't put other people in harm's way."

The bathroom is too small, too poorly constructed to contain our conversation. I wonder how many people can hear how many words. I glare at him, halted by the competing things I want to say.

"And then there's the matter of your mom," he adds. A little reluctantly but a little too gladly.

"My mom."

He looks away mid-sigh. Calculates. Looks back at me.

"A lot of people think she had something to do with it."

You weren't really surprised, were you.

You reacted. Even felt it. Raised your eyebrows, took a breath in, let the blood warm your cheeks. The anger was real, and you let that fool you into thinking the shock was too.

But didn't his words meet a thought already half-formed in your mind? Wasn't that seed of doubt already there?

Wasn't it his daring that really got to you?

"Something to do with what," I say. It's low, deadly, as close to a growl as a whisper can get.

He considers his options but not seriously. He knows he has to go through with it. He made his choice already.

"Come on, Eran," he says quietly. "If you think about it objectively and honestly, do you really think you could be married to someone planning a suicide mission and not have an inkling?"

"Why would he tell her?" My response is quick enough to surprise even me.

"Why wouldn't he? People don't get married to strangers anymore, Eran." He speaks faster, more urgently. "Just think about it for a second. What's more likely? That a devoted father and husband who loved his family killed himself without even telling his wife? *Or* that a husband and wife shared a set of beliefs, they talked about it extensively beforehand, and she gave her blessing?"

Zack finishes speaking but doesn't feel finished. He holds his breath, as if wanting to say more but not knowing what. Then his shoulders sag, and his voice softens.

"Pretend we're talking about strangers instead of your parents. What would you believe? Honestly."

your parents

Pluralizing that word like it's nothing.

There is silence, then a burst of muffled voices. Services have ended. Zack and I stand and stare at each other, quiet, as the chatter of dozens of people fills the hallway on the other side of the door. They are filing out of the sanctuary, toward the social hall, but Zack and I stand and stare.

More than anything, I wish I could think of something to say.

Instead I slap a hand against the bathroom wall, as hard as I can. The feel of it, the *smack* of skin on drywall, the way the thin wall shakes from the impact, is all so satisfying. It's sudden and explosive enough to make Zack jump a little, and that's satisfying too. My heart pounds its own way against my chest. Someone, probably a few people, heard it. I don't care. I don't care.

"Eran, good lord," Zack manages, somewhere between startled and cross.

"Fuck you," I say through my teeth, and turn around and walk out.

* * *

We were just attacked. Less than an hour ago. Shoved onto the hot cement by some great white ape, gas spilled all over us.

I repeat this to myself, over and over. Silent but lips moving, like an incantation under my breath.

We were just attacked. Someone just attacked us.

Most of the wine's already gone in the social hall, but I find a forgotten thimble. The challah is stale tonight, but it stops me from chewing my lip.

It lets me feel angry without looking angry. Lets me hide out in the open.

But a few moments later, the hairs on my arms stand on end. I snap out of it and realize there's no one standing near me. No one but Eema.

I look around, cautiously, and notice for the first time that a couple people are looking at me. Looking at us. Surreptitious glances, eye contact broken the moment it's made.

It's not obvious to the point of being absurd. It's the kind of thing you might not notice till you notice, and then can't not see. Subtle enough to give everyone plausible deniability.

It feels like that first day back at school, actually.

Eema is next to me. Around us, a bubble of empty space.

I look at her, and she looks up at me.

"Maybe —"

"Two weeks in a row, Eran." I almost jump. Rabbi Cassel, suddenly next to me, voice easy, smile light. "Your mother's habits are rubbing off on you. Or is that wishful thinking?"

His voice is loud. It's always loud, but right now that volume has purpose, I know.

Rabbi Cassel is a nice man. In that moment, staring out at that sea of stony faces, I feel a wave of profound gratitude.

"Maybe," I say. But I give him the hint of a smile before I turn back to Eema.

"We should—"

"Yes," she mutters into her paper cup of lemonade. The keys are already in her hand.

Eema doesn't listen to the radio, so there's just the hum of tires on asphalt, the occasional drumbeat of a bump in the road.

I clock our twelve-minute trip backward, finding my landmarks in reverse. It's night, and Kiley Springs looks different at night.

The reporters who followed us there were gone by the time we left. I don't think anyone's following us. I still look behind me through the back windshield every couple minutes.

"Why do you still go to the synagogue?" I blurt out. The silence is killing me now, and I need something to take my focus away from what just happened. "You're an atheist anyway. You always have been. Why do you bother?"

I already know the answer. She's told me before, thousands of times.

It's important to stay in touch with your Jewish roots, Eran.

I wait for these words, but Eema lets three seconds pass, then five, then eight. I realize with a start, just before she speaks, that I'm getting a different answer this time.

"They welcomed me. Us both, when we first moved here. I did not know how badly I needed this until it happened."

She keeps her eyes ahead, hands firmly in place on the steering wheel. There is the noise of the world outside, but the windows are rolled up, and it's quiet with just the two of us, breathing, waiting.

"It was a small way to connect with my old life," Eema says, finally. "A little piece of home that I could keep. I do not know if I could have made it without this."

The car slows. We are turning on our street, heading into the snake pit. I don't know what happened to the rest of the trip.

"Perhaps it would have been wiser not to remain Jewish," she says. "Perhaps I should have chosen non-Israeli names."

She points the car straight ahead, gliding toward the crowd, the lights.

"But this I was unwilling to do."

The police, the reporters, the group of protesters emerge slowly into view.

They welcomed me. Us both.

Well, not anymore.

Some of those faces tonight weren't friendly.

Some were, but I've known all of these people for years. And some of them were looking at us like strangers.

The thought pulls my mind back to what Zack asked.

What if it were strangers instead of my parents?

parents

What would I believe if I'd just heard about this instead of lived it? Would I think she had nothing to do with it? Would I assume she knew?

The crowd in front reluctantly makes way for us. I can barely hear the shouting through the windows of the car. So much of the chaos is blocked by our little cocoon.

I answer Zack's question and close my eyes against the wave of guilt that comes, hot in my chest like indigestion. I can taste it.

The garage door closes behind us, pushing it all out, leaving me with just this guilt, overwhelming and bitter.

Eema still smells like gasoline.

DEVORAH

The young lawyer helped write the speech, of course.

The sentiments are mostly hers, the words mostly his. It was necessary, to have someone translate her thoughts. But also to add pieces that needed to be said, that she wouldn't have thought of, that he intuited from experience.

She worried about it. Wouldn't people know? Wouldn't it be obvious? Wouldn't they find it disingenuous, exactly at the moment she needed to project authenticity?

He reassured her. They will understand these as your words, even if they know you didn't write them, *he told her.* You are speaking them. You're putting your name to them. And a name is what makes a person.

The young lawyer returns to this theme often, she notices. This idea of names, of the importance of them.

How much weight a name can carry. How solid it is, how it is one's earliest piece of identity. The first glimpse someone sees of you, meeting you for the first time.

She thinks of her name, and her son's. How they both carry her dead husband's name, dragging it like a weight behind them. And in that moment, the seed of an idea is planted.

If a name carries baggage, if a name links one's history to one's sense of self, what happens when a name changes?

The question, out of nowhere, disrupts her thoughts. She pauses in the middle of a sentence for what feels like an eternity. Years later, watching the footage on television, she will be surprised to see it was only a slice of a second. She will see the slightest twitch in movement in the young lawyer behind her, but only he would sense the moment. No one else would notice.

She pushes the thought out of her mind as she reads. It is the first time in days and days that she has felt excitement and possibility, but now is not the time.

Her familiar worries return as she continues. Despite the young lawyer's assurances, she cannot help but think that she doesn't sound like herself, and that everyone can see this.

"I do not know what ultimately drove Dani," she whispers into the dented microphone. "He could not control his passions. He saw evil where there was none. He convinced himself of intent where there was only everyday circumstance. He imagined adversaries. What he did, he did for a made-up cause he let consume him."

The words, not hers, taste all the more bitter, knowing she would have written them if she could.

JADE

XIII

She feels like an intruder.

The neighborhood doesn't look quite like hers. The houses aren't brand-new, but they are newer, built within a narrow palette of brick colors she finds stifling. The lawns are cut short without exception, raked clean, edges trimmed. Jade senses a strict set of rules for this subdivision.

Still, there are similarities, undeniable when viewed from a distance. The way two different cities can look the same to a small-towner seeing them in photographs. The layout isn't much different from her street: homes set forty feet in, grass front yards, one or two trees, lots divided by driveways rather than fences. Sidewalk running across, even and unbroken, leaving a strip of grass and rounded curb to buffer against the street. Mailboxes with flags.

Jade thinks about this, about the defining role of perspective, as she walks these unfamiliar streets. She wonders if people peep out their windows at her, curious about the presence of this unknown black girl among their homes. She makes small adjustments to her posture. Hands shoved deep in pockets, elbows locked playfully, a small bounce in her step, a welcoming smile fixed on her face.

Then she feels ashamed. In her mind's eye, she sees her ma clearly, the disapproval set in her expression, indistinguishable from the pride she always carries, the conviction of self. "What are you doing, Jade?" mind-Ma asks, and Jade shakes off the bits of facade she hoped would make her look easygoing and non-threatening but that made her more tense.

She relaxes her arms, her shoulders, her smile, and looks coolly around. The woods lie still and quiet to her right; the street to the left is empty.

Then she hears the light jingle of collar tags, and Declan rounds the corner with a blue heeler leading the way.

She gives Declan furtive glances and catches him doing the same.

Jade was surprised when she got his text, at first. The suggestion to meet wasn't weird, exactly. But unexpected.

But the more she thought about it, the more it made sense. They witnessed the world finding out about Eran together. They were the two he told about his father, in that bathroom.

And now, Eran has cut him off.

Still, Jade feels herself settling into her guarded mode.

"Why 'Sky'?" she asks now.

Declan shrugs. She decides the gesture looks good on him. "Her maiden name's Blue. So I guess Sky was a logical next step, but a couple notches more creative, you know?"

Jade tries a low whistle. Sky allows one ear to turn back, but her focus stays on the path ahead, the grass and trees and birds and squirrels she thinks she sees.

"'Maiden name'?" she asks.

"The name she had at the shelter." Here Declan rolls his eyes.

"Blue. Because of the breed." He tosses the hair out of his eyes. "My aunt's dog was named Snickerdoodle when they got him. Snickerdoodle. Can you imagine? Because he was a Labradoodle with a cookie-colored coat. Part Labradoodle, anyway. Like, I get it, and it's halfway creative, but that's not a name you give a living thing with a twelve- or fifteen-year life span, because the novelty will wear off by next Tuesday."

Declan takes his first pause for breath. Jade can see how he and Eran are such good friends.

"Not that my aunt did much better. Ended up naming him Poppy. I do not know why."

Jade smiles and thinks about the rare instances she suddenly realizes a new friendship will last, and the little thrill that recognition always gives her. She suspects those moments come less frequently the older people get.

When will she stop meeting people who matter to her?

She decides immediately: never.

They round a bend in the narrow path of the woods, creek hugging the trail to the left, and Jade detects that they have danced around the topic long enough.

"So," she says, hoping Declan will take it from there.

"Yeah." He sighs. "I think he thinks I was hiding it from him. Which I guess I was, but I didn't see any sense in telling him what Mom said. You know how he is." Declan gives her a sideways glance. "Or maybe you don't. But once he gets going . . ."

"Yes," Jade says, "I've noticed."

Declan takes long, loping strides, hunched over but not ungraceful. They match the mixed air of frustration and guilt he gives off.

"I don't know why he's mad at *me*, though. Mom told me she didn't want me to talk to him, and I completely ignored her. What else could I have done?"

"Maybe he expected you to change your mother's mind," Jade offers. Declan surprises her by nodding.

"That's basically what he said when he went off on me. But how? I can't control her."

Sky pauses, one paw raised in the air, listening, and Declan and Jade stop to watch. She lowers her head, ears perked, then darts to the right, startling a squirrel that spirals up the nearest tree, scolding Sky on the way. The dog's movements are slowed by weight and age, but Jade is surprised by her deftness.

They continue on.

"I tried arguing with her, but that didn't work, so I just went behind her back. Best I could do, thought it was enough, at least I was fighting it. Right?"

"He might not be mad at you at all," Jade says. "How long has he known your mom?"

Declan considers. "I guess as long as he's known me. Four years."

"Has she always been nice to him?"

He nods. "Yeah. This wasn't really like her, to be honest. She's usually pretty great with all my friends. Not, you know, like trying to be all buddy-buddy or super cheerful; that's not really her shtick. But she's not standoffish. She jokes around with him."

"So," Jade says, "maybe he's really just mad at your mom. And maybe he was putting all that on you, since you're his friend."

Declan turns to Jade and looks at her full-on for the first time. She looks back at him. Sky notices the pause in step, watching the two of them expectantly over her shoulder.

Then he smiles and turns back to the front. "Here we are." He bends low, pulling off one shoe and sock, then the other, tossing them carelessly to the side, and rolls his jeans haphazardly to mid-calf. It makes Jade think of Tom Sawyer.

She removes her own shoes and socks, but methodically, sitting on the rock edge of the creek, placing them neatly beside each other. When she's done, they both step down into the creek.

Sky wags her tail and follows, sensing adventure, perking her ears against the steady trickle of water.

Jade feels it cascading over her toes. It is cooler than she expected, bringing some relief from the heat that even the shade from the trees couldn't supply.

They walk down the center of the stream to a point where it widens into a shallow pond, never more than a foot deep. Small rocks prick the soles of her feet here and there, but most of the creek bed is smooth mud that squishes between her toes, soft and soothing. The water comes just up to her rolled-up pant legs. Once or twice a ripple in the surface licks the tips of those jeans. Jade wonders if they'll smell of creek water later. Minnows swim around her ankles, just visible in the murk.

Behind them, Sky leaps through the water, pouncing, wagging her tail. Ahead is a wide, low rock that sticks out a foot or two from the center of the pond; this is where they head now.

Jade climbs up first, sitting on the rock to anchor herself as she pulls Declan up beside her.

They sit. From here the woods spread out before them. It's impossible to imagine the houses and streets and cars and joggers and strollers, all yards away, hidden by the trees.

Declan shoves a fist into his pocket, straightening his leg and turning a little to the side to reach in all the way, and pulls out a handful of small stones, smooth and flat. He lays them on the rock between the two of them. Jade pokes through them and chooses a pinkish one, speckled like peppered salmon.

She tosses the first one. It skips five times. Sky perks up, tracking the sound, and makes a move to follow.

"No, girl." She stops, glancing at Declan and flicking her tail, before peering again in the direction the stone flew.

"So, what's your story?" Declan asks, tossing his own. He's left-handed, Jade notices.

"My story?"

He kicks his feet in the water, where they hang. "I feel like you've gotten a pretty intense crash course on Eran and me, but I guess we don't know that much about you."

"What would you like to know?" Jade asks, slow, still guarded.

Declan blinks, not sure what to do now with this new power he's been granted.

"Have you always been in Kiley Springs?" he asks finally.

"Since I was six." She tosses another stone. It veers to the right and crashes into the bank on the third skip. "What about you?"

"I was born here. Donovan was born in Austin, but my parents moved here when he was a few months old." He sighs, drawing it out, and Jade suspects he's dramatizing. "I can't wait to get out. There's no way I'm applying anywhere in Texas. I want to go as far as I can, preferably out of the country. This world is so huge! So vast, so much to see, I can't imagine limiting myself to the same country, much less the same state, once I have a choice in the matter, you know? Where were you before six?"

The question is such an abrupt shift that it's a few seconds before Jade registers it. "New Orleans," she sputters.

"Really?" He looks at her a moment, real interest in his eyes. "That's awesome."

"Mm," she answers, and he catches the noncommittal tone. "I mean, I don't really remember much of it. We left about a month after Hurricane Katrina."

"Oh, wow," Declan says. There's a real note of reverence there. He lets three seconds pass, staring out into the water. "I wrote an essay on Katrina in history last year," he adds, but Jade gets the feeling this is filler for something else he wants to say. Or ask.

"Did, uh . . ." he starts.

"We were fine," she answers him. "Our neighborhood didn't flood much, really. But Ma didn't want to stay, though I think she hated it before the storm. Either way, she won't talk about it." Jade tosses a stone a little too hard. She picks up another, weighing it in her hand, but changes her mind and places it back in the pile. "The only reason we even waited a month was because of Father. He loves New Orleans and couldn't bear to leave it, even in ruins. But Ma put her foot down."

She weighs her own words like she weighed the stone, wondering if the full truth will seep out of the seams.

239

"It's fine now though, right?" Declan asks. But she can hear the uncertainty in his voice and wonders if he makes a habit of self-doubt.

"Sure. But Ma would never allow it. And now my sister and I have roots here. It would be weird to leave." She lets out a one-syllable laugh. "I thought about applying to Tulane, just to upset her."

Declan turns to her, trying to read her expression.

There is more, of course.

About being caught between Father's love of New Orleans and Ma's hatred of it. About that battle leaving her uncertain of a piece of her identity, ambivalent about the where of herself.

More, about Ma refusing to even hear questions. About the chilling effect it's had on Jade, too afraid to ask about her own past and the resentment that's created.

She feels Declan watching her, wondering if he can sense these things, wondering if he will ask a question that leads to more.

Instead he asks, "How old are you?"

The question is so unexpected, the tone so strangely accusatory, that it takes Jade a moment to answer.

"I'll be eighteen in a month."

Declan frowns. "Oh. Then, no. You weren't six."

"What?"

"You weren't six when you left New Orleans," he says. "Katrina happened in 2005, so you would've . . . I guess it would've been right around your fourth birthday."

She's thrown off by the abrupt pronouncement, enough to doubt herself for a fraction of a second.

Could she have been that young?

No, she answers immediately. They moved when she was in kindergarten. She cried a messy goodbye to her best friend, Arabel, the day before they left. It's one of her only memories of that time.

But even when tiny, doubt is persistent.

Could that have just been daycare? Pre-K?

No. Kindergarten. She remembers Miss Humphrey in Kiley Springs, welcoming her. All the other kids already there, eyeing her with distrust, this new girl in their territory.

Jade rubs a thumb over a smooth black stone, calculating. In all this time, she realizes, she's never actually bothered to research the hurricane on her own.

She frowns, submerged in this new uncomfortable thought.

Declan doesn't seem to notice. He tosses another stone.

XIV

She tries to keep those thoughts at bay the rest of the day with mixed success. They're gone during dinner and an unexpected text exchange with Eran, but sneak back here and there at night. They stay just out of reach now, leaving her alone on the roof.

She hugs her knees.

Jade likes hiding in plain sight. She likes the feeling of privacy even while out in the open, concealed only by the inattentiveness of others. She likes it on the roof. People don't look up.

She feels her sister's presence a second before she turns over her shoulder. Sapphire leans out the window, elbows on the sill, face resting in her hands, framed by the light of Jade's bedroom behind her.

"You staying up?" she asks, keeping her voice low. Their parents are light sleepers.

"For a while longer, Saph," Jade says.

"Okay." Sapphire stands up quickly. "I'm goin' to bed. Night."

"Saph? Can you turn the light off when you leave?"

Her sister holds a question in the corner of her eye, but drops it at Jade's even stare. "Okay." She bounds out of the room, flicking the switch, and now the moon is Jade's only source of light. The darkness feels warm.

She watches a man across the street taking a small terrier for a late-night walk. The dog stops short, sniffing at a flower patch. The man looks around guiltily while the terrier lifts a leg.

Jade smiles. No one ever looks up.

The man and the terrier go on their way, tiny dog-collar jingle following their steps.

Earlier, in the quiet of her room, it had only taken a few seconds. She wondered again why she'd never looked it up before.

The date was in a sidebar on the page. August 2005. As soon as she saw it, she realized she'd been hoping Declan was wrong.

Jade waits another minute in the silence, then scoots to the edge of the roof. She dangles her legs over the side, just above the fence that separates her front lawn from the backyard, and lowers herself down.

She fingers the car keys in her pocket as she walks around the side of the house to the driveway. Her father's Prius, chosen for its near-silent engine. The beep it makes when she turns it on still sounds impossibly loud.

Jade imagines for a moment her parents' reactions if they were to catch her. Anxious indignation for Ma, disbelief with a little amusement for Father. That last bit then making her ma even more on edge. Jade scowls at the steering wheel and pulls out of the driveway.

The drive is quiet. It feels wrong even to turn the radio on.

She snuck out of the house just once before, the summer after freshman year. She and Delia, then living closer by, rode their bikes from separate directions and met at the neighborhood pool. They had found a vulnerability along the fence — a low stone ledge that hugged the facility wall, giving them a boost to the top. They climbed over and swam in the pool for half an hour before leaving.

Delia's parents were waiting for her when she walked in, clothes still soaked. She told Jade later that she saw the lights on as she rounded the corner to her street and considered turning around. But what would be the point?

She didn't give Jade up, though. Jade always admired that.

She parks the car now on the curb of a foreign street. Some of the magic is lost, having switched a bike for a Prius, but there is still something undeniably conspiratorial about the moment. She sits in darkness and feels like a spy. Like a different identity.

How old am I?

There it is. The thought comes from nowhere but is not entirely unexpected. It's the first time since seeing the date on the back of the photo that she's allowed herself to think it.

But if she was three in that photo, and six when they left New Orleans, then she's two years older than she thinks.

Jade sees movement outside, a welcome distraction from her thoughts. Eran emerges from the darkness between two houses, walking quickly and a little hunched over. Jade holds her breath, half expecting a gunshot. But he climbs in the passenger side without incident.

"Hey," he says, once he's buckled in.

Jade looks at him. "Where to?"

A sharp knock on her window cuts off whatever answer he may have given. Jade jumps in her seat, embarrassed even in mid-yelp by her skittishness. A flash of light disorients her, blinding her for a few moments, until she hears Eran swear.

"Jesus! Go!"

Jade moves as if on autopilot, hitting the ignition button, moving to drive, pressing the gas. She is both surprised and pleased by the small squeal the tires make from the sudden acceleration.

They're already half a block away when her senses catch up with her, and she registers what's happened. For a split second, she thinks of the man at the park, but this felt different.

"Was that a reporter?" she asks, willing her heartbeat not to sound in her voice.

Eran grunts.

"They must've figured out how I was slipping past without them noticing."

Jade parses this sentence.

"How'd they even know you were getting out in the first place?" she asks.

Eran takes too long to answer. Jade is surprised to learn she can hear guilt in silence.

"I came back through the front door last time. Don't go left."

"Through the —"

"It's my house, right? Why shouldn't I be able to go in and out of it? We didn't do anything wrong. We shouldn't have to be under house arrest because of something someone else did fifteen years ago."

Jade glances in the rearview. There are no headlights, yet, but a pursuit feels inevitable. She makes a series of turns onto unlikely side streets, which feels excessive.

"What happened?" she asks finally.

"There was a commotion. There are protesters out now, did you know that? People with zero sense of irony telling me to go home." He trails off, and Jade thinks for a moment he's finished. "My mom slapped a guy."

"She *slapped* someone?"

"Backhanded him clear across the face." Eran shakes his head. "My mom isn't exactly a friendly person, but that kind of thing is so not her. I've never seen her do anything like that."

Jade has never met Miss Sharon, but she has seen her on the news and online. She is a small woman. Jade tries to picture her backhanding a stranger, but can't quite make the image stick.

"Then someone shoved us to the ground at a gas station." He tries to hide the tension in his voice.

"What!"

Eran exhales. "We went to the synagogue last night. Someone followed us. Walked up while we were filling up on gas and got in our face, then pushed my mom and me both to the ground. Someone called the police before it got worse."

Jade stares. "Did they arrest him?"

"Guy left pretty quick, but reporteres were there so there are pictures. Police stopped by when we got back to take a statement." He pauses, considering. "Didn't say anything about my mom slapping that first guy, though."

"Eran . . ." Jade doesn't know what to say other than his name.

"It's fine. I'm fine." He lets out another short breath. "I dunno where to go. Not like there's anything going on in Kiley."

Jade taps the steering wheel with her thumb. She wonders if she should say more, but sees the subject change and his tone as clear-enough signals.

"I have an idea."

The pool has closed for the season. She parks in the small lot to the right, in front of a separate jungle gym for small children. Behind that is a tennis court that looks ominous in the still dark.

She wonders if Delia will be upset.

The ledge running along the wall is as she remembers it, and Jade makes it over the fence easily enough. She is surprised to see that Eran is clumsier than she is, but he gets over without too much trouble.

On the other side, she feels shy suddenly.

"Is it clean?" Eran whispers. It feels wrong to speak in normal tones when it's so quiet.

"Yes," Jade whispers back. "They maintain it all year, so parents don't have to look at a swamp while their kids are on the playground." She believes this, anyway. The water is still and clear.

Jade puts her shoes and socks neatly beside the leg of a wooden table by the water; Eran throws his in a pile nearby, like Declan at the creek. Phones and keys sit on the table. They wait a moment in silence, as if on the edge of an awkward juncture, and then Eran takes his shirt off self-consciously. He is thin, Jade notices, but not lanky.

She hesitates a moment, then takes off her own shirt, trying to project the casual confidence he lacked. She wears a bra underneath.

He looks doubtfully at the pool's edge.

"Is it cold?" he asks.

Jade shrugs. "It's still warm out here, isn't it?" She walks up to the water and touches it with her big toe. It's actually cooler than she expected, but it's too late for that now. She squats down, hands on the ledge, and lowers herself in silently.

Jade pauses underwater, then opens her eyes. The world is a deep, shimmery blue, punctuated by bubbles. The chlorine stings, but only a little.

She feels a pulse in the water, a flutter of more bubbles, and turns. Eran's hair floats as if weightless, losing the wavy patterns it holds when dry. His eyes are shut, so she watches. Two small bubbles guard his nostrils. His skin is ghostly in here, made pale by the blue around them. He hangs in the water loosely, arms out, knees slightly bent, and waits, letting his body drift.

Then he waves his arms and breaks above the water.

Jade watches him kick lazily below before joining him above.

"There's a drive to kick us out of town," he says. They sit next to each other on the side of the pool, feet dangling in.

Jade knows, has read the petition circulating online. WE THE UNDERSIGNED in a large banner headline, the words underneath just as urgent and aggressive. It was written with mixed anger and glee.

"Like this is some old Western and we're the bad guys or

something. Do they really think a petition's going to do anything? Or that they can make us leave?"

Jade senses a hint of uncertainty in this last bit. Eran churns the water with his feet, leaning back on his hands. The ripples rise and fall against Jade's calves, tickling a little.

"No," she says. "I think it's just supposed to be a show of force. To see how many people are on their side. It's intimidation." She leans forward, dragging a finger in the water, watching the lines of its wake draw outward behind its path.

"It's not just one side against me, though," Eran says. "Half the tweets after my mom slapped that guy were talking about how violent Israelis and Jews are. Like some of these people get that the rednecks are wrong, but don't really care that much because of who they're targeting."

Jade grimaces. "But there's a GoFundMe set up for you too now. People at least on your side."

Eran grunts at this. Jade wonders what that means.

"What do you do all day?" Jade asks.

"Go crazy."

She looks over, watches water drip from his hair and land on his shoulder, running down his collarbone. He doesn't meet her eyes, keeps them focused on the water.

"Mostly TV. Video games. The school started sending me homework instead of making me pick it up, which is fine but kind of ballsy when they won't let me in in the first place. I try to avoid my mom. I try to avoid thinking about . . . about everything. I met up with Riskin, did I tell you?"

Jade raises her eyebrows and sits back again. Eran flicks his eyes up and gives a small smile. "When I snuck out. I went to his house."

"How was . . . that?" she asks.

"It was okay. I mean, it was weird. Guy likes his bourbon. And he's super unnerving. But he . . ." Eran shifts, looking for words. "He made some good points."

Jade watches him lose himself in his thoughts, feels her own thoughts rising back up.

Why would Ma and Father lie about my age?

Eran pulls his hand up to scratch absently at his shoulder, staring at a point in the water.

Wouldn't I remember the extra two years?

She wonders if Eran is thinking about the gas station again.

They are right next to each other, inches away but miles apart, lost in and overwhelmed by their own problems even while hanging out together.

Eran lowers his hand back in place behind him, partially covering Jade's by accident, bringing her back to the present. He murmurs an apology and shifts his hand, but not enough. They're still touching.

Jade stiffens at first, but then forces herself to relax. It's only two overlapping fingers, just a couple square inches of touching skin. She has to fight back the nervous laugh she feels bubbling deep in her chest.

His skin is surprisingly warm.

There is something he's not telling her, she thinks, watching him. Something on his mind that he isn't ready to say.

*   *   *

Church is more restless than usual.

Jade is a suburban Baptist, and their church has always been quiet and reserved, like a man who has attended the wrong funeral but stays in stony discomfort, too polite to leave.

At least, her parents are Baptist. Jade isn't sure what she believes anymore. She's seen the same first hint of doubt pass over Sapphire's eyes too, during sermons and prayers and readings. But Sapphire likes the hymns.

Today there is whispering, fidgeting, clearing of throats. Jade tries to look around, but Ma gives her a delicate nudge each time.

She doesn't know why she's here. Why doesn't she ever put up a fight when Ma announces they're going?

She waits. There is a sigh of relief when the minister begins the weekly announcements that mark the end of services. He seems to notice and reads through his sheet with a clip to his voice.

Her family skips the after-church cookies and sweet tea each Sunday, and for that Jade is grateful. Ordinarily she pulls on her father's hand as they walk down the aisle past the pews to the exit. Otherwise, he would stop to chat with every familiar face he sees. But today she drags her feet.

People stand in small circles in the church lobby, speaking amongst themselves. She knows this is not unusual and reminds herself under her breath. But knowing and truly believing are different things, so she can't help staring intently at them as she passes. She snaps her head from group to group, trying to make out the words.

An older man peers at the bulletin board near the front door. Jade looks at him too, and then follows his gaze, and her stomach drops. She stops in her tracks, turning toward the board.

"Jade?"

She ignores her father, staring instead at the pale blue flyer tacked among birth announcements and prayer-group schedules.

PROTEST

6 PM MONDAY, SEPT. 16 • AVERY PARK

NO TERRORISTS IN KILEY SPRINGS

There are words below this, a brief paragraph of explanation, but Jade's vision is obscured by the word "terrorists."

XV

There's a protest against you in Avery tomorrow.

She reads and rereads this sentence, weighing each word, then holds her thumb down on the tiny Delete key, erasing it in reverse.

Next to her, Sapphire watches the world slide by, humming a hymn to herself.

Jade types out her text again and hits Send this time.

"Whatcha doin', Jade?" Her father's eyes meet hers for one second in the rearview mirror.

"Nothing."

His response comes back as they pull into the driveway.

i know

Jade looks around their section of the table, reading expressions: Delia, Declan, Bonnie. All three are the same, or near enough to make no difference. Variant shades of worry, though Declan's, strangely, is tinged with excitement. She wonders if her own face betrays her as easily.

The paper in front of them is of the same pale blue, same words splashed across. There's a small tear in the corner where

Delia ripped it off the outside wall of the choir room, near the school entrance.

They found others throughout the morning, then the postings online.

"Doesn't that at least narrow it down?" Bonnie directs this to Jade.

"Some," Jade says. "But there are a ton of kids at this school who go to my church. Plus," she adds, face sagging with the realization, "that doesn't mean whoever put it up at my church is organizing it, just that they got hold of a flyer."

All four look at the paper again, absorbing this wrinkle.

"Should we go?" Delia asks.

Declan turns to her, mouth partly open. "I cannot tell if you're joking."

She shrugs. "Friends close, enemies closer? I dunno."

"It might be good to see what we're up against." Jade secretly doubts this, but in the moment it feels important to defend her friend.

"You guys make it sound like we're at war or something," Bonnie says. But she pushes her hair out of her eyes, and Jade sees the uneasiness there.

Delia opens her mouth but is distracted by movement to the side.

A girl rushing by stops suddenly at the end of their table, nearest Declan, as if something had caught her eye. She wears a canary cardigan drawn tightly over a pale blue shirt buttoned to the top, tucked into short-shorts with a too-large belt, carefully curled light brown hair above. She's chewing gum, which looks out of place with her outfit. Jade recognizes the face but can't remember a class she's ever shared with her. It's a big school. She looks like a Lacie, Jade decides.

The girl smirks and gestures with her chin at the blue flyer on the table. "You guys should come," she says, as if in challenge.

"Lissa!" Bonnie says brightly. "I didn't recognize you with your legs closed."

Declan chokes on his water, covering his mouth to keep from spitting it up on the table. He struggles for breath through rasping coughs as Delia closes a hand over Bonnie's, favoring her with a pointed look.

"Bonnie, we don't slut-shame," she admonishes in the patient tones of a veteran elementary school teacher. Jade has a moment to admire her friend's consistency, even now.

Bonnie glares at Delia, but Delia stays resolute. There is a gentle tug-of-war, and then Bonnie sighs and rolls her eyes before turning back to the girl.

"Lissa, I'm sorry," she says in a flat tone. "I did recognize you, even though your legs were closed this time. Will you ever forgive me." It's dripping with disdain, but Delia lets it pass. She knows which battles to pick.

Lissa just chews her gum, considering Bonnie with an expression that Jade is surprised to find she can't fully unpack. She thinks there might be an ounce of amusement there, well-covered by competing thoughts. In the end, Lissa snorts, shrugging, and turns to leave.

Bonnie watches her walk away and digs her fork into a soupy pile of green beans. "You know, she actually used to be kind of okay, back in middle school. Funny how people can turn out."

As she eats her green beans, Declan punctuates the silence with one more cough.

"Anyway," Bonnie says, jabbing her fork at the flyer. "We going, then?"

Delia drives. Their houses are scattered, but Jade's is closest to the park, so Delia picks her up last. Declan and Bonnie left the front for her.

Jade plays absently with the door leather, hyperaware of how quiet the ride is. No one says anything. She sneaks glances at Bonnie in the side-view mirror, wondering if the look of sick anticipation is really there or if she's projecting.

When Delia turns onto the main road that leads to the park, Jade's stomach drops. She wonders how much is anticipation, how much is from other thoughts she can't seem to push out of her mind.

Can I trust Ma and Father?

A moment later, the car slows to a stop. It only registers with Jade when she looks up and sees they're not near a traffic light.

"Whoa," she hears from behind her. In the side-view mirror, she sees Bonnie gaping forward, head sticking halfway out the window. Jade looks past the mirror, in the far distance where the road curves to the right, toward the park.

"Oh," she says.

"What's up?" Delia asks, unable to see the stretch of cars from her vantage point. Declan strains to look from his spot.

"Dele, there's traffic all the way to Avery," Jade says softly. "And the park is packed."

Delia grimaces at her steering wheel.

They leave the car at a Starbucks and walk the rest of the way, along the road, past apartments and businesses. It takes fifteen minutes. With every step, the noise from the park grows in subtle shades, reaching a fever pitch when they're still dozens of yards away, crossing the lot of a large hotel facing the lake.

Jade tries to estimate the crowd, but her vision is obscured by news vans, traffic, trees, and shrubs. Police cars line the road hugging the park, as they did with the SJC protest, but in far greater numbers. The flashing lights give her a headache, so she looks away, at Kiley Lake on the opposite side. The water looks peaceful even now. Seagulls fly overhead, agitated by the presence of so many people. Ducks gather at the shore.

A police officer waits near his car outside the slice of park nearest them. He nods as they approach.

"Trying to get to the protest?" he calls out. The sun reflects off his glasses, blinding Jade for a fraction of a second.

"Yeah," Declan says. "Uh, sir."

The officer shakes his head. "Have to go through the entrance, but I'm afraid they're not letting anyone else in, anyhow."

Bonnie looks past him, at the mass of people. "They're not?"

"No, ma'am. Too many in right now." He gestures behind him with a nod. "If people leave, we can start letting you folks in, but I don't expect that'll happen anytime soon."

"Oh." Declan doesn't seem to have anything more than this.

"Can we watch from here?" Jade asks.

The cop turns toward her, and she stares at two versions of herself in his sunglasses. "Well, 'here' is private property, so no," he says after a moment, gesturing around them. Jade turns, considering the Marriott to their right, surrounded by a moat of parking lot. "But if you find a spot where I can't see you, what can I do?"

Jade turns back, startled. They all look at the officer now, watching for a sign that he's joking. He only looks back, expressionless, then shrugs.

"Okay," Bonnie says. "Guess we should . . . go."

They hesitate and then turn, walking back the way they came.

When they're thirty feet away, Jade turns to look over her shoulder. The cop stares after them, then makes a point of turning away to face the park, his back to them.

"Okay, now," Bonnie, also looking over her shoulder, says with a giggle. They turn left as a group, heading to the side of the hotel. The lot curves around to the back, facing the water, and they emerge in a corner near enough to the park to see most of what's going on, but far enough to be concealed.

A metal railing runs along the back edge of the lot. Bonnie climbs up and sits on the top bar, which makes Jade nervous. The water is on the other side.

She leans against the railing. Someone long ago painted it a tasteful light blue, but the hotel hasn't done much upkeep. Here and there the paint has chipped away, revealing spots of rust the size of half-dollars.

The sound of the crowd mirrors the sound of the lake, she

thinks, rolling in and out like waves. The four of them wait together, chatting to pass the time. They watch the swollen crowd milling about. It is densest toward the center, where they can just see the back of a stage that has been set up. A couple trees obscure most of the view, but Jade sees giant speakers on the sides. A few people stray toward the shoreline where it is least crowded. A small child chases some of the ducks.

It's ten minutes before the sound of the crowd suddenly overtakes the waves, building slowly into a distinct cheer. They look up just as microphone feedback blasts through the speakers, and then a man's voice welcomes the crowd.

It is a raspy, dried sound, this voice, but full of energy — the sound of leaves crunching underfoot. A man who has been speaking, or yelling, too long for his vocal cords to handle, but who has no intention of stopping now. Jade caresses her own neck absently. It's not exactly unpleasant to listen to, but it does make her throat tickle. She can't see the man except for a piece of his shoulder and the back of his head when he happens to move between the leaves. He wears a crisp, pale blue button-down, no discernible patterns from this far back. She can't guess his age from the lost voice, but the hair is white, balding at the crown.

His speech builds, growing more vigorous, and Jade frowns.

"We have been lied to!" he shouts. There is more feedback on the word "lied," startling a seagull and sending it flying out over the lake. Jade watches a child on the shoulders of his father, covering his ears with his hands as the man goes on, spouting more throaty admonitions against deceit and duplicity.

"Look," the man says, softening his tone suddenly. "I don't

know these people personally. I've never met them myself. They may be very nice people."

Some in the crowd boo at this. "Terrorists!" one man calls out, followed by a couple shouts of assent.

"But!" the speaker continues, his voice picking up again. "But the bottom line is this: *We. Don't. Know.*" He enunciates each word carefully, conspiratorially, and his audience cheers, sensing where this is going. "They *might* be nice people . . . or they might not. They *might* be patriotic, or they might hold other allegiances." His volume grows again, from raspy to gravelly to husky. There is discipline to this slow crescendo. "Avi Shamir and his mother *might* be loyal to America . . . or they might be loyal to their father and husband. They might be terrorists like he was, and *we can't take that chance!*"

There is such flow to his speech, Jade thinks, even in its dryness. Like a finely ground substance that behaves as a liquid: the grains of sand that make up and then reshape the desert dunes they inhabit, waves of them across an arid landscape.

She listens with growing queasiness to the ebb and flow between the man's speech and his parched audience. They drink it up, this not-liquid, and want more. They just want to hear the right words, so he gives them up freely.

He knows he has them. Do they realize it? Jade wonders. Do they care?

For a long while, the crowd's cheering remains steady, loud, sustained, like radio static. Jade leans away from the sound, just a little, without realizing it.

Then a subtle shift, and a pattern emerges, just discernible.

They're chanting. Jade listens closely, but it's a few more seconds before enough people join in that the words become distinct.

SEND THEM BACK!

She chews her lip. It's an old nervous habit, one she's been trying to stop. She makes no attempt now. Send them back where? New York? Israel? Is there any place they would find satisfying, or is it just a broad desire to have them go away, to exert power?

Then the man, his speech done, moves fully from behind the trees that were blocking her view, and Jade's heart clenches.

She wonders why she didn't recognize the white hair, the balding spot on the crown. Even the shirt, the same he wore to Balderdash night the weekend before last.

She wonders how many crisp blue shirts Mr. DeVos owns.

XVI

How long has she known him? How often have the DeVoses spent an afternoon in their house? She can't recall a first memory of the man. In her life, he is an always-been.

Jade feels suddenly dizzy and realizes she hasn't been breathing. She inhales a little too deeply and a little too suddenly, and pretends not to notice Delia's curious glance. Then she registers another man at the podium, a smoother voice over the speakers.

"Whoa," Delia says, turning back at the sound of this new man.

"What?" Declan asks, flat but apprehensive.

"That's . . ." Delia strains to listen, tries to see around the trees. "I'm pretty sure that's Doug Abbott."

They wait, expecting more, but Delia is focused on the man's voice.

"Oh, right, Doug, of course," Bonnie says, breaking the silence.

Delia elbows her, but in a halfhearted, distracted way.

"He's a staffer for Darryl Hirsch," she mutters. "Adviser or policy director, maybe? Something. Guys, this isn't good."

The weight of what Delia says hits Jade a half second before her last sentence makes it plain. Darryl Hirsch, the governor.

Even still, her mind returns to her neighbor.

She sits in silence, feeling guilty that she cares more about Mr. DeVos's being there than she does about the governor's staffer.

"Hey," she says after a minute. "We should go."

They don't say anything on the walk back to the car. Delia keeps her head down, lost in thought, hands shoved in pockets. Declan stares at nothing, lips barely parted. Bonnie checks her phone the whole way.

Jade knows what they're thinking about. It feels like a betrayal to be the only one thinking of something else, like she is keeping a secret from them.

Worse, her mind has associated this new anxiety with the growing disquiet she's felt over the photo she found. She switches back and forth between these two things, linked but unrelated, like running into a fire to escape a flood.

The ride back to their houses is mostly quiet, except when Bonnie announces that Governor Hirsch has responded.

"Says Doug Abbott went with his blessing," she mutters, looking at her phone. "Agrees with what he said, stands by him, et cetera . . . Here: 'I don't think any Texan should have to worry that their neighbor may be a terrorist. While it is the Shamirs' right — presuming their true innocence — to live where they please, it is also anyone else's right to protest and make their distress known.'" In the side-view mirror, Bonnie glares at her phone. "'Presuming their true innocence'? He's adding fuel to this on purpose."

No one says anything for a minute, until Bonnie adds, "What a twat."

The rest of the trip is silent.

There is so much on her mind that she doesn't want there.

Classes are useful distractions. In choir they progress through another section of Haydn's *Te Deum*. It is alternately soothing and energetic, this music, an oscillation Jade finds comforting. She and Delia are altos, so their voices live within the harmony. Many girls are drawn to the melody, she knows, but melodies bore Jade.

Choir ends and, with it, the escape from her thoughts. Her face sags as they leave for lunch. She can feel Delia's curious glances. Her friend knows her well enough to understand there is more behind her anxiety than the fact of the protest and the governor's response. Jade will have to tell her.

At least about Mr. DeVos.

She faces forward as they walk down the hall to their lockers. Jade parts her lips slowly as she takes a long, deep breath, summoning the determination to tell Delia. It's funny; she's not even sure why her shame about her neighbor runs so deep. She knows it is his failing, not hers.

"Dele —"

"Whoa." Delia stops in her tracks as they round the corner, tripping a boy behind her and almost sending him tumbling. Jade follows her gaze, and the air escapes her lungs like a beach ball deflating.

She sees Martin first. They were in fourth grade together, back when he had short cropped hair, blond and spiked. It's longer now, unkempt, nearly covering his eyes, matched by the thinnest bit of hair on his upper lip he refuses to shave. Not quite a mustache, though maybe it would pass if his hair was darker, if it showed up more starkly against his pale skin.

Martin and a half dozen others, handcuffed to the push bars of the school office doors.

Two campus police officers, looking helpless. Dr. Pham and one of the vice principals, Mrs. Connor, faces taut. Kids crowding around, some taking videos with their phones, some laughing, some reading from identical yellow flyers, most just watching with the same stunned expressions.

Martin makes eye contact with Jade and grins. It is the same grin she remembers from fourth grade. With his free hand, he picks up a flyer from a stack near him on the floor, and holds it out.

WE DEMAND THE PROMPT RETURN OF

MR. GENE RISKIN

A TRUE ASSET TO THIS SCHOOL.

WE REJECT TREATING STUDENTS LIKE TERRORISTS.

WE WILL REMAIN HANDCUFFED TO

THE OFFICE UNTIL OUR DEMANDS ARE MET.

"Tell your friends," Martin says, his first words to her in years, and flicks his head back to get the hair out of his eyes.

Behind him, on the other side of the glass doors, one of the sophomore English teachers glares at the handcuffed students, his exit barred by them.

"Jesus, this —" Dele only mutters these two words before Mr. Lagunov, incredibly, begins pulling the door open, dragging Martin and three others inward by their arms.

The uproar is instantaneous.

"Ow! *Owww*, what the hell!" the girl to Martin's left screams. Martin himself scrambles to gain purchase with his feet, but these are polished tile floors, smooth and flawless.

"Gerald, stop!" barks Dr. Pham, and it takes Jade a second to realize he's addressing the teacher. Too late, Mr. Lagunov has realized his mistake.

"Are you okay?" he asks the girl weakly.

"Man, that is *fucked* up!" a kid behind Jade shouts, and others join in.

"Excuse me!" shouts Mrs. Connor.

"He's yanking arms out of people's sockets, and you're gonna get on us for swearing?" another boy retorts. The swell of affirmation to this is too loud, too sudden for Mrs. Connor to respond to.

Mr. Lagunov and Dr. Pham hover over the handcuffed kids, checking on them, but the damage is done. The shouts in the hallway swell to a fever pitch. The anger feels dangerous, enough to put the campus police on guard.

Jade's heart skips. She wants suddenly to be anywhere but here. It should be compelling; she should feel rooted to the spot. But right now the idea of being caught in the middle of this mass of fury is horrifying to the point she feels nauseated.

"Let's go," she whispers.

"Now?" Delia says, her eyes still on the crowd. "But it just got—"

"*Dele!*" Jade snaps. Her friend turns, surprised. Jade knows she sees her own desperation.

"Yeah," Delia says. "All right."

"It's just, there's so much anger everywhere already," Jade says later, when she's nearly stopped shaking. "It's gotten to me."

It's not exactly a lie, but she feels too robbed of energy for the full truth right now.

The protest.

Martin.

Mr. DeVos.

The photo.

The hurricane.

She cycles through these like a short playlist on loop, skipping each song after the first few seconds. Tired to the point of distraction by the same melodies, over and over and over.

She can't escape it at home, either, even when she tries.

This is her favorite time of day, at the peak of golden light. For just a few moments, every color is richer, more saturated, warmer, deeper. Everything is more brilliant, the most ordinary things given new glory before the night saps their luster. Jade sits at the opening to her garage, trying to hold on to this moment of bright green grass and deep and brilliant pink sky, when the back door opens behind her.

"There you are." Ma could sharpen knives with that tone.

Jade finds herself more angry by reflex than afraid, something she's not used to. She turns her head but stays seated. This is Ma interrupting her time, after all, not the other way around.

Her mother considers her, licking her lips. The shadows harden her expression, but in a different light she could look agitated; fearful, even.

"You were with that boy."

That boy, she keeps calling him, as if a name would make him real.

"What do you mean?"

"Don't," Ma snaps. "There's a photo of you in the news. Driving him in your father's Prius, in the middle of the night."

Jade's stomach drops. That reporter, the night they went to the pool. The reporter who snapped a photo right as she picked Eran up after he snuck out.

She tries to remember her expression, what her face must have been like as the flash went off. Mouth and eyes open in surprise. Would there be a glare in the driver's-side window, emphasizing the dirt and grime, overlaying it on her face and hair?

Stop.

She swallows the shame that has already begun calcifying in her throat.

Any other day she might let it win out, but too much has already happened. There is no reason to be embarrassed. She did nothing wrong.

She forces it down, into her chest, her arms, imagines it flowing through her and being repurposed into her own strength.

"Yes" is all she says back.

"Jade!" Ma barks, surprising them both. "Are you out of your mind?"

"I'm not the one acting crazy," Jade says.

"You're grounded!" Ma hisses. Jade opens her mouth, but Ma is faster. "*You cannot do this.* It is *so* dangerous for you. To be involved with him, no matter what he is or isn't."

Jade glares at her ma a moment, then turns her full body around to face her. The golden light warms her back. No one ever talks about sunset, no one her age, but she doesn't know why.

"What do you think he is, Ma?"

Ma takes a step forward, the shadows shift, and the hardness in her expression nearly dissolves. She is worried, afraid, imploring. She looks old.

"It doesn't matter, Jade," she says. "I don't care what he is. I don't care about fault or fairness. I care about you, and I care what this could do to you." Ma makes her muscles rigid, anticipating. She pulls at the stones of her bracelet. Blue, green, foggy rainbow. "Tell me you won't see him again."

Jade wonders when her ma became this.

"I'm sorry I took Father's Prius," she says finally.

"Jade." Ma breathes out. "Please. Tell me you won't see him again."

Jade turns herself back around, to face the last of the light before it goes.

She hates lying.

"I won't, Ma," she says.

She stares at the last of the sun, resentful that she's lost the taste for sitting out here, that even this sliver of relaxation was taken from her.

When it goes, Jade makes up her mind and stands.

She swings open the back door too hard, letting it hit against the wall and slam behind her. She stalks down the hallway, up the stairs. It is five angry steps to her desk drawer.

Jade looks at the photo again, at herself on this little plastic tricycle somewhere in New Orleans. Ma will be angry, but so what? Jade will be angrier. She snatches it up and hurries downstairs.

In front of the closed door to her parents' bedroom, she pauses for the first time.

You sure you want to do this?

Yes.

She reaches for the doorknob, and then hears Father's voice from the other side.

"You've been hard on her lately."

Her hand, an inch from the brass knob, unable to move.

She measures the silence. Just as she wonders if Ma's reply is too quiet to hear, it comes through.

"It's her birthday this week. It's been on my mind is all." Ma's voice is haunted. "She would be twenty."

Jade's breathing stops; her heart nearly does too. Her fingers, cartoon-inflated in the doorknob reflection.

"I know, hon," Father says. "My mind too."

"If we'd —"

"No." Father is fast, firm and gentle at the same time. A practiced maneuver. "We had no control over it."

There's quiet. Jade's lungs burn while she waits in silent agony. Then Ma's long sigh in response, and nothing more.

She moves as if underwater. Pulling her hand back takes all her concentration, all her strength. She takes a step backward, then another, a third. Eyes still on the doorknob. All her answers are behind that door, and now she can't get away fast enough.

My birthday is a month away. This thought in defiance, as if grasping on to what truth she knows.

The last of her strength breaks Jade free of whatever it is that holds her. She is only just able to keep from falling to the floor.

The stairs make her dizzy. She does not know how she makes it to her room, but a moment later she closes the door behind her and collapses on her bed.

In and out, in and out, long deep breaths under her pillow. Trying as hard as she can to get the air she needs without making a sound. Her chest aches.

It must be minutes. But eventually breathing brings her enough calm to feel in control of her own body.

I have to get out of here.

She thinks this seconds before her phone buzzes.

No text, just an image. A little blurry, but Jade can make out what must be a huge crowd being directed, shepherded away. Dozens of cars, police, flashing lights. The ghost of Eran's image, holding a phone, the reflection in what must be his living room window.

The sky in the image is a shade of pink that left the sky not long ago. This was just taken. She peers at the image closely, finds bald patches in the crowd where the road shows through.

Now a text: They're clearing the street.

Then another: Come.

I won't, Ma.

It is the easiest thing in the world to say yes.

XVII

The entrance to his street is packed. She turns onto the street behind his house, but reporters are there as well. Word has gotten out about his sneaking out the back.

Jade drives past them, hoping no one recognizes her from the other night. She slows down on the next street, and then the next, but the curb is full of cars. It's another minute or two before she finally finds a spot three blocks from Eran's, squeezing the Prius between two pickups, and sets out on foot.

She squeezes her hands into tight fists and then releases. Squeeze, release.

It's almost full night now. The yellow streetlamps corrupt all the colors around them, making everything look dead.

A police officer stops her at the entrance to his street.

"No more protesters."

"I'm not a protester," she says, looking past him at the crowd. The road is completely obstructed now, teeming with onlookers. How do Eran's neighbors get in and out? she wonders.

"No more *people*," the officer says in a clipped voice, betraying a hint of impatience. "We're past capacity. Sheriff is clearing all nonresidents out now."

Jade raises her eyebrows, hoping her own impatience doesn't show through. "Can I watch from here?"

He hesitates, favoring her with a mistrustful look, but can't find a reason to decline.

"From there." He jerks his head toward a spot across the intersection behind her. "There'll be traffic coming out, so stay clear. And don't try to enter this block."

Jade turns, eyeing the place he indicated, then gives him a nod before walking over. It's the place two sidewalks meet, at the corner of the next block. There's no bench, so she leans against the stop sign.

She texts Eran.

I'm at the intersection with Paloma Drive.

Then she remembers and walks back to the cop. He cocks an eyebrow.

"What about the next block over?" She peers down the side street, trying to make out the name on the sign. "Oak Chase."

"What about it?" he asks.

"Are you clearing that out? There are a bunch of reporters there too."

The officer looks at her long and hard, then reaches over to the radio on his shoulder and presses a button.

"Burnick? Send a car over to Oak Chase, street behind the house. Kid's telling me media has set up there too. Check it out?"

He doesn't take his eyes off Jade, and it's a moment before she realizes he's going to say nothing more. She gives him a cool look and walks back to her post, and waits.

*   *   *

She's surprised how long it takes. The protesters are first, mostly by foot; they wander back to the cars they've left on other people's streets, choking the roads. Several narrow their eyes when they see her. She tries to guess which are just genuinely curious at her presence and which recognize her from the photo.

The reporters take longer, dragging their feet as they pack their equipment, hoping for last-minute breaking news that never comes. Eventually they roll down the block like a gaudy funeral procession, leaving only the police and a few stragglers behind.

The police are last, or most of them. One car stays behind, in front of Eran's house, just visible from Jade's corner. Two others park outside either entrance to the block, guarding against those who would sneak back.

You're free.

There are only a couple other cars on the curb now, which Jade assumes belong to his neighbors. A few of those neighbors are outside now, surveying their newly evacuated space, checking their lawns and property for damage, gossiping with one another or talking to the lone policeman on duty. They frown at the spread of litter on the street. It sparkles in the yellow lights, little plastic and glass gems in an asphalt sea.

The difference is startling. It is a residential street in a suburb, so the emptiness shouldn't be so remarkable. If anything, it's what Jade's street looks like even now, minus the garbage and residual air of excitement. But her mind still holds on to the image from a half hour ago, the mass of people, the road thick with noise and anger.

275

She's still watching when she sees a lone figure emerge from Eran's house, tall, stooped, awkward. He walks to the sidewalk and turns toward her, silhouette breaking here and there against the lamps, doing his best to ignore the stares from his neighbors.

He walks up to her, looking both ways as he crosses the road even in the near-perfect silence of the evening, and stops short three feet away.

Eran looks over his shoulder at the surly officer, then back to Jade.

"Hey."

She nods.

"It's quiet."

She nods again.

Eran smiles. Jade doesn't. He turns around, slowly, as if taking everything in. When he's facing her again, his smile is wide and bright, skirting on the border with laughter.

"It's so quiet," he says again.

Now he does laugh. There's something sharp in it, like a small burst of feedback from a speaker.

But it's a laugh. She tries to remember the last time she heard it.

Then a crack of thunder. They both look up.

"Hear me out."

He says this to the sky, still facing up as if taking stock of the night clouds, then looks back down.

"Let's ride bikes."

*   *   *

Eran is already in the full swing of things when the first drop hits.

"When was the last time you rode one?" he asks, but it's not really a question. "Two years ago for me, before I got my learner's permit. I haven't pulled mine out since I started driving. But I saw it in the garage on the way over here, and I had the strongest urge to take it out. You remember what it feels like, to ride as fast as you can, getting places you can't in a car or can't quick enough on foot?"

Light drops hit her eyelashes, making her squint. But every now and then one lands on her lips, cool and soothing enough to make it worth being out here.

"And look, I know it's about to rain, but doesn't that make it better? Isn't it more fun to ride in the rain, when it's still too hot out for the wind to freeze you? When it pours, it's like swimming anyway — it feels great being in a thunderstorm, and even better when you're moving through one at top speed."

This is the old Eran, she thinks.

Almost.

"I've been cooped up inside for a couple days, and now the crazies are finally gone, and I want to get out and you can use my mom's bike —"

"Eran." Jade cuts him off. "I'm in."

She watches him hurry back to his house as she waits.

But she's still on edge from before, still feeling manic from what she overheard, and this has left a residual boldness in her that makes her energized and daring. So she texts Declan.

* * *

She braces herself when she sees Eran's silhouette emerge again, now walking two bicycles, one on either side of him.

There is no hiding Declan. He made it in under five minutes, just threw his bike into his mom's car and drove over without asking, parking just a moment ago. The knowledge that he will be seen, that Eran will understand what's happening while still too far away to say anything, batters her nerves. But it can't compete with her determination today.

The burden of two bikes makes Eran slower, prolonging the moment of anticipation. It tastes metallic but not unpleasant.

There is an instant where she wonders if he will just stop, just turn back around without saying anything, but he walks up to them both without breaking his stride.

He stands, resting a palm on either set of handlebars.

"He's not coming," Eran says finally, looking only at Jade.

"Then I'm not either." She doesn't hesitate.

Eran says nothing, just stares at her, and her patience breaks.

"What are you fighting?" she snaps. "All he's done so far is try to support and help you, every step of the way, going against his own mom and choosing you over her. How do you not see that? You have plenty of enemies already, Eran. Stop making more out of the friends you have left."

That last bit hit harder than she meant it to. She winces internally but tries not to let it show.

Eran looks at her with a stony expression, but she can read surprise there too, and something else: the smallest hint of shame.

Then another crack of thunder, and it begins to pour.

Jade watches the rain pelt Eran's hair, matting it down, taking away the waves and curls. He smiles and pushes one of the bikes to Jade. She catches it.

"Fine," he says to her. "Everyone can come."

He moves as if to get on his bike.

"Eran," Jade says, now more measured. She hopes it sounds kind, that she isn't pressing her luck. "You should apologize to him."

"It's fine," Declan mutters, embarrassed.

Eran freezes, blinking, then closes his eyes for a moment. When he opens them, he addresses Declan. "I'm *sorry*."

Jade stiffens at the sardonic tone before she senses there is no hostility there.

Eran rolls his eyes, making room for a tiny smirk as he swings a leg over the seat. "Get your bike before Mom here grounds us."

He takes them to the greenbelt, then past that; to the subdivision park, then past that.

They stop at the far edge of the park, near a low wire fence. The grass gives way to mounds of tan dirt, turned to clay in the rain.

"They're building another subdivision next to mine." Eran lifts his bike over the fence, then steps across it. "Let's go."

The lightning starts only a couple minutes in.

It illuminates their new world in flashbulb glimpses, lumines-cent photographs that burn into the backs of their eyes, leaving a glow when the darkness rushes back in. They pass through acres of mud and bright orange cones, tractors and excavators and concrete mixers abandoned at the first drops.

It pours now, a roar of water drowned out only by the cracks of thunder close overhead. The rain stirs up the dust, giving the outdoors a smell that both stings and comforts.

Jade can't remember ever being this soaked. Her phone is in her pocket, protected only by a layer of saturated denim. She doesn't care.

It's a Houston thunderstorm, a real one.

She loses track of where they've been and where they're headed. They just follow Eran along a path that winds around construction equipment and half-dug foundations that all run together after a while. He yells directions they can't hear over the storm, so they keep close behind.

She barely feels the water anymore, the way you do when you've been in a pool so long you lose your point of reference.

Every now and then, she catches Declan's grin. She wishes she felt like smiling, but this is the closest she's gotten yet.

They find a field of giant concrete pipe sections, laid about like an elephant graveyard. They leave their bikes out in the rain and climb inside one of the pipes. Declan first, then Eran and Jade.

It's cozy, but not uncomfortable, and it's dry.

Outside the rain pounds against the concrete, a series of tiny beats that merge into one continuous rumble.

No one says anything for a minute or two. All of them just enjoying the not-quite-silence.

"My mom says she didn't know my dad was planning anything."

Eran's words bounce off the rounded concrete in front of him, a jarring echo that overtakes the rain outside.

"I don't know if I believe it."

Jade hears that burst of feedback louder now. That thing on his mind, the sharpness laced into his laugh.

She almost says something but listens instead.

"Zack asked me a question." Eran tilts his head at Jade. "A friend from my synagogue. Goes to a different school. Declan knows him. Anyway. Zack asked me on Friday: If this weren't me, if it were about some random strangers, what would I believe?" He pinches the fabric of his wet jeans, making and unmaking creases. "Would I trust her when she said she didn't know anything? 'What's more likely?' is the way he put it. It's a good question."

Jade scans the texture of the concrete, looking for patterns.

"I've been thinking about it the last few days, and I don't have an answer. Or a good one. If this were just someone I'd read about? Yeah, I'd probably think she was lying. I know she was never charged, but people get not charged all the time even when they're guilty. Because of a lack of evidence or whatever."

She thinks about the way his words accelerate like the rain, each new drop building on the ones that came before.

"But more to the point, how *couldn't* she have known? How could she live with someone planning something like that, live with him for years, and just . . . not know?"

"You don't trust her?" Declan's question comes with no hint of accusation, just simple surprise.

"Why would I? I mean, isn't that it? She's been lying to me for fifteen years, but I'm supposed to believe her now?" It builds even more. "This isn't a temporary thing, or even just a long time. That is my entire life, my entire relationship with her on this earth, used up on lies. Lies are all I know from her, the only thing she's ever chosen to expose me to. She wants to pull that rug out from under me, then ask me to trust her?"

Jade listens to the words as they run together, imagines his anger as liquid, as a flowing current carrying words like debris, broken and sharp. It's soothing, almost, the ups and downs of his tones, the rush of his river-water voice.

"Well." Declan measures his words. "The guy at the gas station walked right past you, right? He was coming for your mom, not you. He only turned on you after you interfered."

Eran listens, so Declan keeps going.

"Your mom knows what it's like to be a target, and she wanted to keep you from being one too." She can't see Declan but imagines his face as he speaks and pauses. "I dunno," he says finally. "I'm not defending her for lying your whole life. I just mean that trust is easier when you at least know someone's intentions were good."

Jade picks over this, probing her own feelings. Is that true? Do intentions make a difference with trust? Should they? She thinks about Ma and Father, feeling her own face harden.

"I don't see how," Eran says, reflecting her own thoughts. "The end result is the same, isn't it? Even if her heart was in the right place, she still lied for years, and I'm the one who has to deal with the aftermath of it all. Why wouldn't she make that mistake again? How do I know she won't lie to me the next time she thinks it's for my own good?"

Declan doesn't respond, because he can't. Eran knows, so he only pauses a moment.

"And this wasn't some harmless lie. It made things worse in ways she didn't understand. Like with my anger. I've been trying to figure out how to handle it for years, and my thinking was totally based on what I thought was the truth about her and my dad."

He coughs, a throaty sound as wet and agitated as the storm.

"I can't figure out what I want," he says. "Part of me hates getting as angry as I do. But there's still another part that thinks anger can be a virtue, that it gets stuff done, and that's the part that really scares me. Like, what does it mean that I can see first-hand what kind of anger is in my DNA and still want to defend it? What does it say about me that learning what my dad did hasn't cured me of being angry?"

He waits. They wait together.

"At least before, I had an out. I figured my anger came from my mom, and the cure must be on my dad's side. I figured that was why it was hard for me to get better, because the cure was never around. And now it turns out I had it backward — my mom was the cure, and even though she was the only one around, it *still* didn't work on me."

Jade thinks about the power of anger, the power of patience, the limitations of both. How many times has she wished she had confronted her ma but deferred instead? But how many times has she discounted her own ma's anger, watched it wielded like a cudgel and promised herself never to do the same thing?

The outline of the photograph is visible in her jeans pocket. It must be soaked through.

"What does that mean? That I'm unfixable?" Eran asks the wall. "That I'll just be like him no matter what?"

Jade glares at the concrete but holds her feelings in check. Then she sees it, the glimmer of an answer to his question.

"Anger can be a virtue, but only if you can control it," she says. "Isn't that what makes us, anyway? What we decide, rather than what we're born into?"

She surprises herself with this last bit, this thought that escaped her lips unguarded. It hits a little too close to home, so she redirects.

"Maybe that's how you and your dad can be different."

She keeps her lips parted for more, but decides this is all she has to say. It's the only thing she's said since they climbed into the pipe.

Jade will think about this moment years later. The three of them, waiting out the rain in a grimy section of concrete pipeline, talking about things they didn't expect to have to deal with at their age.

In three years, ten, forty, she will think of this moment. When her granddaughter asks her about high school, what it was like, she will think of this moment.

She will think about sheltering from a thunderstorm, soaked, with two new friends who would come to mean the world to her.

But she will also think about how she listened and didn't speak. She will think about how there was so much she could have said but chose not to.

She will think about that decision, wondering what led her to keep silent about what she was going through, what she was dealing with. She will think about why she deferred, again.

She will wonder and know the answer at the same time.

You can want trust before you're ready for it.

She knows this, but it doesn't make it easier to understand.

Outside, the rain has let up. Jade looks at the circle of darkness to her right, the entrance to their pipe, and watches the water slow from a cascade to a steady stream to a trickle. She can just make it out.

They don't speak for minutes, just sit in the quiet of a wet night.

Her back aches and her legs are cramped. She doesn't want the moment to end.

"Let's go back," Eran says after another several minutes of silence.

There is sullenness in that voice but also calm. He can't hide it.

XVIII

The ride back eases her transition into the real world, and for that she is grateful. They bike slowly, almost lazily, in no hurry without the rain, no one wanting the night to end.

In middle school, she and Father would sometimes go see a movie together at Bay Creek Mall, just the two of them.

Jade loved those afternoons. She loved the total darkness of the theater, the way it would envelop her, the way she could be in a room with dozens of strangers and the darkness would be a cocoon.

She loved how the movies would pull her in, make her totally forget where she was and who she was. For two hours she was someone else, somewhere else, somewhen else.

She dreaded the walk back to the car, emerging into blinding daylight. It was jarring. "How'd you like it?" Father would ask, every time. "Good," she would answer, every time. It was embarrassing—not the question, not the answer, but the fact of inhabiting her real skin again so suddenly, when her mind was still elsewhere. Walking through a giant parking lot outside a suburban mall, fifty yards from an Applebee's, while she still imagined phoenixes and new planets and ancient civilizations and magic. Viewed side by side, movies made life seem like a sad punch line. She was too young to be able to articulate it, to understand those feelings, but she still felt them. It was hard not to.

They ride back now, through excavation sites that look almost mystical in the gloom after a storm, and Jade says goodbye to the evening, slowly. It's not the Bay Creek Mall parking lot. Jade is given the time to let go.

"There you are!" Father says as the front door opens. "Where have you been all evening?"

Jade makes some quick calculations from his pointedly upbeat tone, from Ma's forced calm. Ma is conceding something to Father, making good on some earlier promise. It would be risky to tell the truth, but Jade hates lying.

Then she sees Mr. DeVos, relaxing on the living room couch near his wife, and she deflates.

So many things have been on her mind, she nearly forgot about this one.

"Dele's house," she says, staring at him.

"Well, this is good timing," Father says. "Join us for Scattergories. The DeVoses brought some games."

Jade closes the door slowly behind her, eyes on her neighbors.

"That sounds like fun. Excuse me for a second, please." She turns quickly, before she catches a glimpse of confusion on their faces.

In the closed-off stillness of the bathroom — warm yellow light, smell of clean towels, heart beating fast — Jade asks her reflection several questions.

How long has her family known him?

How can she not trust him after all these years?

What about Sapphire?

Ma?

Father?

If they trust him, what does it say if Jade doesn't?

Can someone make a terrible mistake and still be a
good person?

Does she have a responsibility to call those mistakes out?

Is she even sure what is and isn't a mistake? Who is she
to decide?

Then why is she so angry?

Why did the sight of him make her hands shake?

Can she really be wrong about something this clear?

No. She is not wrong.

But.

The DeVoses have been there as long as she can remember.
They are as much a part of her life here as this street, this house,
the frayed yellow curtains in her room. They are as familiar as
sitting on her rooftop, as reliable as ham on Sundays.

Mr. DeVos helped her up when she skinned her knee, age six.
Convinced her that she could still learn to ride a bike and that it
didn't really hurt anyway. She stopped crying as he said the words,
like they were magic.

He had them over for a cookout for her twelfth birthday
party, spent an hour looking for a piñata beforehand. She'd always

wanted a piñata, even if she secretly thought twelve was too old for one.

He taught her swear words in Dutch, making her promise to keep it a secret from her parents. He helped her with trigonometry, because he used to teach it. With history, with economics, with her SATs.

Still, her heart pounds. She forces her hands not to move.

Mr. DeVos is a good man. But good men can be wrong, even badly wrong.

He has an open mind and is a good listener. He deserves some faith. She owes him that much.

She will tell him, she decides. But not today.

Jade stares at her reflection, waiting for it to smile back at her.

Today is for Scattergories.

"Book title that starts with the letter *K*," he says. "Jade? What'd you put?"

Jade blinks at her empty sheet a few times and looks up at Mr. DeVos's sly smile.

"You're an asshole and you're wrong about Eran Sharon."

Jade drinks in the shock and discomfort and hurt she sees in Mr. DeVos's eyes. It is both satisfying and terrible, a delicious pain. No one says anything for a moment, until Sapphire breaks the silence.

"That doesn't even begin with *K*."

"Jade!" Ma hisses.

Jade turns her fire toward her. "Do not," she snaps. "Where have *you* been the last two weeks? Where have *both* of you been?" she asks, folding Father in with her eyes. "You know there's a drive to kick Eran and his mom out of the city?"

"That has no chan—"

"I *know* it won't happen, Ma. It's not about it happening—it's about the fact that people are trying, and you guys are just sitting there letting them. And this man"—she points at Mr. DeVos without looking at him—"is leading the charge."

Jade pauses long enough to hear her voice echo, just barely, off the high ceiling of the dining room. She glares at her neighbor. He looks back, too stunned to react.

"Eran is my . . ." She swallows. "He's more than a friend. What you're doing to him and his family is evil. He was two years old when his dad killed those people. It destroyed his mom and turned his life upside down. And you're going to blame him for that?"

She turns back to her parents. "You know what it's like to know nothing about where you came from? You know what it's like when your parents won't tell you the truth about it, no matter how much you ask?" Something flickers in Ma's eyes here. "And then suddenly learn it all at seventeen? And then have an entire country hate you for it? And you guys want to laugh and play Scattergories with the guy causing all this."

There's some quiet.

"You said 'parents,'" Ma says.

"What?"

"You said 'parents,' with an *s*. 'You know what it's like when

290

your *parents* won't tell you the truth.'" Ma's expression is something Jade hasn't seen before. "Who were you talking about?"

For just a moment, Jade is silent, even now impressed by Ma's sharp perception.

This thought, the final click of a gear holding everything in place.

You still have it with you. It's in your pocket.

It's time.

She presses the valve that releases it all.

Jade pulls the photograph out, wrinkled and wet, but the image is still good. She holds it out to Ma like a weapon, relishes the look of near agony that spreads on Ma's face as she registers what she's seeing.

"You've been keeping it from me too long," Jade says, in a voice she stole from her mother. "I need to know. How old am I?"

Ma stares at the photo with a level of misery on her face that Jade finds almost unnerving. She stays that way for a long time, too long, watching the photo as if it were a memory played back to her.

"That's not you, Jade," she says finally.

They go to her parents' bedroom, just the three of them, after Father sends the DeVoses home. A room in the heart of their house, enclosed but not cramped, private but not claustrophobic.

Ma closes the door gently behind them, leads her daughter to the bed. She sits, pats a spot of comforter next to her, too lightly to hear.

Jade doesn't move.

Father sits on the carpet, back against the wall, forearms on his knees.

"I will tell you," Ma says. "If I hesitate, it's because it hurts, not because I'm holding back. I know it's difficult to trust me right now, but this is the truth."

Ma looks down at the photo, gently wiping off the last of the water with the corner of her sleeve. The sadness in her voice scares Jade.

"You had an older sister," she says, tugging a stone of her bracelet. "Her name was Opal."

Jade stands at first, but as her ma speaks, she moves to sit on the bed.

She was an explosion into our lives. A burst of color, of energy, always giggling, always moving. You know how some people seem to laugh at everything, are so quick to joy? She was like that from the start. Every day for two years, there was laughter in our little house. Every day that spirit was pouring out of her.

Then one day it wasn't.

"It's just a cold," they said. "Children get sick. She's tired, but she'll come bouncing back."

She didn't. There were no other symptoms at first. Maybe on another child, it would've looked normal. Maybe it would've gone undiagnosed even longer. Maybe that joy she had carried with

*her up until then added another couple years to her life, if only by
providing the point of contrast.*

*It took a while. Another year to get just the glimmer of an
answer. By then, you were with us too, oblivious to it all.*

*We saw the inside of too many doctors' offices. Opal stayed in
too many hospital beds. She gave too much of her blood to labs, to
faceless women and men running her life through their machines.*

*The same words, over and over: "Congenital. Dormant.
Unclear. Unclear. Unclear."*

Then: "Terminal."

Jade looks at the argyle pattern of her parents' comforter. She
finds a path in the lines that zigzag toward Ma, connect her to
her mother.

It took a full week for the weight of that word to hit us.

*It was more than denial. It was disorientation. An inability
to even understand the meaning, like it wasn't even a word, but
a sound at the far edges of our comprehension. Like seeing a face
you can't recognize.*

*But there was too much to do to fall apart. Opal needed more
and more equipment, more routines at home and at the hospital.*

*We were determined to make her as comfortable as possible,
to pack as much happiness as we could into the little time she had.*

Then Katrina came.

*We were lucky when the hurricane hit. So much of the
city was underwater, for such a long time. Our house flooded,*

understand, but only an inch. We lost power two days, pulled up the carpet to dry underneath. Nothing much to do after that. We were lucky.

But the hurricane made an already-fraught situation even harder. So much was closed down and abandoned. Roads were wiped away. Emergency services tapped out.

Opal needed almost round-the-clock supervision. She had very strict and specific needs, an entire cabinet of prescription drugs. Equipment to monitor, tubes to change out, shots to administer. A thousand ways something could go wrong, a million tiny mistakes that could cost her her life. And we were on our own.

Some days we got her back. Just a flicker. We saw the energy she'd had before; we heard her laughter. Then the next day, she'd slip back in. My little rainbow trapped in the fog.

Some days her pain was so great that nothing helped. All we could do was stay with her as she cried.

There were times that were especially hard on us too. Nights we did not sleep, trying to keep up with a new emergency, some new threat to Opal's life. It very nearly drove your father and me apart. Some fights we had still make me sad to think about. We were young and unprepared for a challenge this enormous.

It went on another year. A steady, subtle decline. Like being nudged, slowly, slowly, over a cliff. It was a drawn-out torture.

There were times, toward the end, that the anticipation became unbearable. I caught myself wishing for it to happen, hoping for an easy way out. I would feel so, so guilty, thinking these thoughts, but that wouldn't stop me from thinking them.

I wish I could say different, but I can't. Those were dark months, waiting for the death of a child we could barely take care of.

Then, of course, one night it happened.

When I heard that long, sustained beep, I was lying in bed, asleep. It pulled me into a half-awake state — or maybe that's a lie I tell myself. I wish my first feeling had been dread, horror, anguish, confusion; anything else but relief.

I think that was what broke me. Those two seconds of relief, while my head was still on the pillow.

Jade has never heard Ma's voice lose its composure before. She has never heard this lack of confidence, so deafening in its absence.

Father watches Jade as Ma speaks, but she cannot meet his eyes.

She finds that she has gripped a diamond of the argyle comforter in her fist.

The guilt came immediately after, of course. The dread, the horror, the anguish, all of it. The shame.

I don't remember burying Opal. I don't remember much from the days after. She was almost seven. She made it longer than anyone anticipated.

I expected despair. I expected the guilt.

But expecting on paper is not the same as living it.

I began to wonder if I had allowed Opal to die. When I was alone, having coffee in the kitchen, sitting on the bus. I would find myself questioning whether I had slipped in my care of her on purpose, subconsciously sabotaging my daughter's fragile life.

Your father tried to reassure me, but it did no good. He assumed I was just grieving, but this was more than that. He's always been able to see the good that's there in a way that's harder for me. He can see past tragedy.

Maybe it was that, or maybe it was because he was taking care of you while I was gone to the world. Either way, Opal didn't stay with him the way she did me.

I saw her everywhere. I would go to the grocery store, and she would be an aisle over, holding another woman's hand. I would go to work, and she would emerge from a courtroom down the hallway. I would go to church and see the back of her head ten pews up. I would rush over in the middle of services and she was gone, and everyone would be looking at me.

You asked about your missing sister, at first. You weren't quite five. But I wouldn't say her name. Couldn't hear it. And when I sensed that you were starting to forget her, I let it happen. It made the shame so much worse, but I let it happen anyway.

I stayed this way for nearly a year. By then, Sapphire was born, but I had forgotten about my two living daughters. Your father could not reach me, but not for lack of trying.

I came to hate New Orleans, associating it not with my family then but the family I had lost, the little girl I had let down.

Your father recognized it well before I did, to his credit.

Understand, he loved that city. It was home to him, and he always thought it would be forever. Even after the hurricane, he thought we could make it work. Maybe he saw things too rosy, but maybe he was right.

But neither of us expected this.

It was his idea to leave. He recognized that I needed that.
So we did.
I couldn't talk about New Orleans.
So we didn't.
And when I finally looked away from Opal, Jade, I saw you.

"I thought I could keep this locked up in the twelve years ago where it belonged," Ma says. Her voice is dry from speaking, from remembering.

"I thought it wouldn't leak out, that it would congeal over time into something I could remove." She looks straight ahead, at the empty wall. "But I think the focus of my guilt and my anxiety just transferred over to you."

For the first time since she started talking, Ma turns to look at Jade. Jade can feel that look even as she keeps her own eyes down, on the comforter. It warms her cheek.

"You were so young, Jade. Delicate, like she had been. I was afraid that I would fail as a parent with you, the way I had with Opal."

Jade lets go of the comforter.

"I know I worry too much about you, Jade. I know I fuss and fret. I know I make it hard on you to learn about your past." Ma takes a deep breath in, lets it out. Jade senses her mother's release in that breath, feels it herself. "There is history there, and I am still trying to fight against it. That's all."

She puts a light hand on Jade's knee. It is dry but warm.

"But that's my history, not yours. Even your father would agree." Jade feels her ma's smile.

"I would," Father says. His low voice pulls at Jade, coaxes her eyes finally to his. He watches her with a still expression. Then, slowly, a smile forms.

"You remember that book of mine you ran across, about the three deaths?" he asks. "I left it on the table. You were about ten or eleven."

Jade doesn't remember. She shakes her head slowly to the right, the left.

"Can't remember the title now. It was open to a page, and you saw it on the table and read what was there. It was a passage about how everyone has three deaths: first when their body dies, second when they're buried. Third death is when someone's name is spoken for the last time."

Father smiles wider now, reliving the memory.

"Your ma and I found you in front of the computer hours later. You were looking up old obituaries, newspaper stories, any name you could find from a hundred years ago or more. Not famous people, but everyday folks — people who were long since forgotten. You were saying their names out loud." Father chuckles. "When we asked you what you were doing, you said, 'I'm trying to keep them alive forever. It's not fair they have to die just because they were regular people.' You don't remember?"

She does, now. She felt the first faint tug when Father listed the three deaths, a wisp of a memory that became clearer and more vivid the longer he spoke. She had been terrified of that passage, had been saddened by the thought that one day she, too, would die for want of her name on someone else's lips.

Ma and Father had shown her the rest of the passage then, about how living forever isn't always a blessing. How many of those people wanted to die, wished people would stop saying their names so they could move on, separate themselves from a legacy they could no longer control.

"You've always been a pretty literal person," Father says. "Like your ma. That was my mistake, not remembering that. So let me tell you what I remember about New Orleans. No rosy stories this time."

Father scratches his chin.

"The truth is, it had its good and bad parts, before the storm. Like any place. The sidewalks were mostly cracked, streets even worse. We called the city, didn't do any good. But those are small things, when you take in the good."

He stares past Jade, getting lost.

"You knew your neighbors in New Orleans. More than here, even. People here are nice on the outside, but only a few of them keep that going past hello. Maybe that's why we were so forgiving of Mr. DeVos, because he's been one of the few real ones." Father looks down now, at the carpet, counting his memories. "But back there, your home was theirs, and theirs was yours. Guy on the corner, sold me a paper every morning, sometimes put in a cup of coffee just because. Barber and I went to the same poker night when I was younger. Block parties every year before the storm; didn't need a permit. That kind of thing."

He grazes the stubble on his cheek with his fingernails.

"Katrina changed that. It was quieter afterward. Not a peaceful quiet, though, a sad quiet." Father lets out a couple beats of a reluctant chuckle. "Quieter in the streets, I mean. It was louder, much louder, in the news. The world was watching us. We were like an exhibit — how are these fools going to survive and rebuild? It was a curiosity for a lot of people on the outside. They had pity, sure, but they were so detached from it. It was entertainment more than anything."

The remembering pulls at the corners of his mouth, like the smile there is too heavy to carry.

"Maybe it was worse that we didn't leave with everyone else. It broke my heart, staying behind. Seeing the ruins, not knowing what would come back." Jade looks at the whites of his eyes, cracked with red here and there. "You get it, though? It broke my heart because I remembered what there was before. Because there was good too."

Father sighs, long and deep, an unusual thing for him.

"I miss New Orleans. Your ma didn't like it much, but I did. That's not rosy, just the truth." He smiles. "But I'm not a fool. It had its problems, same as any other place. It's my old hometown, but it's not home for *us*. Your ma's right about that."

Father flicks his eyes, finally, back to Jade.

"If you're looking for home, this is it, sunshine. You'll find things you love and hate about it. You already have. You'll tell your kids someday.

"But this is the place that made you."

* * *

Jade barely remembers the walk to her own room.

She has never felt relief and sadness in such intensity, in such equal parts, at the same time. She wonders if this is a fraction of what it was like for Ma when Opal died.

She sits on her own bed now.

Sapphire knows enough to come.

She knows to walk in without knocking, that her knock is neither expected nor needed, that she is welcome most in times like this.

She knows not to say anything, that words are useless. She knows not to ask what's wrong, that her sister will tell her when she's ready. She knows to just be.

And she knows to leave when Jade feels she has to be alone again.

Jade watches the door close behind her sister.

She wonders where that tricycle is now. Discarded, donated, washed out into the Gulf with the rest of the hurricane's chaos.

Jade looks at Opal, at her new sister, at this tiny moment captured in the tiny life of this tiny person.

She sits that way for a long time before her phone buzzes. A wall of text. She doesn't know the number, but she recognizes the frenetic energy behind those words.

Jade puts the photo down.

DEVORAH

Her heart skips a beat. There is one paragraph left. The only one she insisted she write herself.

It will be choppy, and imperfect in its grammar, and a noticeable shift of style. The young lawyer tried to help, of course, even if only to correct the grammar. But she insisted this paragraph have her full voice.

None of this worries her. She spent a full day writing and rewriting these few sentences, and still she feels they are inadequate. She comes only to the edge of what she truly wishes to say, but never further.

This is the closest she could come, and it is not enough. So her heart pounds.

"My tiny boy, my Avi," she begins, thinking again about the permanence and impermanence of a name. Her mind moves through the space between her son and herself, marking the path to him. He is only a few steps, a few dozen feet away.

"One day he will learn where from he comes. I do not know when. I do not know how to say to him. I want to put this day off for as long as it is possible."

She speaks slowly now, as if each word is a struggle, because it is.

"I want to care for him, now. He is my concern, only. Not myself." She taps her own chest too hard.

"I want only to move on. For him," she says, shoving the word out through her teeth, with a force that has been absent in her speech until now. "His father committed carnage, yes. This awful sin that destroyed many lives."

There are seven words left.

"But that was Dani. Not this boy."

They are not enough.

So she says five more.

ERAN

XIX

I am aware of some things and not others.

Anger can be a virtue.

I remember crawling out of the pipe, heading back home. I remember my wet bike seat. I remember the giant bulldozer we passed on the way in.

But only if you can control it.

I don't remember the rain letting up. I don't remember saying goodbye to Jade and Declan.

Maybe that's how you and your dad can be different.

The entire way home, I think about what Jade said. About her careful word choice.

Can be.

I forget how soaked I am until the AC hits. It kicks on right as the back door closes behind me. I stand dumbly in place for a moment, as if stunned, and shiver a little when I feel the cold air.

"Eran?" This voice, from the living room. It's not Eema's, but it's familiar.

I take off my shoes and socks, letting the carpet dry my bare feet.

Mrs. Redwood is just getting up from the couch when I walk into the living room.

"Hey." I look at her, not sure what to do. She isn't smiling, which is rare for her.

"Eran," she says, shuffling toward the door. "Your mother had to go. She was trying to get ahold of you. We gotta go too."

I pull my phone out of my pocket, trying to wipe drops off the screen with a wet shirt. "It's dead," I tell her, because I don't know what else to say. Mrs. Redwood nods but looks distracted.

"Listen, Eran. Your mom got a call from your rabbi a few minutes ago. Some idiots busted up your synagogue pretty bad."

I don't react, even internally, because I'm still parsing out what this means.

Mrs. Redwood looks pained, like she's doing something unpleasant but necessary.

"She only left a minute ago. Let's go, kiddo. I'll drive."

I stand there while she opens the door.

"The synagogue?" I manage, finally.

Mrs. Redwood turns around. She looks at me a second, then glances down at my feet.

"You need your shoes. We gotta hustle. Let's go, Eran."

It is twelve minutes to the synagogue.

I've never been in Mrs. Redwood's car. It's ancient. Something from the eighties, long and wide, wood paneling. Is it real wood? Did they use to make cars out of wood? Isn't that dangerous? Didn't they have aluminum and steel in the eighties? Wait. What are cars normally made out of? I get lost in this train of thought and then remember where I am, what we're doing.

Shipley's Donuts, then the Mormon church.

I ask her what she means by "busted."

"I don't know, amigo. Your mom didn't say much, just that she had to go and would I wait there for you."

Valero station, where that guy shoved us down to the ground. I keep my eyes on the spot where I fell, moving my head to follow it as we drive by.

The seats are fake leather. It smells dusty and old, a grandma car. But it's clean. She has a cross hanging from the rearview mirror, swaying back and forth. I get lost in the rhythm for a bit. There's a tape player.

Highway 6.

"Did someone vandalize the synagogue?" I ask.

"I don't know, Eran."

We make it there in nine minutes.

There are red and blue lights flashing as we get closer, playing off the dashboard and the seats and every other surface, making my stomach drop. I look for Eema.

The parking lot is half paved, half gravel. Mrs. Redwood pulls up to a not-spot in the gravel. It's closer.

My door's open before the car's off. I'm out, I'm walking up to the main double doors, and I see it before I really register it.

One of the doors is wide open. The other, still closed, the stained-glass window in its center shattered. Impaled by a giant wooden cross.

I slow down as I get closer to the door. The cross is boxy, as thick as it is wide, an effective battering ram. It is fine wood, I can see, ornamental. I wonder where it came from.

It hangs loosely from the window it was shoved through, its bottom inside, the T of the cross outside, supporting it and keeping it from sliding out. There's still some jagged glass left sticking out of the frame. I scan my memories, but I can't immediately remember what this stained-glass window was.

I look at the floor just inside. There are shards of glass everywhere, thick and heavy. Most are different shades of green, some brown, the rest white, and I remember. The Tree of Life. I loved this window.

"Eran."

I look up and see Mrs. Persky farther inside the entrance hall. And Rabbi Cassel, and two police officers, and a dozen other people. And Eema.

And what else has been done.

There is glass everywhere inside too, but what I notice first is the paper.

It takes me a moment to make sense of it, but then I see the highlighting, and the little colored paper clips they use to bookmark pages for whoever's leading services. These are pages of the siddur, dozens of copies ripped up, pages torn out.

The glass is from framed photos and art that had been hanging on the wall.

Beyond that, beyond this group standing around, is the sanctuary. I walk past everyone. The doorway frames a little rectangle of chaos, a little glimpse, like the frame of a television showing someone else's life, like watching Eema through the door frame at home as she picked through socks. I walk in.

There is garbage everywhere. Rancid, rotting garbage. Food

that had been thrown out days before. They must have pulled it in from the dumpster in the parking lot.

I keep going.

The chairs are in disarray. They're just cheap folding chairs, metal with a vinyl cushion. But they're everywhere, as if they've literally been tossed around. I see bits of fluff here and there, and realize they've taken a knife to the cushions, ripping open the little bit of upholstery they had.

I walk past these, toward the *bimah,* the raised platform with the giant wooden podium at the front of the sanctuary. There are scratch marks all over this, but I'm looking behind it, at the ark, at the ornate cabinet where they keep the Torahs.

How many do we have? I think three. I usually only get a glimpse when they open the ark doors. Except on my bar mitzvah, when I was up there, when the rabbi pulled one out to hand to me, to carry around the sanctuary. I remember three.

One of them is on the floor now, undressed and rolled out, down the two *bimah* steps and across the carpet. Another is still in the ark, but opened and sliced in half down the full height of the scroll. I can't see the third. Maybe they left it alone.

"Be careful."

Eema has followed me in. I look at her, and then past her, to a small group that stands just in the doorway.

My stomach drops. For the first time, I remember where I am, who I am, what it was like the last time we were here.

"Maybe you should leave."

Mrs. Persky is at the front of the group.

I open my mouth to say something I haven't thought through

yet, to draw from the well I always do, but a pinprick of thought interrupts me, makes me stop. A flash image from the inside of a concrete pipe in the middle of a thunderstorm.

Then Eema steps forward. She puts herself between me and Mrs. Persky, between me and the group standing with her.

She's guarding me, I realize with a jolt.

"We are here to help." Her tone is the same. What it was at the gas station, what it was in front of our house. It is firm but resigned, the voice of someone who has come to accept too much, who knows what it is to have to live with something.

How long has she been doing stuff like this? Little protective moves that I found annoying at the time, when I didn't understand what was driving them?

I stare at the back of her head, at the big bushy mass of hair. There's a lot of brown now. She hasn't dyed it in a while.

"Don't you think you've done enough?" Mrs. Persky snaps. I'm taken aback by the ferocity there. She has been waiting to say something, I realize, waiting longer than she wanted to, dying to get this out. "We don't need your help — we need you and your son to go away. We need you to stop attracting all this unwanted attention on us."

She gestures around her at the destruction that fills the room: the overturned chairs, the desecrated Torahs, the damage to the podium, the garbage, the glass, the torn paper. Other things I'm only now seeing: scratch marks on the walls, torn carpet, folding tables snapped in half.

"Why do you think they did this?" Mrs. Persky asks, incredulous. "Do you think it was because of any of us?" There are more behind her now, nodding. Mr. Cohn, who taught us Sunday school through seventh grade. Miss Kaplan, the last rabbi's daughter.

Zack.

I didn't see him arrive, but there he is, a walking punch to the gut. He won't even make eye contact with me. He's just looking at Eema; they all are, daring her to reply, and I feel the first bubbles in the water rise to the top.

Fuck him. Fuck all of them. We didn't do any of this shit. It's been —

Maybe that's how you and your dad can be different, Jade whispers in my ear.

You really thought you'd get better? You really thought you could go a day without fucking it up?

This is what you do.

This is what you'll always —

"Fuck off," I mutter.

"What?" Zack says this, looking at me for the first time.

"Not you."

I walk past Eema. I put myself between her and them.

"We're here to help," I say, low and steady as I can.

I can still feel it, can feel the water bubbling, making my hands shake a little, my voice too. I ignore it. It hurts my chest, but I ignore it.

"We haven't done anything. We didn't do any of this, and we weren't the cause of it. It was done to us as much as it was to you."

My voice is almost cracking.

"If they'd done this to our house instead, you'd be fine with that? You'd be cool with it?"

I wait. They think this is a rhetorical question, I know.

"Would you, Zack?" He looks taken aback at my forcing him to answer.

"No," he mutters, resenting me for calling him out.

"What about you, Mrs. Persky? Better us than the synagogue?"

She glares at me. There is something she wants to say to this, but she's weighing the wisdom of it. So I say it for her.

"I know you think my mom was part of the parade bombing. Or you suspect it."

She scoffs, breaking eye contact. But she doesn't deny it, and that tells me everything.

"She wasn't. I know because I've been watching this eat at her for fifteen years, seeing her carry this huge burden by herself. Accepting everyone's judgment because there were no other options, because she knew there was nothing she could say to convince anyone. She knew she would have to live as a victim without being seen as a victim."

Mrs. Redwood appears behind the group, drawn in by the commotion. Then the rabbi behind her. He looks livid. I can't remember ever seeing him even angry. It almost knocks me off course, but I have too much I need to say to stop now.

"It's just, I didn't know that's what I was seeing until a couple weeks ago, because she was working so hard to keep it away from me. That's been her focus since the day it happened: keeping all this shit away from me."

My voice has been building, growing louder, the stress marks showing. I put all my strength into shoving it down. I just need the lid on for another minute.

This is what you always do.

"How lonely do you think that is? To have something that awful happen to you, and then be blamed for it? To make the choice not to involve the only person that could share the burden because you don't *want* to burden him? That's how I know she wasn't involved. Because the only thing she's cared about since that day is cleaning up after my dad's mess so it wouldn't affect me. She didn't put herself in that situation, my dumb angry crazy dad did, and people like you kept her th —"

"I cannot believe that," Mrs. Persky snaps.

The interruption does it, knocks the lid off the pot, and I know I'm going to scream, and then I think, *Kalamazoo.*

I can feel Eema behind me. Right behind, watching. The bubbling simmers down, the rolling boil dying, and I'm just left with a little heartburn. But a calm voice.

"I'm not arguing this point. I don't care about convincing you, either. I'm stating a fact. You can do whatever you want with it, but it won't change its truth.

"My mom has been surviving for fifteen years despite the best efforts of people like you. She'll keep that up as long as it takes. Me too.

"We're here to help clean up, because this happened to us too."

I take a breath. It comes easy, a miracle. It leaves me with enough control to look directly at Mrs. Persky.

"You're the one who said I should come here more often."

Once you were nine. You screamed at your mother.

Your emotions were too big for you, but it left a mark. A point of reference that you could save for later, to revisit and measure against.

You're older now.

Mrs. Persky doesn't look the least bit cowed. She's an older woman, and I suspect she's not impressed easily.

I don't care. This wasn't for her.

I turn around. Eema is watching me, has been, as I knew, as I felt. She has a look so rare I don't recognize it at first.

Pride. That makes me sad.

I turn back and accidentally make eye contact with the rabbi. My stomach almost drops before I see that he's not glowering anymore. His expression is almost a smile, and at least a little playful, and then I realize it wasn't me who had made him angry.

"Thank you," he calls from the back of the room, booming voice startling Mrs. Persky and Mr. Cohn. "I think we could use all the hands we could get, honestly."

He looks directly at me, and I directly back at him.

"There's a lot to clean up."

Mrs. Redwood claps, once, loud.

"Well, I got nothin' better going on tonight."

XX

We roll up the Torahs first, Rabbi Cassel and Eema and me. It's careful, slow work.

The police ask us not to, just yet. They need to take photos.

"Young man," Rabbi Cassel tells the officer. "Leaving a Torah in this condition would be like leaving your grandmother naked in a snowstorm."

I ask the rabbi what we're going to do about them. The damage is pretty serious.

"There are ways to repair a Torah and make it kosher again," he says. "It's not cheap, but it is necessary."

We'll all have to fast for a while, he tells us. The whole congregation. Standard practice when a Torah so much as touches the ground.

"You seem pretty Zen about this whole thing," I tell him. I pick up the shards of fine wood, chunks broken off the handles of the Torah they rolled across the floor.

"This is not my first synagogue to be vandalized, Eran."

I look at him, trying to guess his age. Sixty-five, maybe seventy.

Declan and Jade show up within twenty minutes. Eema let me use her phone to text them both. It's a Tuesday night so I wasn't sure, but when they both said yes, I wasn't really surprised.

We all work alongside each other, sometimes talking, sometimes not. It comes in waves, a side comment or two that turns into a conversation.

Then we're quiet again, confronted by the work ahead of us, what it means that it even needs to be done.

I steal glances at Jade when she's not looking. She looks distracted when she doesn't know she's being watched. Thinking about whatever it is she hasn't told us yet.

Does she know I sense something? Probably. She's smarter than I am.

We work till near midnight. We're not done. There are only a handful of us, but I'm proud that the people we brought made up about half the crew.

"We will come back tomorrow," Eema tells the rabbi as he locks up.

"That's very nice of you, but please don't feel—"

"We will come back tomorrow," she says again.

I ride home with Mrs. Redwood. I think Eema understands.

We're there by ten the next morning. Mrs. Redwood brings her wife, Jeanie. I've never shared more than a few words with Jeanie, who seems reserved next to Mrs. Redwood but not uncomfortable. She gets right to work, moving faster and more diligently than I'd expect from an old woman.

We clean up glass, we shampoo the carpet, we vacuum, we sweep.

We take breaks. Have lunch. Mrs. Redwood finds a bottle of kosher wine.

"Is this any good?" she asks, peering at the label. "Manny-whozit." The rabbi's look is somewhere between disapproving and amused, but he defers. Maybe because she's a guest, maybe because she's older than him.

"Manischewitz," I say. "It's supposed to be sweet, but I think it tastes like rubbing alcohol."

"You've had rubbing alcohol?" She smirks and pours some into a paper cup, swirling it around like she's some kind of connoisseur.

She takes a sip and tilts her head back, as if considering.

"This is both wonderful and terrible at the same time," she says finally, to the ceiling.

"I told you."

"No." She points at me with the pinkie finger of the hand holding her cup. "You said it was like rubbing alcohol. This is better."

We go back to work.

The police took photos where they could, but we make sure to take our own before we move anything.

We take inventory of the damages, marking carefully the number of chairs slashed, the square footage of carpet that's been torn up or irreparably stained.

Victorious Lutheran Church calls us. We learn where the cross came from. They saw it on the news.

We drive it over. It's only a quarter mile away.

They are relieved but apologetic, as if this was their fault. We end up comforting the pastor, making it clear their church was vandalized too. The cross was crowbarred off their front door, leaving foot-long splinters where it came apart.

There's a moment where I have to stifle a laugh at the absurdity of his guilt. He's a nice man.

Mr. Rosen teaches me how to patch holes in the drywall. I take over when I've gotten the hang of it.

Jeanie finds me.

"Hello," she says, and I think she's come for supplies or to help or to ask where the bathroom is. But she just stands there, with her peaceful, self-sure smile, and I see that she's come for me.

"Hi," I say. For the first time, I realize I only know her as Jeanie.

"You're avoiding your mom."

I put the spackling paste down.

"Sorry?"

Jeanie only smiles with her lips closed, no teeth. If you don't know her, it looks forced and polite; if you do know her, you know it's just that she's pretty chill.

"No biggie, just something I noticed." She lets her smile pull wider, just a hair, just enough to notice. "Thought you might want to talk about it. We're here if you do."

Jeanie walks past me, still with that smile, and disappears into the social hall.

I turn back to the hole I'm smoothing over, thinking of my Snoopy bank, the little crater in the wall my last big bout of anger left.

* * *

Declan and Jade come by right after school. I don't even think they stop home first.

They bring Delia and Bonnie, and our little team grows.

"The school's been getting a lot of bad publicity," Bonnie says, tying up another bag of trash.

I look at her. I've been out of the loop.

Declan nods sagely. "Martin Krauss's dad is the PTA treasurer, or secretary or whatever. He was already super pissed about how they handled that whole handcuff protest thing at the school and was raising a big stink about it." He looks around. "Then word got out about this place getting trashed, and it's sorta been turning people to our side."

I don't look at him. Something about the way he talks about "sides," like it's a football game, compounds the gross feeling I got when I was reading tweets and comments that were alternately against us or sympathetic.

Like after the governor said his thing. People either attacked us because they loved the governor or were supportive because they hated him. It had nothing to do with us. What he said was just everyone's cue as to which side to take.

"Oh, Kyden Wheeler got suspended," Declan adds.

This takes a second to register.

"Who?"

"I don't know him," he says more softly. "I think he was in your PE class though, from what I heard?"

I stare at the twist tie in my hand. The guy who shoved me against the changing room bench.

I smile to myself. Dr. Pham actually went through with it.

*   *   *

We stop for the day around six in the evening.

"Hey." Declan nudges me as we're locking up. "Come over? I finally got *Injustice 2.*"

I glance over at Jade, but she's a ways off, not looking, keeping us at arm's length or beyond.

"Won't your mom be mad?" I ask.

"Seems likely."

Declan always picks Flash, because he likes grabbing his opponent and running back in time to smash him against the Sphinx. I think it's kinda weird, but it makes him laugh every time.

I play Harley Quinn because I like her hyenas.

"Where is she, anyway?" I ask.

"Out. With Don."

"When are they getting back?" I ask.

He shrugs.

"Aren't you worried about that?"

He shrugs.

I can't tell for sure if he really isn't worried, but I know why he invited me over, and I know enough to just appreciate it.

But when we hear the garage door open, I glance over, looking for any signs. He doesn't even react.

Donovan walks in the room first, carrying two grocery bags in each hand. He pauses for only a second when he sees us.

"This should be interesting," he says, and disappears into the hallway toward the kitchen.

A moment later, I hear his mom toss her keys on the dining room table and follow the sound of her shoes against the carpet. It's eleven steps before the fridge door creaks open, then the crack and hiss of a can. It'll be Diet Sprite.

I turn my head to the living room entrance, timing it to her arrival, and brace myself.

"No. Absolutely not."

Declan pauses the game and turns to look at his mother, eyebrows raised expectantly.

"What exactly do you think you're doing?"

"We're playing *Injustice 2*," Declan says.

Donovan walks in from the kitchen to watch, leaning against the door frame, holding his own Coke.

"Do you think that's funny?" his mom hisses. "What did I tell you about speaking with him, much less inviting him over to our house?"

"I don't really —" Declan began.

"Mom, he's right in front of you. You can at least treat him like a human being." This from Donovan, behind her.

She turns, surprised. Declan trails off, whatever he was about to say forgotten.

"You remember when Dad filed for divorce, how everyone in your church group reacted?" Donovan says.

Mrs. Knowles's lips tighten more than I've ever seen them do. I hold my breath. Donovan looks unfazed.

"They all just straight-up shunned you. They blamed you for it, even though it was really all Dad. And it happened when you were at your lowest point. You said that was one of the worst parts of the whole thing. Right? Being blamed for something that someone else did to you."

Donovan shifts his position to scratch his shoulder.

"Come on, Mom. You've known Eran for four years, and he was just a baby when it happened. He may be a huge, worthless, annoying, shit-stirring tool, but that doesn't make him a terrorist."

Donovan takes a sip from his Coke and walks out.

Mrs. Knowles stares at the empty door frame for the longest five seconds of my life, then follows him without looking back.

Declan unpauses the game.

I think about Donovan, about Kyden Wheeler. I think about the reactions from other people, the PTA, the GoFundMe, and I wonder if our luck is turning.

I think about Jade, about whatever she hasn't told us. I think about Eema, and what Jeanie told me.

There's an email waiting for me from Dr. Pham when I get home.

XXI

I watch him through the windshield.

He closes the front door, adjusting his backpack as it slides off his shoulder. He spins on his heel quickly, turning toward me, and flashes two Kit Kat bars, shaking them in the air. He's like Oprah telling me I won a car.

Declan shimmies a little as he walks around the front of my shitty Fiesta toward the passenger seat.

I glance over at the window to his living room, catch a glimpse of curtains moving.

"Did you, like, buy those ahead of time?" I ask as he climbs in.

"Yeah!"

"What's your deal with Kit Kat?" I ask, engine idling.

He shrugs. "I like Kit Kat."

It's so weird being back.

Coach Flynn is still subbing for Riskin. When I realize he's just having us take notes from the textbook, I zone out. Is this all they've been doing since Riskin got canned? What a waste.

There are kids in there who talked about me to the press. Jillian, T.J., Kristen. I haven't seen them since everything happened. I don't even look in their direction. I don't care to see them.

I relax a bit in the classes I have with Declan and Delia, and especially at lunch with the full group, even though I don't eat anything. The rest of the day I avoid eye contact.

Not out of fear or anticipation.

Mostly out of disinterest.

I thought once I was back in school, I'd either be drinking in everything that I'd missed or else in hiding. One of two extremes. But it's neither. Instead it's this apathy I can't shake, this sudden understanding of how much of the right now doesn't matter, that next year I'll be in a different city anyway, that I'll never see most of these people again.

Before she decided she hated me, Declan's mom would sometimes talk about old friends of hers. People she kept up with on Facebook (of course, Facebook). She'd tell us how "fun" it had been to watch her high school friends get married and buy houses and have babies and watch those babies grow into toddlers and kids and teens. They would all post photos on specific milestones, comparing life stories without ever meeting again in person.

"These are people I probably would never have talked to again," she told us. "It's a nice way to keep up and see how they're doing."

She showed us some of her posts from like ten years ago, Declan and Donovan just little kids.

I wonder if that will be us, on Instagram or something else instead. I wonder if all these kids I see in the halls today will be in touch with me a decade or two from now, indirectly, through some medium that doesn't require a lot of real effort or investment. I wonder if they'll remember the last two weeks, if they'll think of me as that guy whose dad was a terrorist, if they'll care after they have their own babies and houses and lives.

I doubt it.

Today I think about perspective.

Today I think about how much I've gone through in the last two weeks, how much it will affect me in good ways and bad for the rest of my life. Today it's so easy to dismiss those looks I'm getting in the hallway, the rumors and the stupid high school drama.

It's so ridiculously weird, being back.

Still. More people come to the synagogue that afternoon and evening. Other congregants, including Zack, though we avoid each other.

But some people I don't recognize. Volunteers who tell us they heard what happened.

Some I do recognize but didn't expect: the pastor from Victorious Lutheran and others from his church. It's spreading.

There's a news van parked out front. I keep my distance, watching it like it's a hornet's nest. But no one ever approaches me.

I sit in the tiny kitchen by myself, on a break, drinking expired apple juice. It's only two months past, and I looked it up and the Internet said that was fine. It tastes okay, and sell-by dates are all a scam anyway.

A professional team came to replace sections of carpet. I don't know if we hired them or if this is pro bono or what. I don't know where the money would've come from. I'm sure the synagogue has insurance.

When we were thirteen, Zack and I experimented with the ancient microwave during Friday services, putting different objects we found in for a few seconds at a time.

I sit in a little folding chair and try to remember again what the smoke looked like in here, how much Zack's terrified expression made me laugh.

The door opens. Eema closes it behind her.

"You are by yourself."

I run this sentence through a filter, scanning for hidden tones and their implications.

"Yes," I say.

"It is important to take breaks. You need water."

"Apple juice is fine."

"You need water." She turns, having found something to do, and grabs a fresh paper cup. I listen to the white noise rush of water as she holds it under the faucet, timing it by its rising pitch. "You should stay hydrated while you work."

I take the cup because she's making small talk, and small talk means she's leading to something more.

"Eran." She looks at me full-on. "You are not a stupid boy. But you sometimes do stupid things."

I don't react. Part of me wants to roll my eyes, more of me wants to laugh. But she holds my gaze, not letting me look away, telling me with her eyes that this isn't it.

"I used to say this all the time when you were little. I would meet mothers of other children, some stupid, some not. These mothers, every case, they will not want to hear that their perfect son or daughter has done a stupid thing. I tell them, 'My Eran commits stupid acts constantly,' and they look at me with their polite American smiles and hold back what they think."

Eema leans on the counter right next to me.

"I knew what they think. They think I am a tired mother or a cruel mother. They think it must be the culture and wonder if Israel is run amok with angry women screaming at their sons." She laughs here, a slow, rough laugh, like steel wool scraping wood. It's been so long since I've heard her laugh.

"I am tired, but I am not cruel. I understand why these mothers hate to scold their children. It is the same reason I hate to scold you. But I love you, Eran. This is why I am stern."

She puts a hand on the back of my head, under my hair, like she used to when I was young. I'd forgotten. Her skin is calloused but warm.

"We spend our lives making mistakes. Every day we each find failure in dozens of ways, big and small. Is it not better to learn from them? And how do we learn if we refuse to see them, if we cannot stand to admit them? When a child runs into the street, that is a stupid thing. You tell him, you make sure he knows, because saving his feelings will not save him from a speeding car.

"Do you see?" She searches my eyes. "There is no reason to be delicate with mistakes, to see them as a great defeat. They are like . . ." Her lips twitch. "Like bowel movements, unpleasant but good for you. Something no one likes to talk about even as it happens to everyone, every day. We all do stupid things."

She looks at me long and hard.

"Eran, it is so with me too. I have been stupid. But my mistakes are greater than any you have made, all the worse for my age. They lasted fifteen years. They put such burden on you, when I thought I was saving you from it."

The wall clock ticks twice. Eema locks eyes with me. I can't look away.

"I should have told you. It is my fault for being so weak, to think that you were as well, that you needed to be shielded and protected so."

She pulls her hand back. It gives me a chill, no longer feeling the surprising warmth of her touch.

"Eran. I am sorry."

We look at each other. I blink first, look away.

I nod once, short and quick. Play with the rim of the paper cup. Look back at her.

I scan that face, the premature wrinkles and lines, and my eyes wander back upward.

"You quit dyeing your hair."

Eema tilts her head, just a bit.

"Of course. They found me. What was the point anymore?"

She raises her eyebrows at my look of confusion.

"You think it was vanity all this time? That I didn't like the color?"

Eema gives me one of her rare smiles, a gift, and then walks out.

I toss back the water and throw out the apple juice.

* * *

In the overflow student lot. Ricochet of pebbles off the under pipes of my car. Flashes of that day with Declan, trading off the BB gun, Declan nervous as usual, me careless and overconfident as always.

I turn the engine off.

"Here we fucking go," I say, still a habit, and unwrap today's Kit Kat before we climb out of the car.

I don't want to be here. I don't want to see these people today.

But I walk toward first period anyway, slow as I can. Ignoring the stares.

Outside the door, I stop, take a deep breath. Prepare myself.

Then I walk in.

"Ah! Mr. Sharon," Riskin says from the front.

It stops me short. I just stare at him. I'm taken aback by how familiar he looks standing there, but how unexpected. It's funny how a person can look both out of context and in their natural place at the same time.

"You're here," I say, for lack of anything better.

He raises an eyebrow.

"Seems we both are."

A second goes by.

"Have a seat. We're going over mob mentality today, and how the will of the majority has been used to oppress marginalized groups throughout history." He looks so satisfied to be saying this.

I blink, then smile, then nod, then turn toward my desk.

333

On the way, I make eye contact with Jillian and take satisfaction in the frightened openmouthed expression on her face.

Bonnie's hair is bright yellow. This might be the sunniest I've ever seen her.

Jade is the last to join our table today, carrying her tray like it's a prison meal. I watch her carefully as she sits. She looks down as she approaches, and when she finally makes eye contact, the smile is thin and bland. Same as yesterday.

There's nothing in front of me again, but the rest of them know why. I've allowed myself the morning Kit Kat, but otherwise I'm fasting.

I'm not religious, just as Eema is not. But that synagogue took me in. As they did Eema.

We're quiet for a few minutes. It's funny: this group of us has been through so much, it's as if there's nothing left to say.

But I know there's something more to it, and after those couple minutes, I've lost interest in pretending otherwise.

I don't say her name, just watch her until she looks up. When she does, I raise my eyebrows and tilt my head a little, pointing with my eyes.

She nods.

"We'll be back in a bit," I say, standing up.

"No," Jade responds. "Let's all go."

They bring their lunches. There aren't really any places to sit in the bathroom, but we find spots. Jade on top of the trash can,

Declan and Bonnie against the sinks, half leaning, half sitting. Delia and me on the floor.

It's gross, but it's quiet, and it's strangely comforting.

Jade takes a moment. All of us wait, no one really eating anymore.

Then she tells us about her sister Opal.

She tells us about the date she found on the back of an old photo.

She tells us about the life-support machines, about the hurricane.

She tells us about Ma, about Father, about their secrets. About this tug-of-war they've played with her memories without realizing it. About knowing too much and too little about New Orleans.

"I didn't know till now what place really made me," she says at one point, and I think of Eema.

She tells us about how parents can strike too hard when they mean to protect, can insulate and shield so much they do more harm than good.

She tells us about good intentions, how those can only cover so much.

I don't normally listen, I know. My instinct is to talk, to act, to do, to conduct; I am a constant whirlpool of movement that leaves little room for others. Maybe my subconscious saw listening as too passive. Maybe this is at the heart of what I've been trying to change.

It's so easy to listen now. I don't think it's any sudden, magical improvement I've made on my end. I think that will take a long time, maybe a lifetime.

I think it's Jade.

I wonder if she knows how much power she has.

When Jade is done, I let out a long breath and look around.

Bonnie, Declan, Delia — they watch her with apprehension, and for a moment I'm confused.

I look back at her, at the sadness in her expression, and realize they don't understand that she's finished. They don't understand why, if she's finally learned the answers to questions she's been asking all her life, she's still so sad.

They don't see the relief engraved into the sadness, embedded and inseverable, like melted gold used to repair cracks in pottery.

It's so familiar to me that I can't not see it.

It's not perfect, and it's not over.

It's just better, that's all.

I think that whenever someone stares at me in the hallway. When there are whispers, too quiet to be innocent, too loud to be ignored.

I think it whenever I'm by myself the rest of the day, Declan and Jade and Bonnie and Delia in their own classes in different areas of the school. We reunite when we can, but when I'm alone, I think of that word.

I think it when I get a rare smile, from another acquaintance or sometimes just a kid I don't know.

I think it when I think of Kyden and Dr. Pham and Zack and Jillian and Declan's mom. I think it when I think of going back to the synagogue after school, of another day of repairing, fixing, improving, making better.

I still have my own sadness, and my own anger, and the bit of distance left between Eema and myself. So does Jade.

But we'll be fine, because every day it'll get a little better.

We'll be fine.

Mrs. Bennett shoos us away at the bell. "Don't y'all go drinking, it's only two-thirty."

She gives me a small pat on the shoulder as she walks by. I smile at my desk and gather my stuff.

Declan and I head toward the front entrance after our lockers. We find Jade right outside, waiting on the bench swing like she said she would be. Back to us, swaying lightly.

The swing is older than we are, I know. A relic of a far-back decade, when the school was freshly built.

But I love it. It's so out of place and unnecessary and a little rickety, and I love it.

I keep my eyes on her as we walk up and around the swing. On her curly hair, bobbing just a little in the breeze. The way the light brightens it here and there, turning it from dark brown to light to golden, casting playful ragged shadows on the grass below her. The smooth brown skin of the back of her neck, vulnerable and clear.

The bench creaks as she swings, an unending, lazy pattern. I can hear it over the talking and yelling and laughing from thousands of other kids around us, the idling engines, the car doors slamming in the parking lot. Over all that, the creak of the swing as we get closer.

When we're even with each other, she turns, and she smiles.

DEVORAH

She lives a lifetime in two seconds.

This is not our fight.

She wonders where those words came from. She wishes she hadn't said them. She is so happy she did.

This is not our fight.

She can almost hear them echoing out from the speakers at the base of the platform, can see the sound waves bend from her voice. She watches those words travel at the speed of light around the world, picked up from the cameras in front of her.

This is not our fight.

She sees reactions across the country, in other parts of the world, reflected in the faces in front of her. Surprise. Anger. Indignation.

Understanding.

This is not our fight.

Those words echo out in a pulse, like the ripples in a pond racing away from a dropped stone.

This is not our fight.

After two seconds, she recognizes something. An end to this trance her small crowd has been in.

She grabs the paper and pulls it off the podium as she turns away. The movement breaks the spell.

It is like when she entered. The small crowd erupts. Flashes of light, camera clicks, questions, shouts, fervent movement. She ignores it as she did before, but this time with some peace in her heart.

This time, when she walks those steps between the podium and her house, the strangers are behind her. Each step takes her farther from them. Closer to her son.

She opens her front door, and Avi is the first one she sees, and she smiles.

Shalom, Eran,

she says, to herself,

to him.

ACKNOWLEDGMENTS

Thank you to my editor, Liz Bicknell, and my agent, Brianne Johnson, two of the most talented people I know. After five years, my heart still stutters (in a good way) every time I see an email from them. And special thanks to Bri for the *kintsukuroi* imagery, an idea you didn't even know you gave me.

Thanks to Allison Hill and Miriam Newman, Readers One and Two and so much more, who helped push this story and its characters to be richer. Thank you to Matt Roeser, Anna Gjesteby Abell, Tracy Miracle, Lindsey Yanow, and everyone else at Candlewick who worked on this book behind the scenes.

Thank you to my writing group, Zack Clark and Preeti Chhibber, for hammering out some of the first bumps.

I asked a thousand different friends questions about their various professions. Thanks to Aruna for medical answers, Elisa for answering a random email about lawyers, Rachel for insight on old memories and childhood amnesia, her daughter Rosie for examples of toddler speech skills, and Brittany, Larry, Mel, and others for fielding my many questions about public school teachers. Thanks also to Catherine for weather help and Emily for a bit on churches. I'm sorry if I got anything wrong.

Thanks to Dan for letting me borrow a little from our own childhood. Sorry I caved and admitted we microwaved that Styrofoam.

Thanks to my brother-in-law, Declan. Sorry, it's just such a good name. Thanks to Kathryn and Bill for naming him. And thanks to David Tomczak for the first hint at his on-page personality.

Thanks as always, Mom and Dad. Mom, I got only the flattering or eccentric parts of Eema from you. And of course thanks to the rest of Damien's and my combined families, who are pretty forthcoming about their pride and encouragement, even when they make fun of me.

Thank you to Jas Walden, who I think would have loved this — if only to see some bits of our own synagogue in the story.

And then there's Damien. This became a story, almost accidentally, about trying to be better. Thank you for giving that to me.